BE KIND, REWIND

MELISSA BROWN

Be Kind, Rewind

A 90s Nostalgic Romance
(Spotlight Video Book 1)

By Melissa Brown

BE KIND REWIND

A SPOTLIGHT VIDEO

MELISSA BROWN

Cover Design: Michelle Preast Illustration & Design

Editing: The Ryter's Proof

Published by: Lady Boss Press, Inc.

CHAPTER 1

Naomi

October, 1994

"*F*oreskin Gump?" I shouldn't have said it out loud, but I couldn't help myself—the words came tumbling out of my careless mouth before I could stop them. It was my first day at a new job, and I should have just nodded and stayed quiet like a good little employee. But instead, I stared, eyes wide, unable to remove my gaze from the large, white VHS box on the shelf. On its cover was a nerdy guy sitting on a bench while a woman with a low-cut, black dress lifted her leg to him...showing her lady parts.

Still stunned, I asked, "Is this...um, is this for real?"

"Yeah," the assistant manager said, his pale cheeks reddening with each second that we stood awkwardly in the tiny room marked *Adults Only* separated from the rest of the store with a simple, pink curtain.

No wonder Marley calls this "The Pink Room."

"Unfortunately, they didn't waste any time getting that one made," he said.

"Wow," I said again, ignoring the little voice in my head telling me to shut my damn mouth.

"An-y-way," he said slowly, gesturing for us both to leave the room, "I'm not sure if Heather covered this when she hired you, but one of the requirements to work here is to restock the adult videos when they're returned...which is often. Will that be a problem?"

"Um..." I said, swallowing hard. I was no prude, but everyone had their limits when it came to boxes covered in pictures of dicks. Personally, I'd have no problem never setting foot in that room ever again. But obviously, that wasn't an option. And I really needed this job.

"Not a problem," I said, not as convincingly as I'd hoped.

"Are you sure?" he asked, running his hand through his dark hair. "Because your *friend* avoids it like the plague. Not sure I want to deal with *two* of you."

I resented the way he talked about Marley, a girl I'd met in English Lit who always smelled like bubblegum. We didn't know each other that well, but she was friendly, and she offered me gum at the beginning of each class. One day I'd vented to her that my checking account was getting dangerously low, and she suggested I apply to work at Spotlight Video. She'd worked there for three months and loved her job. She said it was the best place to work on campus and had made a bunch of friends during the twenty hours a week she spent there. Unlike Marley, though, so far I wasn't impressed. And this guy, Ben, although incredibly good looking, wasn't nearly as nice as Heather, the general manager who'd hired me just a few days before. In fact, he was a total buzzkill.

Buzzkill Ben.

I chucked to myself, and Ben narrowed his eyes in suspicion.

Way to go, Naomi. Piss off the sorta-kinda-boss on your first day.

Clearing my throat, I shook my head. "I can return the porn to the shelves. Not a problem, sir."

Ben paused for a second, one eyebrow raised. He looked utterly annoyed. "Sir?"

"What? Too formal?" I asked, trying to be just a little bit playful and lighten the tension between us, but *Buzzkill* wasn't having it. He was all business.

"Is this your first job?"

"Well, not if you count babysitting my siblings."

"I don't."

"Okay, then yes. It's my first job. But I love movies."

"Right," he said with snark. His bright blue eyes were gorgeous yet dismissive and cold. "Who doesn't?"

His smart-ass reply stopped me in my tracks, so I decided to take his question literally...just to have a little fun with him. "I'm sure there must be *someone*. My room-mate doesn't own any movies. Not one."

Ben sighed with an elongated blink. Clearly, he was not amused. But I was.

"What's your point?"

"I don't remember," I said with a casual shrug and a laugh.

I wonder if the pizza place next door is hiring.

"Hmph," he muttered as I followed behind him to the large front desk where two of my new coworkers were standing at their respective cash registers. They were arguing about something, but I couldn't quite figure out what about, at first. "Guys, lower your voices. There are customers in the store."

"Fine, fine, but first you've got to settle this," said the bigger guy with a chestnut ponytail spilling down his back. The skin on his nose was oily, and he smelled a little like the deviled eggs my mom made every Easter.

Ew.

Ben looked irritated once again. The big guy, who I think everyone called Sully, was oblivious and continued, "Oompa Loompas."

"What about them?"

"Creepy, right?" the other guy asked, looking directly at me. He was tall and slim with bony shoulders. But his eyes were deep brown, and he had a boyish grin. Not my type at all but definitely cute.

"Hush, Emmett," Sully said. "Don't sway the judges."

"I have no opinion on Oompa Loompas," Ben said, shaking his head. The phone rang, and Ben grabbed the receiver, turning his back to all of us as he graciously asked the customer what he could do to help them.

I leaned in toward Emmett. "Totally creepy."

"I know, right?" Emmett said, raising his hand for a high-five. I happily obliged.

"But, doesn't everyone think so? I mean, who's sitting

4

there watching *Willy Wonka* and hoping the little orange guys come out for another rousing musical number while some kid is presumably doomed off-camera? Not this girl."

Sully threw his hands up in the air. "Are you kidding me? Those guys were badass. Didn't you see how they rolled that blueberry girl out of the inventing room? Classic, man. Classic."

"Okay, I'll give you that. But they aren't at all how the book described them," Emmett said.

"And that matters why exactly?"

"Authenticity is important," Emmett said with a shrug.

"Whatever, Polaroid," Sully said, rolling his eyes.

"Polaroid?" I asked, but they both ignored me.

Emmett crossed his arms in front of his chest. "No, I'm serious."

Sully turned to me, rolling his dark brown eyes again as he tipped his head toward Emmett. "He takes this stuff way too seriously."

"Don't even get me started on taking things too seriously. You're *majoring* in taking things too seriously," Emmett snapped at Sully, eyeing him from head to toe. Sully was dressed all in black. Black t-shirt, black jeans, and even black socks tucked inside his worn navy sneakers.

"What's with all the black?" I asked, raising one curious eyebrow.

"I don't like your tone," Sully said, crossing his arms in front of his chest and leaning back into the gray and black speckled countertop. We stood in silence for a moment as I waited for him to answer my question.

He didn't.

Ben hung up the phone. "Get back to work, guys. Emmett, show Naomi how to check out a customer. Bryan—"

"Sully," Sully corrected him.

"Fine. Sully, check in the returns. And don't forget to rewind them if the customer didn't."

"And give them a big ol' fine when they don't? Let's say...fifty bucks?" Sully asked with a shit-eating grin and wide eyes.

"Don't confuse Naomi," Ben said, shaking his head, turning his attention to me. "We don't do that."

No duh.

But I simply nodded, pressing my lips into a thin line.

"I have to call corporate, so I'll be in the back. Emmett knows what he's doing. He'll show you the ropes."

"Thanks," I said, relieved to watch him walk off the main video floor.

"He's intense, huh?" I asked, wrinkling my nose at Emmett.

"Ben's okay."

"He seems a little...stuffy."

Emmett shrugged again. "He just has a low tolerance for bullshit. And this place can be a revolving door, especially during the winter."

"What do you mean?"

"Well, Sully and I have been here for a year, right, Sully?"

Sully didn't turn to face us, but he gave a thumbs-up as he scanned in the VHS tapes.

Emmett scratched the back of his neck. "But a lot of

people get the job and just stop showing up after a month or so. Their classes get hard or whatever and they just stop coming to work. Ben has to track everyone down, which is almost impossible. Usually, he just leaves a bunch of pissed-off answering machine messages that are never returned."

"That sucks."

"They should have a word for that," Emmett said.

"What do you mean?"

"Like when you blow someone off by disappearing. You know, when you're like nowhere to be found and you leave someone hanging. They need a verb for that."

"You mean aside from disappearing?"

"Yeah, that's…tired. Something more interesting."

"Maybe one day they will."

"Maybe." He shrugged.

"But, FYI, I really need this job…and I don't see that changing anytime soon. And I'm sure Marley won't disappear either. She always volunteers in class and is the first person to turn in her papers. She's good people."

"Good. Yeah, uh…Marley's cool."

Sully laughed under his breath as he grabbed a two-foot-tall stack of videotapes and left the front desk area, biting down on his lower lip as he raised both eyebrows.

Emmett, his cheeks pink, shook his head and muttered, "Butt munch."

"Hey," I said, moving in closer and lowering my voice. I didn't want to piss anyone off on my first day, and I knew I was already on thin ice with Ben. "Why *does* he wear black?"

Emmett rolled his eyes. "He's in mourning."

"Oh no," I said. "Did he lose one of his parents or something?"

"You would think so, wouldn't you? But no. Not even close."

"So, what's his deal then?"

"Kurt Cobain. When he died, he stopped speaking to everyone. Took like a vow of silence or something. Heather told him he had to speak to the customers or she'd stop putting him on the schedule. So, since that day, he's talking again, but he's been wearing nothing but black. It's like his own little protest or something. It drives Ben and Heather nuts, but he's not breaking the dress code, so technically he can't be busted for it."

I remembered the day Kurt Cobain died...I was still in high school. It was a spring morning, I knew that for sure, but everything else was hazy. I remembered Courtney Love reading his suicide letter and MTV had to beep her out because she was dropping f-bombs left and right as she yelled at him. I sat on my couch, stunned. He was one of the biggest stars on the planet when he died. But he did. And he'd been gone for months.

"Kurt Cobain died in the spring, right?"

"April. Sully never lets any of us forget it."

"But it's October...how long is he going to be '*in mourning*'?" I asked, using air quotes around my last two words.

"No idea. We'll see what happens." He reached into the pocket of his jeans and pulled out a pink container of Bubble Tape. "Gum?"

"I'm good, thanks." Emmett ripped off an extra-large piece of the powder pink gum. After about a minute, he smelled just like Marley. "So, should I not mention Kurt Cobain around him?"

Emmett paused for a second to scan the room, looking for Sully who was still placing videos back on the shelf. "Probably a good idea. He'll talk your ear off if you do. He thinks Courtney Love had him killed."

"Wait... so...what, she murdered him and made it look like a suicide?"

"Bingo."

"Wow. That's really out there," I said with an amused laugh, turning to find Sully just a few feet away from the front desk with daggers in his eyes—all pointed at me. If they were real daggers, I'd be just as dead as Kurt Cobain. But somehow, I didn't think Sully would mourn me.

"Something funny?"

"No, I—"

"Show some respect."

"For Kurt Cobain?" I asked incredulously. I mean, I liked Nirvana just as much as any person my age, but their lead singer wasn't someone I revered. Not even close. "He was okay."

"Okay? *Okay?*" Sully's forehead wrinkled with rage as the register of his voice deepened. "Kurt Donald Cobain was *the* most talented musician to ever walk the planet Earth."

Wrinkling my nose, I recoiled, and a sardonic laugh jumped out of my mouth.

"What?"

"Well, I mean...you don't *really* believe that, do you?"

"Careful," Emmett warned, gritting his teeth.

"What about John Lennon? Jimi Hendrix? Elvis?"

Sully shook his head. "Puh-lease. Don't insult my intelligence."

"That's funny," Emmett said.

"What?"

"Naomi gave the exact same examples as Ben."

"No, she didn't," Sully argued.

"No, I remember it very clearly. You were standing where Naomi is now and Ben was asking you to wear something else besides black. You scoffed, and a very similar conversation started. And Ben used those *exact* examples. In the same order, too."

"Ugh, you and your memory, Polaroid."

"Memory?" I asked, looking between the two guys.

"He's got that photographic memory or whatever. You can't get anything past him. And who cares if she came up with the same examples? That doesn't mean anything."

"Well, it means that *other* legendary musicians come to mind for a lot of us," I suggested.

"Whatever. As my little, annoying sister, Brittany, says, *Talk to the hand, New Girl.*" He held a hand up and walked away, his ponytail swinging like a pendulum.

Emmett nudged me with his arm. "He gives everyone a nickname. Don't take it personally."

"Don't worry, I won't. Besides, I can think of a lot of names that are a *lot* worse than that."

"True," Emmett said, grabbing videotapes from the drop slot. "So, are you a freshman like Marley?"

"Yep."

"Cool. Major?"

"Performing arts. Musical theater."

"So, you want to be an actress?"

"Yep," I said with confidence. "All my life."

"Nice. I could see that. You seem like you might have a flair for the dramatic."

"Just a bit," I said, raising both eyebrows playfully. "And you?"

"I want to be Steven Spielberg," Emmett said, his eyes bright and determined. With that simple sentence, I could tell he was just as passionate as I was.

"I love that," I said.

"People always laughed at me when I said that…'til I came here, that is. Now I've found my people."

"Did you always want to go here?" I asked, already knowing his answer even before his head started to nod emphatically. For so many of us in the Midwest, Lurie University for the Performing Arts was the ultimate place to prepare you for a career in the arts. And the fact that it was located in gorgeous Evanston, Illinois certainly didn't hurt. One quick ride on the "L" train, and you were in Chicago. I couldn't think of a more perfect location. "Me, too. Total dream school."

"What was your Plan B?"

"Didn't have one."

A satisfied smile crossed Emmett's face. "Me neither."

"I guess I would have gotten a job and tried again mid-year."

"Same. My mom was really on my case to apply to other schools, but I told her this was the place. This is where I needed to be."

"Thank God we both got in, huh?"

"No shit," Emmett said before clenching his teeth and locking eyes with a customer. She waved him away with a smile before rounding the corner and wandering down another aisle of videos. "I've got to work on that."

With a laugh, I smiled. "Probably. But I'm guessing most of the customers are students here, right?"

"At least half of 'em, yeah. But we do get some of the luxury condo people, and they can be a little snooty."

"Blech," I said, grabbing videos from the box and placing them in a row for Emmett to scan.

"I have a feeling you're going to fit in really well around here."

"You know what, Emmett?" I asked with a smile as I looked around the small video store. "I do, too."

CHAPTER 2

Ben

November, 1994

"You're late," I said, not even looking up from the pile of videos on the countertop. It was Sunday, which meant that it was time to prepare the new releases for rental on Tuesday.

"I knoooow," she said, dragging out the word.

"Again."

"I know," she said, pausing as she stood next to me. "Sorry."

When she didn't move, I turned to face her, feeling uneasy as she stared at me.

"What?"

"I have to put my purse away." She gestured to the cubby beneath me, where all of the female employees dropped their stuff, despite the fact that we had lockers in the back room for that exact purpose. Lockers I had to beg corporate to give us just six months earlier.

"Oh," I said. "Right. So, what's your excuse this time?"

"It's so nice to see you, too, Ben. How *are* you?" She rolled her eyes.

I ignored her sarcasm. "Really, though...why are you thirty minutes late?"

"You wouldn't understand," she said with a sigh.

"Try me."

She shrugged, narrowing her eyes. "I'll tell you later."

"You're impossible," I said, getting back to the new releases in front of me.

There was something about Naomi Parker that irritated me. I couldn't quite figure out what it was. Maybe it was the fact that she wasn't intimidated by any kind of authority, which meant that every time she made a stupid mistake, blurted something crass out in front of customers, or strolled in thirty minutes late, she really didn't give a rat's ass. And as her boss, that sucked. Or maybe it was how dramatic she got over movies, gushing about all the hot actors that she dreamed of working with one day—when she left Illinois for New York or Los Angeles.

Or maybe it was the fact that her personality—her entire presence—was so much bigger than my own.

Whatever the reason, she drove me up the wall during every shift we had together. And it didn't even matter that she was probably the most beautiful girl I'd ever met in person. Never mind the fact that her strawberry blonde hair always smelled like coconut and a tropical flower I couldn't quite place. Hibiscus? Orchid? Never mind her piercing blue eyes or the pair of freckles that sat upon the apple of her right cheek. Never mind that she had more confidence in her pinky finger than most college girls had in their entire bodies. Because none of those things mattered when it came down to me doing my job and doing it well. Besides, I wasn't supposed to date employees.

"Ooh, it's what's his name..." she said, grabbing the box for *Speed* right out of my hand.

"Keanu Reeves."

"Right. But I always think of him as Ted 'Theodore' Logan."

I stared at her blankly.

"Don't you remember Bill and Ted? *Strange things are afoot at the Circle K*," she said with wide eyes.

"Oh...right."

She tapped the VHS sleeve. "I wanted to see this in the theater. Have you seen it?"

"Yes," I answered simply before holding my hand out and gesturing for her to give the movie back to me so I could cover it in plastic and blast it with the heat gun to seal it up. Naomi and I locked eyes, and then she ignored me, flipping the cardboard sleeve over to read the synopsis.

Total pain in my ass.

"Naomi."

She held up a finger. "One sec."

"Naomi," I said again, this time my voice was stern, a little more 'assistant manager-ish.'

"Ben," she said with raised eyebrows and a mocking

tone. She was being playful and flirtatious, and I had to admit that a small part of me loved that side of her. If I were being honest with myself, she pulled me in by my balls when she teased me...which was often. But there was no way in hell I was going to let her know it. I couldn't let her see the effect she had on me in those small moments. Ninety percent of the time, she drove me crazy...but the other 10 percent made me feel off-balance, off-center. And that unsteady feeling frustrated the hell out of me. I didn't want to like Naomi and most of me didn't. But that other 10 percent wasn't controlled by my brain...and that other 10 percent was, let's just say, awfully stubborn.

"I need that back." I huffed. "Anytime this century would be great."

"Ugh, take a chill pill, Ben. I'm a slow reader."

"Or maybe you just like staring at movie stars."

"Maaaayyybe," she said with an over-the-top wink, dropping the sleeve in front of me on the counter. "Speaking of which, the girls on my floor went to see *Interview with a Vampire* on Friday night. Have you seen it?"

"I've been working all weekend. What do you think?" I shot back, shaking my head.

She ignored me, lost in her own little world.

"It was amazing. What I wouldn't give to be in a Brad Pitt-Tom Cruise sandwich. Delicious!"

"Nice." I shook my head while slipping a piece of styrofoam into the empty *Speed* sleeve and covering it with the plastic. Before picking up the heat gun, I gestured toward the box of empty sleeves at my feet.

"Grab someone and take those to the back, okay? They need to be broken down and recycled. Garbage comes tomorrow."

"You bet. But seriously, one day I'm going to work with one of those guys...preferably Brad. He's just... yummy." She pinned her name tag to her black dress that was covered in bright gold sunflowers. A black choker necklace was pressed tightly to her neck. She was gorgeous. There was no denying it.

"Plus, Tom Cruise is a scientologist," I said, scrunching my nose. "They're a little nuts... and he might try to convert you."

"A what-a-tologist?"

"Scientologist."

"I have no idea what that word means."

I laughed. "I'll tell you later. To the back room, please. Make Sully help you."

"Fine. Just as you were getting interesting..." She wiggled her eyebrows, and the scent of coconut wafted in the air as she grabbed the closest box and started walking to the storeroom. I heard her call out to Sully, and within seconds, he was at the desk, grabbing the second box.

"So, managers are allowed to take these bad boys home, right?" Sully asked, grabbing a tape already encased in its thick plastic clamshell.

"That's right. One of the many perks of my position."

"Sweet," Sully said, placing the tape back on the counter as Naomi rounded the corner.

"Maybe I could take one home?" she asked, looking eager with wide, bright blue eyes.

Before I could reply, Sully rolled his eyes. "You're not a manager, New Girl."

"So? Ben *is*, and if he says I can take one, then it's fine. Right, Ben?"

"You would think so, wouldn't you?" I said, slightly amused.

"No way," Sully said, his eyes wide. "I've been working here for over a year, and I've never been allowed to take home a new release. You've been here what—a month? Hell, you don't even have a shelf on the picks wall yet."

It was true. We had a wall of employee picks where each employee was able to choose five of their current favorite films, and we switched them out each week. Customers could follow employees who had a similar taste in movies, and it made the employees feel like their opinions mattered. Even though I never took credit for it, the employee picks wall was my idea. I'd gone to Heather and corporate with my proposal, explaining how it would be good for staff and customers alike, and they agreed.

"That reminds me," Naomi said, totally ignoring Sully's point. "When do I get a shelf on the picks wall? Marley said she got hers after just a couple of weeks."

"That's because someone else quit the day she started. When someone else quits, you'll get a shelf."

She placed her hands on her hips, looking betrayed. "Seriously? That could take…months."

I shrugged. "There's no more room."

"What if I *made* room? Could I have picks then?"

"The store has a set number of shelves, Naomi."

She rolled her eyes, shaking her head. "I know that, *Ben*."

"So…what's your plan?"

A crafty smile crossed her lips. "I'm not sure yet…but I'll think of something."

"While you're thinking, maybe bring some more sleeves to the back room."

"Oh my God, I've got it. I've got it!" she said, jumping on the balls of her feet.

"What?"

"You'll see," she said, grabbing another box and sauntering to the back room.

"She's up to no good," Sully said, joining me at the counter.

"What else is new?"

The bell above the front door rang, and Sully and I turned to see Dutch, our resident pot-smoking Deadhead/Phish-head/Rusted Root groupie, enter the store. Just like Naomi, he was late. Very late.

Shocker.

"You'll *never* believe what happened to me," Dutch said, approaching the counter.

I shook my head. "Save it, Dutch."

"No, Ben, I'm serious this time. My roommate locked me out, I swear."

"If you were locked out, why didn't you just come to work?" I asked, turning to lean against the counter.

"I had to change my clothes." He looked down. "You know, to look presentable or whatever."

Sully and I looked him up and down. Wearing a black t-shirt and a loose, open flannel shirt, he wasn't exactly the picture of professionalism. As he joined us behind the counter, his baggy jeans came into view and were fraying at the bottom after months of being dragged under his black Doc Martens.

"What the hell were you wearing *before?*" Sully asked, raising one eyebrow.

Took the words right out of my mouth.

"You don't wanna know, man. Trust me," he said with a laugh before running his fingers through his greasy hair. The scent of patchouli wafted past me. Not my favorite scent. Dutch wasn't our most reliable employee at Spotlight Video, but he was friendly with the customers, loved to talk movies with anyone with a pulse, and was really good-natured most of the time. And people loved his picks. The movies on his shelf were almost always checked out.

"Geez," Sully said.

"You're one to talk, man," Dutch said to Sully, looking annoyed. It was hard to annoy Dutch. Most of the time, he just loved everyone, but Sully had a way of ruffling everyone's feathers. As my grandfather would say, Sully was a mixer.

"What is that supposed to mean?" Sully asked, crossing his arms in front of his chest. His standard move during a confrontation.

"Well, I mean, no offense, but you look like a mortician or something."

"I'm making a statement."

"And just exactly how long will this statement last?" I asked.

"I'm not breaking the dress code," Sully fired back. "I checked."

"I know. You've told me that many times."

"So?"

"So...don't you think it's time? I'm sure Kurt appreciates your dedication and all, but..."

"But what?"

"But," Dutch jumped in, "if you ever wanna get laid again, you need to ditch the black, dude."

Sully shook his head, scratching the zit on his forehead. "I don't need help in *that* department, thank you very much."

Dutch chuckled under his breath as he attached his name tag to his flannel. "I'm just saying..."

"Yeah, whatever, man. I have no trouble with the ladies, believe me—."

Fed up with the conversation, I interrupted, "Why don't you guys return some tapes to the shelves. It's dead in here now, but things will pick up in an hour or so."

"I call the porn," Dutch said, waggling his eyebrows and leaping toward the return box.

"Ugh, don't linger back there," I said. "Last time you were gone for at least fifteen minutes. And you only had a few tapes to put back."

"*And* remember we can see you," Sully said, gesturing to the tiny monitor on the desk. When the store first opened, Heather said there were some...issues with a few men visiting the adults-only area, so they had to install security cameras.

What some guys will do to save a buck.

"Some of the titles are hard to find," Dutch said, his cheeks reddening.

"Sure, they are." I chuckled.

Both guys walked away with stacks of videos in hand,

and I quickly got back to work preparing the week's new releases.

* * *

A LITTLE WHILE LATER, the return box was empty, there were no customers in the store, and Dutch was zoning out watching *The Empire Strikes Back* on the TV above the registers. He sat with his elbows digging into his thigh muscles as he stared up at the screen as wide-eyed as a little kid.

"Find something to do, Dutch."

"Wait, wait…here's my favorite part." He bit down on his lower lip, and I glanced at the screen, knowing exactly which part it was before he even rattled off Yoda's famous line.

"*No, there is another,*" he and Sully said in unison before giving each other a high five. "Best movie line ever, man."

"No way," Sully argued. "I mean, it's good. But there's better."

"Such as?" I asked, genuinely curious what Sully thought could top Yoda's iconic line.

"How about *Terminator*? '*I'll be back!*'"

"Lame!" Dutch said, shaking his head. "*Terminator* sucks, man."

"Says the guy worshiping a Muppet."

"Show some respect, man. He's a Jedi Knight."

"You guys are reaching new levels of nerdiness, you know that, right?" Naomi said just as she proudly strutted back to the counter.

"Okay fine," Sully said. "How about this one? *You're gonna need a bigger boat.*"

"*Jaws?*" I asked. "Yeah, that's a good one."

"No way," Naomi said. "That's not it."

"Because you've never seen it," Sully scoffed.

"Sharks don't interest me," She said matter-of-factly, like she couldn't be bothered.

"Then you tell us, what's the best movie line in existence?" Sully pressed.

"*Nobody puts Baby in a corner!*" she said proudly.

"Oh my god," Sully threw his head back in laughter. "That is *so* lame."

"*You're* lame, Sully. *Dirty Dancing* is a classic. Johnny Castle is all that *and* a bag of chips. And that line will never get old. Mark my words." She then turned her attention to me, drumming her hands on the counter. "Are you ready?"

"Ready for what?"

"The big reveal of course."

"What are you talking about?" I asked, playing dumb.

"Are you serious?" She huffed, cocking one hip to the side as she drummed her fingers against the counter. "We *just* had this conversation, like, twenty minutes ago. You said if I made room for my picks shelf, I could have one."

"Oh, right...that," I said, joining her on the other side of the counter.

"Well, come on!" She grabbed my arm and dragged me to the picks wall...only it was no longer the picks wall.

"Oh no," I muttered. "What did you do?"

"I...renovated the picks wall. See, I shifted these two sections just a tad and created the picks *corner.* See? Now there is almost double the space for our picks! And if we hire more people, they can have shelves, too."

I had to admit, it was smart. I studied her creativity, genuinely impressed.

"So?" She pushed against my forearm. "Say something!"

"I'll have to make sure it's okay with Heather."

Her blue eyes fell. "Seriously? That's all you have to say?"

"What do you want me to say, Naomi? I have a boss, and it's up to her what goes and what stays."

"But I mean...look at it. I didn't mess up the new release wall at all, I just shifted it. Customers will still be able to find everything, and our picks will just be a little closer together, but it can be divided amongst more people. Don't you see?"

"Yes," I said, my expression impassive. "I see all of that."

"What is your problem?"

"Excuse me?"

"You. You're like...devoid of enthusiasm."

"It's just employee picks, Naomi," I said, turning to walk away.

"No." She grabbed my arm and turned me back around. "It's more than that. You have a problem with me."

"Okay, maybe I do."

"So...what is it?"

I sighed in exasperation. "Why were you late?"

"What? Seriously? You're still on that?"

I cocked my head to the side, placing my hands in my

pockets, and shrugged. "You said you'd tell me later. It's later."

"I was running lines with my scene partner."

"What? For a play?"

"*Othello*. I got the part of Desdemona." She paused, tilting her head toward me as if I should know the significance of that name. I didn't.

"I don't know the story."

"She's the female lead. It's a Shakespearean tragedy. It's kind of a big deal. The director said no freshman has ever gotten the lead before."

"And why wouldn't I understand that?"

"What do you mean?" she asked, looking confused. "I never said you wouldn't understand it. It's Shakespeare— once you get used to the language, it's pretty easy—"

"No," I interrupted, "earlier you said I wouldn't understand your reason for being late."

"Oh." She shrugged and then shook her head, looking detached. "I don't know. You never believe my excuses."

"Because that's all they are...excuses."

I struck a nerve. Naomi stomped her foot and balled her hands into fists at her side. "Oh my God, what is your problem?"

"You," I said matter-of-factly.

"Me?"

"Be better than your excuses, Naomi."

"What?" She glared at me, and I swear I thought fire was going to shoot out of her ears. She was pissed, but I didn't care. I had a point to make.

"Be better than your excuses," I said again, my voice calm and composed.

She opened her mouth to speak, both of her eyebrows raised high as she stared at me with wide eyes. She was flustered and unsure of what to say next. And I had to hold back a laugh because the shoe was finally on the other foot. Naomi flustered me, frustrated me, and left me speechless a lot of the time. But finally, I'd turned the tables.

And it felt damn good. For about two seconds...and then reality set in.

"It's time for my break," she said, narrowing her eyes and walking to the back room.

"Ben?" Sully called from the front desk, and I stood frozen, watching Naomi walk away from me. She turned back after hearing Sully call my name, and for a second, when I saw the crushed expression on her face, I almost asked her to wait. I almost told her I was an idiot and that her 'renovation' was genius. I almost apologized for being such a tight-ass around the store, for never just going with the flow and letting people have fun. And I almost explained to her that I'm not always like that...that 'Assistant Manager Ben' annoyed me almost as much as he annoyed her.

Almost.

But instead, I turned and walked back to the desk to answer Sully's question and continue my day as Assistant Manager Ben...even though that guy was such a fucking asshole.

CHAPTER 3

Naomi

"Shit," I said under my breath as I finally hopped off the campus bus a block away from Spotlight Video.

I was late. Again.

Be better than your excuses, Naomi.

I'd made the mistake of stopping at the student union to check and see where I landed in the lottery for Tori Amos tickets. She was coming to Assembly Hall, and I was just dying to see her live. The union was not only out of my way to work, but I had to take a separate bus to get there, only to find out that they weren't posting the numbers until the next day. By the time my second bus showed up, I knew I was going to be at least ten minutes late for my shift.

"Shit, shit, shit," I muttered as I hurried off the bus and

hustled down the block, not even paying attention as my shoulder rammed into another person. A person with rock-hard muscles. A person I saw every day at rehearsals.

"Oh, God, sorry, I—Jamal?"

Jamal Stevenson was my counterpart in the theater program. The Othello to my Desdemona. He was as talented as he was gorgeous. And I felt like an idiot for literally crashing into him on the sidewalk of Green Street.

After the initial impact, Jamal's brow was knitted, but as soon as we locked eyes, his expression relaxed, and he pulled me in for a hug.

"Whoa, Naomi. Where's the fire, girl?" Even as surprised as he was, his voice was gravelly, deep, and steady. In other words, sexy as hell.

I grimaced, and I could feel the heat radiating from my cheeks. "Sorry, my fault. I'm late for work."

"Oh, right. I can't believe you even have time for a job." A dimple formed in his left cheek as he smiled at me, his deep brown eyes even more alluring than when he was reciting Shakespeare's words on the stage.

"I know, but my checking account was in dire straits."

"Ah, I see."

Not wanting to discuss my lackluster finances, I quickly changed the subject. "Where are you off to? I don't usually see you around here."

"I'm meeting some friends at Kam's for happy hour."

"Nice," I said, running my fingers through my hair. For just a second, I imagined myself blowing off work, inviting myself along, and having drinks with Jamal and his friends. My heart jumped just a little bit at the thought. If I was honest with myself, I had a little crush on Jamal. I mean…the man was built like a God and had the cocky grin of the boy next door. He was the best actor in the program, hence his role as Othello. "Well, have a shot of tequila for me. I'll probably be putting pornos back on the shelf all night."

"Well, that sounds like an interesting Wednesday. Maybe *I* should get a job there," he said with a wink.

"Maybe," I said, my voice cracking against my will. I couldn't help it. He was just that beautiful. "See you tomorrow morning for rehearsal?"

"Yep, bright and early."

"Great." I smiled, patting him gently on his bicep and resisting the urge to squeeze his taut muscle before hurrying to the store. Holding my breath as I pushed on the heavy glass door, I realized sneaking in was futile since the bell would alert everyone to my presence anyway. And Ben would inevitably look disappointed in me…yet again.

We hadn't spoken since the night he told me to be better than my excuses. And as much as I wanted to pretend those words didn't hurt me, that I was impervious to his sourpuss attitude, the truth was I couldn't get those words, or him, out of my head. And the last thing I wanted to do was to apologize for being late. Again. But it seemed that would be my fate.

I was all ready to rattle off some joke about *Groundhog's Day* and how every time I was late, it was really all just happening on the same day. Over and over again. I would make him laugh, and he'd stop giving me such a hard time. Hell, maybe we'd even become friends.

Yeah, and monkeys might fly out of my butt.

All ready to set my plan into action, my eyes searched the store, but Ben was nowhere to be found.

"Hey," Marley said from the front desk. She was scanning in videos, and Emmett was organizing them alphabetically. They both smelled like bubble gum. She lowered her voice, "Don't worry, Ben's not here today."

"He isn't? But he always works Wednesday nights."

"Not today. He and Heather switched a couple of their shifts."

"And where's she?" I asked, looking around the almost empty store. "Smoke break?"

"Back room, fighting with her boyfriend."

"Ooh, is he here? I've never seen him."

"No, she's on the phone. He lives in Missouri, remember?"

"Oh, right."

I could never understand long-distance relationships. To me, they were doomed to fail, which is why I promised myself that if I was dating someone when the time finally came for me to leave the Midwest and start my acting career, that I would do it alone. No guy was going to hold me back from my dreams.

"She's saving on those long-distance minutes," Emmett said with a wink.

"Smart." I nodded. "I'm surprised Ben hasn't turned her in to corporate," I said with a smirk, and Emmett shook his head, pressing his lips together in a thin line.

"What?" I asked, making a sour face.

"You're too hard on him. I told you, he's a good guy."

"Yeah, well, you weren't here the other night when he humiliated me."

"What happened?" Marley asked.

"I don't want to talk about it."

"That's convenient," Emmett said before grabbing a stack of videos and walking to the beginning of the new release wall.

"Are you sure you don't want to talk about it?" Marley said, lowering her voice and leaning in closer. I nodded and patted her on the shoulder.

"Thanks, though. How's your day?"

"Well, I was kind of hoping you'd do me a favor."

"What's that?"

She pulled out the list of overdue videos and handed it to me. "Second one down."

"Yeah, the guy has three late pornos. So what? Just leave a message on the machine. It's not a big deal, we do it every day."

"I can't. Not with this guy."

"Why not? Ex-boyfriend?"

"How did you know? I broke up with him a year ago, and I don't want to sound conceited or anything, but I don't think he's over me. He'd be so embarrassed if I made that call."

"Well, not embarrassed enough to avoid renting porn at the place where you work. You'd think he'd just return them on time to avoid the shame of the call."

I looked down at the paper and read the title aloud, trying hard to hold in my laughter, knowing there were customers in the store, "*The Whore of the Rings* 1, 2, *and* 3?

Geez, he really went for it, huh? I mean that's a whole trilogy of hobbit sex."

"Naomi."

"I wonder how big Gandalf's *staff* is." I cracked myself up, throwing my head back in laughter. But Marley didn't even crack a smile.

"Get it? His *staff*? Come on, Marley, that's gold. There aren't even *real* movies for those books yet—which is a shame, by the way—"

"Naomi." Annoyance was plastered across her normally sweet face, and I knew it was time to stop.

"Sorry." I clenched my teeth, still amused by the guy's taste in porn. And a little impressed with the movie studio if I was honest.

"Okay. So, will you call him? Please?"

"Marley, doesn't he know you work here?"

"Guess not. I've never seen him in the store."

"Fine. But this is the first *and* last time. Next time that hobbit rents a bunch of porn and forgets to return it, you're calling him. No ifs, ands, or buts."

"Thank you."

"Not so fast. In exchange, if Heather asks, I was here right on time. Five o'clock on the dot."

"Fine, okay," she said, but she wrinkled her nose, and I knew immediately that she'd just ask Emmett or Sully to make the call for her. I'd come to learn that Marley bribed others in the store to return tapes to the pink room so that she wouldn't have to do it. She kept Emmett stocked in Bubble Tape, which explained why they always smelled exactly the same. Sully was a little harder to please and demanded she bake for him. Since Marley had grown up in Evanston and still lived in her parents' fancy condo, she had access to a gourmet kitchen and brought him brownies, cookies, and cupcakes every single week. Dutch quickly caught on to Sully's method and started demanding baked goods from her as well, even though he loved going to the pink room whenever possible. And Marley acquiesced. Anything to avoid the dreaded porn.

I, myself, had gotten desensitized to our adult materials over the past month. I had a system for the pink room. I alphabetized the titles and kept my focus on finding each one's location. As soon as the final tape was tucked behind its display box, I got the hell out of there and didn't look back. I returned videos to that room once per shift so no one would give me a hard time. And if Dutch was working the same shift, I just passed them to him with a wink and a smile. He thanked me every time like I was doing *him* the favor. No cupcakes or bubble gum necessary.

Unfortunately, Dutch and I weren't always on the schedule together…and I was sure there were plenty of pornos in the box.

"When'd you get here, New Girl?" Sully asked as he approached the counter.

"I've been here a while, right, Marley?"

"Yep," Marley said, her cheeks bright red. "Five o'clock. Right on time."

"That's a first," Sully scoffed before playfully nudging my forearm.

"You know I've been working here for over a month, *Bryan,*" I said, enjoying using his first name. I figured if he could give me a nickname, then I could do the opposite by ignoring his.

"Sully."

"Right." I closed my eyes tight, pretending to have forgotten. "I'm not sure 'New Girl' really fits anymore. Maybe you should come up with something new...or here's a thought, maybe just call me Naomi."

I gave him a playful wink. Sully and I got off to a rocky start on my first day, but since then, we'd found common ground and could stand to be around each other. He challenged my movie picks more than anyone in the store, and I kind of liked that. I gave him shit right back, of course. You could say we had an accord.

Sully narrowed his eyes at me while taking a long pause. When I raised my eyebrows and tilted my head forward, urging him to respond, he finally shook his head and said, "Nah."

"Alrighty then," I said in my best Ace Ventura voice.

Sully raised one eyebrow, pointing at me dramatically as he rested the other elbow on the counter. "Ace."

"What?"

"That's your new nickname. Ace."

"My impression wasn't *that* good."

"Good enough. I mean...I *could* call you Gandalf if you prefer." Sully tilted his head to the side.

"You heard that, huh?"

"Of course, I did. This place is the size of a shoebox."

"I mean...it was funny."

"It was. I'll give you that. So, I'll be nice and let you choose."

"Between Ace and Gandalf? You've got to be kidding."

"Nope. Dead serious."

"Fine." I threw my hands up in the air and decided to take control of the situation. "Gandalf it is."

"Wait. What? Gandalf? Really?" Sully lit up like a Christmas tree. Obviously, I impressed him with my devil-may-care attitude.

"Go big or go home, right?" I shrugged.

"You realize you'll have to explain your little wizard dick joke to everyone who asks, don't you?"

"I'm not embarrassed."

"I'll give you five bucks every time you can tell that story with a straight face."

"Are you sure you want to make that deal?" Marley asked just as Emmett returned to the desk. "She *is* a theater major."

"Oooh, that's right," Sully said, nodding as he rubbed his chin between his thumb and forefinger. "Just a dollar then."

"Cheapskate."

"Hey, man, I'm a poor college student. I eat ramen every single night."

"Because you *love* ramen," Emmett said, shaking his head. "You've already gone through two hot plates since I've known you."

Emmett and Sully had been roommates since arriving on campus the year before. An odd pairing for sure, but it seemed to work for them. I think if my roommate worked at Spotlight Video, I might have to kill her. But that was a whole different story and one I wasn't interested in telling.

"You're not supposed to have hot plates in the dorms, you

know," I said with raised eyebrows, pretending to care one iota about dorm rules. I didn't. I just liked giving Sully crap.

"Ask me if I care," Sully scoffed.

"All right, all right," our boss, Heather, said as she approached the desk. Heather was a tall and slim thirty-something with a blonde pixie haircut. She wore her bangs pulled back with a barrette and was always wearing concert t-shirts under overalls. Heather was adorable and much more tolerant of her employees than the assistant manager, who shall remain nameless.

She tapped her fingernails on the counter as she eyed each of us. "There is way too much to do for you guys to just be standing around talking. Emmett, there's a customer who needs help renting a video game console. Show her how to do that, please."

"You got it." Emmett turned and walked to the video game corner of the store.

"Marley, the children's department is a disaster. Please organize the titles because they're all out of order. I think some of Dutch's friends messed with the tapes last night. Little shits."

"You should ban them from the store," Sully said.

"I wish." She shook her head. "Oh and, Marley, just to be safe, make sure those little fuckers didn't slip a porno in with the Disney movies. We cannot have that happen again—we'll end up on the news or something."

"Really? They did that."

"I can't prove it was them, but yeah. It was a few months ago. I think Dutch's friends had a little too much fun killing time while he was closing the store. Therefore, he's currently on my shit list. But Ben has a soft spot for him, so there you go."

"A soft spot? Ben?" I asked, regretting it immediately when Heather tilted her head to the side in confusion.

"Yeah, why?"

"Oh, um...nothing." The truth was I couldn't imagine Ben having a soft spot for anyone, considering how annoyed I seemed to make him.

"Naomi, man the desk, please. And when a girl named Jennifer comes in, send her to the back room. She should be here soon."

"New employee?"

"Hopefully. If her interview goes well—I need more people for the holidays since so many of you are going home."

"True," I said, scrunching my nose. "Sorry."

She shrugged. "Par for the course. We're a campus store, I'm used to it." Heather turned to walk back, then stopped in her tracks.

"Bryan."

"Sully," he corrected her with an elongated blink.

"Whatever." She rolled her eyes. "Clean the bathrooms, please."

"Ugh." Sully threw his head back in disgust. "Again?"

"But you do such a good job," she said with a wink. "Thanks a bunch!"

"Grrrrrr," Sully said, baring his teeth at Heather, who ignored him completely, returning to the back room.

"Sorry, Sully," I said. "One of these days, I'll switch with you."

"Really?" he asked, looking hopeful. "You'll clean the bathrooms while I man the desk?"

"Hmmm," I said, tapping my chin. "On second thought...no."

He shook his head and sighed loudly. "Pain in the ass," he muttered before walking to the supply closet to grab the gloves and bleach.

Holding back my laughter, I walked to the return bin and started pulling tapes out to scan them in. The bell above the door rang and I heard a soft voice say, "Excuse me."

I popped up, and with a smile, I greeted her. "Hey, welcome to Spotlight Video. What can I do for ya?"

The girl was petite with dark brown hair pulled into a braid, a simple nose ring, and deep brown eyes. She was adorable. "I have an interview with Heather."

"Oh, right. You must be Jennifer."

"Jenn," she said. "With two Ns."

"Got it. Nice to meet you. If you head straight toward the new releases, you'll find her in the back room. Second door on your left."

"Thanks."

But then she didn't move. She bit down on her bottom lip and stared at me. For just a moment, I paused and waited for her to say something else. She didn't.

"Is there something else I can do for you?"

"No, um...yeah, I guess. Is, um..." she looked around, pulling on her braid as she glanced around the store. "Is Ben here?"

"Ben? Assistant Manager Ben?"

She lit up, and for reasons unknown, I was overcome with feelings of irritation.

"Yeah," she said, "I met him last week, and he suggested I apply. I just wanted to, um…thank him for getting me the interview." Her face was so bright, so full of hope and enthusiasm.

It made me sick.

"Oh," I said. "Well, you can thank him yourself when you get the job."

Her face dropped, and I realized that I sounded bitchier than I'd intended.

"Because you will," I said with a fake smile, and Jenn with two Ns smiled in relief.

"Here's hoping," she said as she crossed her fingers and walked toward the back room.

I stood and watched her walk away, wondering why the hell I was so bothered by her presence. Why I hated hearing Ben's name come out of her mouth. Why I suddenly wanted to march to the back room and tell Heather not to hire her. And wondering why the hell I couldn't get Ben's hostile, yet somehow sage-like words out of my head. Like a bad cassette recording, I heard his voice over and over again: *Be better than your excuses, Naomi.*

Ugh, I said to the Ben inside my head, *shut up already!*

But, he didn't. He only got louder.

CHAPTER 4

Ben

"*O*h, my Gooooooddddd!"

Just as I was placing a *Barney* video back on a shelf in the children's section, I heard a girl outside the store shrieking in terror.

"Booyah!" Sully yelled, throwing both of his hands up in the air. "She never saw it coming!"

Dutch and Sully were total opposites and didn't get along most of the time. But every once in a while, they teamed up to play pranks on other employees, and sometimes, customers. They thought it was hilarious to scare the customers returning videos to the slot. Dutch would sit next to the return bin waiting for Sully to nod when a customer approached. And when he did, Dutch would extend his arm into the bin, grab the tape, and freak out the customer on the other side of the glass.

"Sorry, Ben, it's just..." Sully began but was laughing so hard he couldn't speak clearly. He held on to the counter to try to catch his breath.

"It's too freaking hilarious," Dutch said, hopping up from the floor and giving Sully a high five. "They never see it coming, man. Never."

"We can't resist," Sully said, his face red like a fire hydrant.

"Try," I said, shaking my head.

"Who's coming in tonight?" Sully asked, attempting to change the subject. As he struggled to catch his breath, he bent down to check the paper calendar that hung next to the video sensors, away from customer view. "I have a psych paper due tomorrow. Totally forgot, so I... kinda need to get out of here early."

"I didn't know you were taking psych. Do you even have a textbook?" Emmett teased from one of the registers.

"No. Textbooks are for suckers. I learn intuitively." Sully shook his head.

"What the hell does that mean?" I asked.

"It means he flies by the seat of his pants," Emmett said, shaking his head.

"Hey, psych isn't my major, so I don't really give a rat's ass. And I go to class and pay attention. I don't have your memory, Polaroid, but I do just fine."

"What *is* your major, Sully?" I asked, realizing I had known him for over a year but had no idea what he was studying or what he was planning to do with his life.

"Script writing."

"Movies?"

"Of course," he said proudly, "I write them, and Emmett directs them. Dream team right here, baby."

"His stuff is good," Emmett said with a nod. "Really good, actually."

"You have to say that—he's standing right there." Dutch laughed, grabbing videos from the bin and scanning them in. "And you're his roommate. That's entrapment."

Everyone paused. I wasn't sure about everyone else, but I was shocked the word entrapment was in Dutch's vocabulary.

"You keep using that word," Emmett said with a Spanish accent, waving one finger in the air. "I do not think it means what you think it means."

"*Princess Bride!*" Dutch yelled with pride in his eyes. "You can't *ever* get one past me."

"Whatever. We both know I can wipe the floor with you. That was an easy one," Sully said, glancing again at the calendar. "Naomi and Jenn are coming in an hour. Maybe I'll call and ask one of them to come in early?" He raised one eyebrow, hoping for my approval.

"Or you could just head out. We'll be fine," I said, knowing that three of us were more than enough people to handle the dinner hour. It was a Tuesday night, and even though it was a new release day, it was one of our slowest nights of the week. I had no idea why Heather insisted on over-staffing every single Tuesday. Maybe in the suburbs, people were lining up on Tuesday nights to rent videos, but in a college town, it was just another weeknight, and I had to find things for the guys to do.

Most of the time, we just ended up talking about movies and giving each other shit.

"Really? You don't care if I leave, like, right now?"

"Nah, we're fine, right, guys?"

Emmett and Dutch nodded.

"Thanks, Ben. By the way, that Jenn girl has got it bad for you."

"Jenn with two Ns," Dutch chimed in before making an exaggerated kissing face.

Morons.

I shook my head. "No, she doesn't. She's just a nice girl."

"Riiiiight." Sully shook his head. "I mean, don't get me wrong, she seems nice, but I'm telling you, the second that girl walks through the door, she's got her eyes on no one but you. And have you seen that nose ring? Dayum, that's hot."

"You keep talking like that and Ben's gonna open up a can of whoop-ass," Emmett said with a smirk.

"Again." Sully scoffed. "Riiiiight."

"I thought you had a psych exam," I said, feeling my cheeks grow hot against my will. I knew Jenn had an innocent crush on me, but I was hoping to avoid talking about it with the guys. She was cute, yes. But not my type at all. "And the rest of you morons need to find something to do."

Dutch tapped his hand against the counter. "No whoop-ass necessary, Emmett. Ben doesn't even like Jenn with two Ns. I'm pretty sure he likes *someone else*."

I knew Dutch was talking about Naomi. Every time she and I had an argument, which was often, he would look at me with knowing eyes like he was some kind of all-knowing love guru or something. I always ignored him. But then again, he also thought Rusted Root's hit *Send Me on My Way* was really called *Simeon the Whale*. Even when I brought in my CD and showed him the actual title and lyrics, he dug in his heels and insisted that it *should* be about a whale and refused to change how he sang along…. Not exactly the brightest bulb in the bunch. But damn, that kid knew his movie quotes.

"Who?" Sully and Emmett asked in unison.

"Jinx," they said again at the same time.

"Double jinx."

"Triple jinx!"

"You guys are ridiculous. I don't *like* anyone. What is this, fifth grade? I feel like we're on an episode of *The Wonder Years*."

"Nah, then we'd say you *'like her,* like her,'" Emmett said with a smile.

"Winnie Cooper she is not," Sully said.

"Dude, can you imagine Winnie Cooper with a nose ring? Holy hell, I'd be all up in her business." Dutch said, scanning in videos as he humped the air.

"Customers, Dutch."

"Sorry, man."

"So, Emmett…" Sully said, tapping his fingers together like Mr. Burns from *The Simpsons*. You always knew when Sully was up to no good. "How's Marley doing?"

Emmett's cheeks turned as pink as the Bubble Tape container peeking out of the front pocket of his jeans. Looking exasperated, he threw his head back, staring up at the ceiling as he shook it back and forth. "I don't like Marley. We're just friends."

"Sure, you are," Sully said. "Is that why you were saying her name in your sleep last night?"

"You're a dead man," Emmett said, glaring at Sully.

"Oh, chill out. She's not here, it's just us. You can keep it real."

"Like I said, we're *just* friends!"

"No way, man. Sorry, not buying it. So…when are you gonna get on that? Marley's cute, and if you don't ask her out, maybe I will," Dutch said, looking all too impressed with himself. He smoothed down the fabric of his ratty Phish t-shirt. "She's got a little bit of a Winnie Cooper thing going on, right?"

The room fell silent, and I'm sure the rest of the guys were doing exactly what I was doing. Trying to imagine sweet, clean-cut Marley with our resident stoner. It was like a puzzle piece that just won't fit no matter how many different ways you try to place it.

"I don't think you're her type," Sully said, scrunching his nose.

Dutch recoiled, looking offended…and offending Dutch was not an easy thing to do. He usually let everything roll off his back. Not this time.

"Whoa. Wait a minute. Why not?" he asked.

"Because she has a *nose*." Sully waved his hand in front of his face and laughed. "And I don't think she's big on patchouli."

"Dude, I just showered yesterday. I'm fresh as a flower."

"Are you sure?"

Dutch paused, his eyes vacant like he really couldn't remember. "Pretty sure."

"This conversation is over. Like Ben said, let's get back to work." Emmett hopped off the register platform and walked around to retrieve a stack of videos.

I didn't really make a habit of paying attention to the different relationship dynamics amongst the employees, so I had always thought Marley and Emmett were simply good friends. But it was obvious to me now that Emmett was way too upset for someone who wasn't vulnerable. And the last thing I wanted was for Dutch and Sully to take advantage of that vulnerability.

"Does he really like her?" Dutch asked, lowering his voice.

Sully started to respond, but I held up my hand, silencing him. "That's his personal business. You guys should really get back to work."

"Yes, Boss," Sully said, "but getting back to our original discussion, you really should let Jenn down easy. Poor girl."

"Sully."

"No, no, hear me out. Starting tomorrow, most of us will be gone. And you'll be working with that girl for *days.*" He glanced again at the calendar, leaving one finger on Black Friday. "Like three days in a row."

Annoyance turned to anger in my gut. "Do you have a point?"

"I'm getting to it, be patient."

"Too late," Dutch said under his breath.

"Enough!" I snapped.

"But, Ben, I was just playing—"

"I'm not talking about this anymore. Jenn is a nice girl and a good employee, so just drop it, Sully. I'm getting really close to writing you up."

Sully's nostrils flared, but he raised his arms in surrender. "Fine. Okay. I'm sorry."

"I thought you had a paper to write."

"I do."

I glanced at the door. "Happy Thanksgiving, we'll see you next week," I said with a dismissive nod. I'd had my fill of Sully for the week. He was a good kid, but he was... a lot to take sometimes.

Sully paused, then nodded in return.

"See ya, guys," he said under his breath before slowly leaving the store.

Emmett stopped near the counter, his chin digging into the stack of videos in his arms with pity written all over his face. "He doesn't mean to be such an ass."

"Yes. He does."

"Okay, fine, but he doesn't mean to take it too far. He just can't help himself."

Before I could respond, the bell rang above the door and Jasper Liu, my best friend *and* one of our best employees, strolled through the door. Surprised to see him, though, I tilted my head.

"Hey. You're not on the schedule."

"Great to see you, too, buddy."

"Sorry. It's...uh, it's been a little crazy around here. What's up?"

"No worries, man. It's always crazy under the spotlight!" Jasper said, tapping his hands against the counter.

"You know it," Dutch said, handing a video to a

customer as she walked toward the door. He then hopped up on the counter, his wool mules tapping against the drawers that housed all the video games. I hated when he did that, he always left scuff marks on the wood. "Plus, Sully was giving him shit about Jenn with two Ns."

"Don't swear, there are customers in the store," I hissed.

"Oh, you mean the crush situation?" Jasper asked, resting one elbow on the counter.

I closed my eyes tight. "Not you, too."

"Sorry, man." Jasper shrugged. "It's so obvious. The girl follows you around like a puppy. Naomi and I were just talking about it the other day."

"Wait," I paused for way too long. "You were?"

Jasper narrowed his eyes. "Yep." He pressed his lips together in a thin line, and I could have sworn he and Dutch exchanged a glance, but I pretended not to see it.

"Anyway, since it's Tuesday, I told Jules I'd pick up a movie. What just came out?" he asked, glancing up at the bulletin board where we listed all of the new and upcoming releases.

Jasper and his girlfriend, Jules, were one of the only couples I could tolerate being around for long periods of time—no baby talk, no PDA. It was nice. And over time, I came to see Jules as my friend and not just Jasper's girl-friend. We'd tried to convince her to work at the store, but she insisted that would be too much time with Jasper. They shared a master's degree program, an apartment, and even a cat. She didn't want to share a part-time job, too.

"Nothing good," Dutch said. "*Little Buddha, Getting Even with Dad* or some shit. No thanks."

"Watch the mouth, Dutch. For real," I said, rolling my eyes and hoping the woman two aisles over wasn't listening closely to our conversation.

"What? You're not a Macaulay Culkin fan?" Jasper said, his voice facetious. "That's shocking."

"You couldn't pay me to watch that, man. I can barely sit through *Home Alone*, but my mom can't get enough of that kid. She makes me watch that freaking movie every year."

"Poor Dutch." Jasper made an over-exaggerated frown. "Your mother makes you watch heartwarming holiday films while you decorate the Christmas tree in your cute little suburban house."

Dutch looked shocked. "Dude. How did you know?"

Jasper shook his head and turned his attention back to me. "You know what part gets me? The ending with the old man and his granddaughter. I'm not ashamed to admit that scene makes me all teary-eyed. Every time, man. Every time."

"It's a good scene," Emmett said, returning to the counter. "Clever use of music, too. Gets you right here." He tapped on the center of his chest.

"You're going to direct, right?" Jasper asked. Jasper was getting his Master of Fine Arts in Stage Design. His dream was to design sets for Broadway shows. And I had no doubt he would achieve all of his goals and then some.

Jasper was special. One of those guys with a magnetic personality. Everyone who knew him loved him. Heather liked to say that Jasper could make friends with a mop. He was just a good guy who was nice to everyone and didn't have a cruel bone in his body. As his boss, I loved how reliable he was. As his friend, though, I appreciated his sharp sense of humor and laid-back nature. We joked that we were yin and yang. I was the serious one, the one who made sure everyone was in line, and Jasper made sure everyone had fun doing it.

"Yep," Emmett said. Everyone in the store knew that Emmett wanted to direct with every fiber of his being. He had dreams. Big ones.

"Stage or screen?" Jasper asked.

"Screen."

"He wants to be Spielberg," I said

"Not Scorcese? Or Tim Burton?" Jasper asked. "I could see you doing something with an edge."

"Nah."

Jasper shook his head. "I mean, c'mon…*Beetlejuice, Edward Scissorhands*. Burton's gotta be one of the most underrated directors in Hollywood, don't you think?"

Emmett shook his head. "He's good, don't get me wrong. And so is Scorcese. But, they're not the best. I want to be the best."

"No pressure," Dutch said with a laugh.

"You've got to believe in greatness if you're ever going to achieve it. I believe in greatness," Emmett said before heading to the nearest register and calling over the next customer.

"That kid is headed for big things, I can feel it," Jasper said.

"I agree."

Jasper glanced at his watch. "I'd better find a movie; I

ordered a pizza next door, and it's probably ready by now. Any suggestions on what to get, Ben?"

"Nothing comes to mind. Check the picks wall."

"Good call. I should update my picks anyway...and I know just what to put on my shelf."

"*Home Alone?*"

"You know it."

"Oh, by the way," Jasper said, pointing toward our monitor for the adult room. "Those girls have been back there the whole time I've been standing here. Might want to keep an eye on them."

"Got it."

And that's exactly what I did for the next forty-five minutes. The girls wandered the room, studying all of the adult videos. Dutch and Emmett joined in, and before I knew it, we were completely engrossed in why these girls were spending so much time in our adult video room and were ignoring the rest of the store. Jasper left at some point, but I couldn't tell you when. I was obsessed with the four girls in the porn room.

"What are you guys doing?" a familiar voice asked as we were huddled around the small monitor.

Naomi.

The three of us turned to see her standing with hands on hips and one eyebrow raised. "What's going on in the pink room? Why are you staring like that?"

The bell above the door rang and Jenn walked in, saying hi to everyone. Naomi didn't budge.

"There are these girls back there...they've been back there for almost an hour," Emmett said.

"So?"

"So, it's weird."

"Why?"

"Only guys go back there most of the time," Dutch said with a shrug.

"So, women can't watch porn?" She crossed her arms in front of her chest.

"No, they can…we're just not used to it. And they've been back there for a *long* time."

"Maybe they're looking for something specific…something unusual."

"Are you speaking from experience?" I challenged her. Even though she didn't bribe people to take videos back like Marley did, she was probably the fastest person in the store when it came to returning videos back there. So, I highly doubted that Naomi was a pornography aficionado.

"Maybe," she shot back. "I'm just saying they have a right to be back there…and to rent whatever they want."

"It is weird, though," Jenn said. "I mean…maybe they're waiting back there to make guys uncomfortable."

"Nah. Guys have come and gone, they don't seem to notice," Emmett said.

"Whatever," Naomi said. "I say leave them alone. They'll pick something eventually."

"Did you get tickets? For Tori?" Emmett asked Naomi. She was a huge fan of Tori Amos and was hoping to get tickets for a small show in the campus's smallest concert hall. According to Naomi, it would just be Tori and her piano. Nothing else. I wasn't a fan, so I didn't really understand the significance of that, but she seemed really excited about it.

"I did. Good ones, too. I was number thirty-six in the lottery."

"Nice," Emmett said.

"Oh, that reminds me, Ben...I can't work a week from Saturday. Can you not put me on the schedule? That's the night of the concert."

"Sure, no problem."

"Thanks," she said with a grateful smile. And I was equally grateful to not feel uncomfortable tension looming between us. Maybe we could finally get past the picks wall/corner night after all. Maybe we could even become friends.

Stranger things have happened.

"And..." she clenched her teeth, "maybe not the next morning either?"

With an elongated blink, I tilted my head to the side. "Anything else?"

"Nope."

"Do me a favor and write it on a Post-It and put it on the calendar so I don't miss it."

"You got it."

"Excuse me," a voice said from the other side of the counter. Dutch and Emmett turned to stare at me. It was the girls from the back room.

"What can I do for you?" I asked as I gestured for all of my employees to scatter. Jenn and Emmett went straight for the return box while Naomi and Dutch moved over to the other registers.

"We're um..." Her cheeks were as red as tomatoes. "We're looking for a certain kind of movie...."

"We know," Dutch said. Naomi nudged him in the arm before giving the girl an awkward smile.

"Maybe I can help?" I asked.

"It's, um…well it's not really PC to say, but um…we're looking for little people videos…that you'd find in the back room…"

"Midget porn?" Dutch said.

"Dutch!" Naomi and I snapped at the same time. Dutch put his arms up in surrender. "Sorry, little dude porn?"

"We heard there's a *Snow White*-themed one, but it's never on the shelf when we come in."

"We can't keep it in stock," I said simply. And it was true. That video was always rented out, and it was one of the top movies we had to call customers about to ask them to return. Heather was looking into requesting a second copy from corporate since it was so popular.

Dutch bust out laughing, covering his face with his hands and turning away from us.

"Can we get on a waiting list or something?" one of the girls asked, looking eager.

"No, I'm sorry, we don't do that."

"You could try a different store," Naomi said.

"Blockbuster doesn't have adult tapes, and they're the only other video store near campus."

"Maybe we could leave our phone number…and you could call us when it comes in?" the original girl asked, tilting her head to the side and biting down on her lower lip—like that was going to influence me. She was cute, don't get me wrong…but I wasn't someone who easily manipulated by flirtatious behavior.

"You can write it down, but I can't promise anything. Like I said, it's really popular."

Naomi passed her a Post-It note and pen, and the girl jotted down her information and handed it back to me. "Thanks."

"Yep. Sorry we couldn't accommodate you guys."

"Some other time," she said with a flirtatious smile. "Come on, girls."

And with that, the four of them left the store, and as soon as they were out of sight, I crumpled up the Post-It and tossed it in the trash.

"Are you crazy?" Dutch said with wide eyes before grabbing the crumpled pink paper. "Those girls were hot. *And* they watch porn."

"Women of your dreams, huh?" I asked, shaking my head.

"Um...yeah!" He shoved the paper into the pocket of his brown corduroys.

"They're all yours, Dutch. All yours."

Naomi and I caught a glimpse of one another, and for the shortest second, I thought I saw relief on her face. About what, though, I couldn't be sure.

But a little piece of me thought I knew.

And her relief made me smile.

Just a little bit. I couldn't be too careful. Dutch was on to me.

CHAPTER 5

Naomi

"Which one do you like better?" My roommate, Sarah, asked, holding up two different plaid flannel shirts from her closet. They were both cute and perfectly in style, and no matter which one she chose, she'd look great.

"What tank top are you wearing?"

"This one," she said, looking slightly annoyed as she pointed to the skintight, white, fitted camisole already on her body. If I was considered dramatic—which I most definitely was—then Sarah was sure to win an Oscar by the time she turned twenty.

"Okay, okay, in that case..." I studied the two options. "The red and brown. Brings out your eyes." Sarah had deep brown eyes that contrasted her golden blonde hair. It was definitely the right choice for her coloring.

She turned back to the mirror, tilting her head to the side. "Are you sure?"

Now it was my turn to be annoyed as this was Sarah's M.O. She'd ask me for my opinion and, almost always, she'd do the exact opposite. It was infuriating. "Why did you even ask me?"

"Ugh, fine, I'll wear that one." Sarah flipped her hair behind her and tossed the blue and green flannel onto the bed. "Thanks for coming with me, by the way. I don't know that many people yet."

Sarah had pledged a coed service fraternity, Alpha Phi Omega, and had just been formally initiated into the organization as a member. That night, they were celebrating all of their new members with a kegger. When Sarah had first told me she was joining APO, I was surprised—she didn't exactly seem like a selfless person, and I couldn't imagine that she was chomping at the bit to volunteer on a regular basis. There had to be more to it. So, I asked her lots of questions, grilling her at every turn to try and find out her true motivation for joining such a group. Turns out, I didn't know my roommate all that well, and she actually enjoyed tutoring at the local grade school every single Tuesday while I was at rehearsals.

People are always surprising me.

"No problem," I said, applying mascara to my eyelashes as I stared in the mirror. Sarah plopped herself next to me on my bed. "I spend so much time at rehearsals and the video store, I really only know a handful of people on campus. I should probably fix that."

"You could join APO."

I shrugged. "Maybe. Isn't it kind of time-consuming? Not sure I can balance it all."

"Yeah, it is. Maybe I'll just bring you to all the parties."

"Member by inebriation?" I asked with a wink.

"Exactly."

"We'll see how it goes, and I'll let you know."

"You think they're going to be losers, don't you?"

I clenched my teeth and paused...feeling my cheeks grow hot. "I didn't say that."

"You didn't have to." Sarah looked smug. And for good reason. Truth was, I had my suspicions about those do-gooders.

"I mean...they volunteer on a regular basis...for *fun*."

"And?"

"And..." I paused, licking my lips. "Who does that?"

"Not you, obviously."

"Guilty as charged."

Sarah rolled her eyes. "You're ridiculous. Besides, some of the guys are hot. Like really hot. There's this one guy, Dave Morris. He's a senior, and oh my lord, he's *beyond* gorgeous."

"Will he be there?"

"I sure hope so," she said before eyeing me up and down. "I call dibs."

"Of course," I said, waving her away. "You know I'm not like that."

"I know, it's just...have you *seen* yourself?"

I rolled my eyes. "Oh my God. Stop it."

"I'm totally serious. Everywhere we go, guys follow you around like puppies."

"Not true."

"Really? The guy who swipes our cards downstairs can't even make full eye contact. Poor sap."

"Pete?" A laugh escaped my lips as I thought of the poor shy guy who worked in the dining hall. Sarah was right about the lack of eye contact. Every morning, I'd hand him my card, his cheeks would turn a deep shade of crimson, and he'd swallow hard before handing it back to me, muttering for me to have a good day.

"Exactly. He proves my point."

"No, he doesn't. He's just one guy with a crush."

"Whatever."

"I'm serious, Sarah. You're a beautiful girl, and you have nothing to worry about, okay? I'm not going to take your man."

"Okay." She jumped off the bed and beelined for her make-up bag. "But just in case, I'm upping my game."

"Now, who's ridiculous?"

"Guilty as charged," she said with a wink before covering her lipstick with a brighter shade of red.

* * *

AN HOUR LATER, we'd walked across campus to the house where the party was being held. It was a large but mostly dilapidated house covered in cracking white paint. If we were little kids, we'd be crossing the street to get away from a house like this. But as the music thumped and other college students lined the covered porch or lingered in the dying grass with cigarettes hanging from their fingers, we felt right at home.

A girl with bright red hair and wire-rimmed glasses

jumped from the ledge of the patio and ran to us with wide, excited eyes, an empty plastic cup in her left hand. "Sarah!"

The girl plowed into Sarah, and she stumbled back. Quickly, I steadied her with my hand. "Whoa."

The girl giggled, pushing her glasses back. "Sorry, you're the first pledge to show up. Other than me, of course."

"We aren't pledges anymore, remember?" Sarah said.

"Oh, right," the girl said, smacking herself playfully in the head before raising her right hand near her face. "Hey, I'm Presley."

"You mean...as in Elvis?" I blurted out.

I really have to stop doing that.

She laughed. "I prefer to think of myself as a Priscilla, but yes. My parents are obsessed...and I was actually born the day he died."

"Ew! Morbid much?" Sarah said, wincing.

"At least it's an ice breaker, right?" I said through clenched teeth. "I mean, how many people can say that about their namesake?"

"Good point," Presley said with a nod. "I like you."

"Oh, this is my roommate, Naomi. She's a freshman, too."

"Are you going to pledge next semester?" Presley asked.

"I'm working on her."

"You should. Lots of hotties."

"That's what I hear."

She linked arms with Sarah and me and led us toward

the house. "C'mon, all the best-looking guys are by the keg. You guys need a drink. And *I* need a refill."

"Lead the way, girl."

When we reached the keg, I had to admit that Presley had a point...as did Sarah. Three impressively good-looking guys manned the keg. One had a bright blue t-shirt over his other clothes. He was tall with blond hair and strong cheekbones. I wanted to swim in his stormy blue eyes.

"What's that all about?" I asked him as I waited for my beer, pointing toward his t-shirt.

"Sober patrol."

"I'm sorry?"

"The t-shirt. It means I'm on sober patrol."

I raised both eyebrows. "I don't know what that means."

"You don't?" the guy asked incredulously. "How did you get initiated?"

"She didn't," Sarah corrected him. "She's my roommate."

"We're trying to get her to pledge."

"Ahh, I see," he said as his dark-haired friend placed a clear plastic cup in my hand. The head on the beer was perfect—not too tall, not too short. It was just right. "Members take turns at parties making sure no one gets too hammered and ends up in the hospital. We also give rides or walk people home."

"You guys really are saints, aren't you?" I asked, finding myself flirting with the sober blond.

"I wouldn't say that," the dark-haired guy said. "But

alcohol poisoning can get us shut down. We prefer to keep everyone alive."

"Sounds reasonable."

"I'm Jeff," the dark-haired guy said before gesturing toward the blue-eyed, sober one. "And he's Mark."

"Pleasure," I said. "Thanks for the beer."

"Anytime," Jeff said as I turned and walked toward the house. Sarah followed close behind me, pinching my arm as she leaned in.

"What are you doing?" she hissed. "Jeff never talks to anyone. Go back and talk to him."

"Why?"

"Ummm...because he's gorgeous," Presley said, rolling her eyes.

"Not my type."

"Are you blind?"

"Nope. But the blond...now he's another story."

"Mark. Go talk to him."

"Girls, the night is young. Besides, I told you I'd be your wing woman," I said, nodding toward Sarah as I took a sip of my beer and looked back at Mark. He tipped his forehead up and gave me a cocky grin.

"Wing woman? What did I miss?" Presley asked, and I pressed my eyes tight.

Shit. Maybe I wasn't supposed to say that.

"Nothing," Sarah said, shaking her head.

"I just mean..." I said, trying to cover my tracks, "that this is Sarah's thing. I want to help *her* hook up, not the other way around."

Presley looked convinced. "Makes sense." She scanned the crowd, arching up on her tiptoes to see better. "You know who's super cute? Dave Morris. I hope he's here tonight."

Sarah tipped her head back and chugged the rest of her beer. I knew immediately what that meant—she didn't want to fight over a guy. Did I think she was just as cute as Presley and therefore had just as good of a chance with this infamous Dave? Yes, of course. But in the short time I'd been her roommate, I could see that self-confidence was not Sarah's strong suit. And she had no interest in vying for his attention if Presley would be doing the same. I attempted to steer Presley in another way.

"Jeff was looking at you, ya know."

Her eyes widened in amazement. "Shut up!"

"I'm not kidding," I said, lying through my teeth while looking back at Jeff. He raised a cup to me, and Presley gasped.

"He's never paid attention to me. Like ever. I think I have a better chance with Dave."

"Your call," I said before taking another sip of my beer and grabbing Sarah's cup from her hand, placing it in Presley's palm. "But I think you should get Sarah a refill... maybe give him a chance to make his move."

"Naomi—" Sarah began, but I ignored her, staying laser-focused on Presley.

With a decisive nod, I patted her on the back. "Go get him, girl."

Presley giggled again and walked quickly back to the guys at the keg. Jeff gave her a polite smile and filled her cup as she tucked her curly hair behind her ear and tilted one hip to the side.

Work it, Elvis.

"You didn't have to do that," Sarah said, sounding defeated.

"Yes, I did." I smiled. "Wing woman, remember?"

She shook her head and crossed her arms. "I can't compete with her. I mean, look at her confidence."

"Maybe we should do a lap around the party and see if we see this infamous Mr. Morris. Then I'll be happy to tell you if I agree. And you know I'm honest to a fault."

"How do I know that? I've lived with you for, like, three months or so."

"And have I ever lied to you in that time?"

"No…not that I know of."

"Exactly," I said with a nonchalant shrug of one shoulder. "Like I said, honest to a fault."

"Fine. Whatever, let's do a damn lap."

I placed my almost full cup in her hand and gave her a wink when her dark eyes looked confused. "Liquid courage."

"Right," she said with a weak smile before taking three large gulps.

"Better?"

"Getting there." She took a deep breath. "Okay, let's go inside."

"Hey, wait up!" Presley called from behind us, and I could hear her approach as we rounded the side of the house and faced the steps that lead to the porch. "Here." She placed another full beer in Sarah's hand, and Sarah passed my drink back to me.

"Thanks," we said in unenthusiastic unison. "We're, uh…going inside. See who else is here."

"Cool. I'll come with you."

Sarah and I exchanged an awkward glance, and Sarah sighed as we followed a few other partygoers into the house. The staircase split and we followed the music into the basement where a DJ was set up in the corner, and black lights glowed in the dark space. Dozens of people danced with glow sticks around their necks as The Beastie Boys blasted through the speakers.

"Hey, ladies, picture?" a forty-something man asked, gesturing for us to lean in. His camera flashed, and he smiled and walked away toward another group.

"You guys hire a professional photographer?"

"Um…is this your first frat party?"

"Kinda."

"Everyone hires photogs. They take our picture and then, in a week or so, he'll drop off the proofs at our office in the union."

"You guys have an office there?"

"Yep, on the student activities floor."

"That's pretty cool," I said. "So can you buy that picture of us?"

"If I like it, yeah. He charges us, like, two bucks per print."

"And they're super cute; they have our Greek letters and the party date on them," Presley added as she bobbed her head to the music and glanced around the room, an obvious determination in her green eyes. Presley was on the prowl.

"Buy me a copy of the one he took, okay? I'll pay you back."

"No need, wing woman," Sarah said with a playful wink. I could hear the relaxation in her voice and knew that the couple of beers she'd guzzled down were starting to have an effect. Glancing at her cup, I realized it was already gone. She squeezed my forearm, and her breath caught.

"That's him," she said softly, and I followed her gaze to a guy with light brown, floppy hair that hung on each side. He was talking with a petite blonde.

"He looks just like Hugh Grant," I said.

"Who?"

"*Four Weddings and a Funeral*," I reminded her.

"Is that a movie?"

"You haven't seen it?" My words were incredulous. *Four Weddings and a Funeral* was my current favorite romantic comedy. Hugh Grant's self-deprecating charm was captivating, and I'd made each of my high school friends go with me to the theater to see it.

I wasn't ashamed to admit that I'd seen it six times.

"I'll rent a copy and make you watch it."

"Okay, fine, whatever," Sarah said before grabbing my beer from my hand and draining the cup. "What do I do?"

"Oooh, there's Dave. Who's he's talking to?" Presley asked, still oblivious to the fact that she and Sarah were interested in the same guy.

"Katie Kramer," Sarah deadpanned. "She's going to run for pledge trainer next semester."

I leaned in close so Presley couldn't hear me and whispered into Sarah's ear. "She's got nothing on you."

Sarah cracked a smile, but then she looked at Presley. Without skipping a beat, I added, "And neither does she. Honest."

I nudged her arm gently, and she sighed.

"To a fault?" she asked, her eyes searching for validation.

"I don't know any other way, my friend."

"Naomi?" I turned to the sound of a familiar voice. And my eyes lit up when I realized it was Jasper, one of my favorite Spotlight Video coworkers.

"Jasper? What are you doing here?"

"Are you kidding? These are my people."

"Really?"

He nodded decisively. "What are *you* doing here? I think I would have noticed if you pledged."

"You're right, I didn't. I'm here with Sarah Evans." I nodded toward Sarah. "She's my roommate."

"Very cool," Jasper said, "'Sup, ladies?"

"Let's go outside and get another beer," Presley said to Sarah, pulling on her arm.

"There's another keg down here," Jasper said, turning his body and pointing to the far corner of the basement.

"Oh, cool. Thanks, Jasper."

"You bet."

They disappeared into the crowd just as a tall girl with curly brown hair approached. "Hey, babe. This is Naomi from the store. Naomi, this is Jules—my girlfriend."

"Great to meet you."

"So, *you're* the famous Naomi," Jules said with a smirk, and I wasn't sure how to take it. Her agreeable voice didn't match her narrowed eyes.

"Jules—" Jasper's face tensed, and he shook his head.

"What? I didn't mean it like *that*," she said with a defensive laugh before running her fingers through her hair, looking like she'd been caught with her hand in the cookie jar.

"Famous? What does *that* mean?"

"Sounds like someone needs to be cut off," Jasper said, reaching for Jules's cup. She quickly stepped aside and pounded the rest of her drink.

I had to respect her tenacity.

"No, I don't!" Jules protested, wiping her mouth with the back of her hand.

He interrupted, "Don't listen to her, Naomi. She's had a few too many."

"Still...what did you *mean*?" I glared at Jules.

"I told her that you're going to make it big in Los Angeles...or New York. That's all," Jasper said, but his expression was conflicted. He was lying to me. Not only was I honest to a fault, but my mom always told me I was a human lie detector. I could smell bullshit from ten yards away.

I rolled my eyes. "Yeah, me and half the campus. Most of us want to be famous, don't we? That's why we go to this school."

"Not everyone has to be in the spotlight," Jules corrected. "Jasper and I are going to design sets."

"Right. And that's awesome. But your dream is to do it on Broadway, right?" I asked, tipping my head forward in annoyance.

"Right." Her expression was vacant.

"In *New York*. That's a really big deal. But how is that any different? We both want to be a part of something. Something big."

"Oh...right. But we'll be behind the scenes, not up on

the stage soaking in all the attention. There's a difference."
Jules shrugged. I realized right then that I liked Jasper and
disliked Jules in equal measure.

"If you say so," I said, resisting the urge to roll my eyes
again.

"I should probably find Sarah."

Jasper pressed his lips into a thin line. "Right. Have
fun."

Making my way through the crowd, I was drawn to
the noisy corner just past the line for the keg. A crowd
had gathered around a ping pong table and plastic cups
lined each side. I smiled, knowing that game anywhere. I
hadn't played beer pong since the spring, but I was pretty
damn good at it.

But apparently, my roommate was not.

I watched as a brown-haired guy repeatedly nailed
every shot he took, forcing Sarah to chug cup after cup.
From my vantage point, I couldn't see his face, and I had
no idea if Sarah had even made him consume a drop of
beer. But mentally, I was adding up the drinks that Sarah
had already had that night, and it made me pause...hoping
she wasn't going to end up puking in our room all night.
She'd told me weeks prior that she had a really low tolerance, and after this game of beer pong, I knew I was going
to have to cut her off. Even if she fought me on it.

Sarah held on to the table, laughing hysterically after
accidentally spilling some of the beer down her shirt.
That's when I heard his voice. And everything came to a
screeching halt as I stared at him, wide-eyed in disbelief.

What in the hell is he *doing here?*

"Maybe we should let someone else play. You look like

you could use a break," he said, rounding the corner of the table and placing a hand on her shoulder.

Ben. Mother fucking Buzzkill Ben was playing my roommate in beer pong. And winning.

What crazy universe had I wandered into?

"Nooooooo," Sarah slurred. "I'm fiiiiiine."

"Well, I'm gonna take a break. I'll get you some water," he said. "Don't move, okay?"

She nodded, and Ben nodded to a friend to take his place at the table. Presley took Sarah's place, and within seconds, the cups were refilled and a new game had begun.

"Naomi?" he said, his eyes meeting mine. "What are you doing here?"

"That's my roommate. She pledged this frat. What are *you* doing here?"

"This is my house. I live here."

"What?" I asked in disbelief.

Buzzkill Ben lived at the party house? Not possible.

"I mean, I do have a life outside the store." He scratched the back of his neck. "I'm going to the kitchen to get your roommate a bottle of water."

"I'll come with you."

I don't know why I followed him through the crowd instead of staying behind to keep an eye on Sarah. Maybe it was because I was realizing there was more to Ben than correcting my every move at work. Maybe I was just a little bit curious to know what he was actually like outside of the store. What he was like in real life.

"So wait, you're, like, a student here?"

"Why do you seem so shocked?"

"Well, I mean...Sully, Emmett, and all the guys talk about their classes all the time. You never do."

He shrugged as we climbed the stairs, the music still thumping behind us. "I guess I just don't have a lot to say about it when I'm there. I'm focused on work."

"What year are you? You're obviously not a freshman or you'd be in the dorms like me."

"Senior."

"Major?"

"Visual effects and motion graphics."

"For real?" I asked as we entered the relatively quiet kitchen where only a couple of people lingered near the fridge. It was at least ten degrees cooler in here than in the jam-packed basement.

"Excuse me, guys," Ben said, reaching in to grab a plastic bottle of Evian. He closed the fridge and turned to face me, licking his bottom lip before speaking. "Why do you sound so surprised?"

"I don't know...that's like special effects for *movies*."

He laughed, shaking his head. "I'm aware."

"Well, yeah, sorry. Of course, you are." My eyes were wide as I stared at him in wonder. This wasn't the Ben I knew. He was...different.

"I dare say you seem impressed, Naomi."

"I mean...yeah, I kind of am. Here I was thinking you were going to be an accountant or something."

"Hey, my dad's an accountant. It's a good job."

"Sorry, but you know what I mean. You're just so business-like all the time."

Ben shook his head. "When I'm at *work*."

He had a point. I'd never seen Ben outside of the video

store. I had to admit to myself that I knew basically nothing about the guy outside of that setting. Hell, I didn't even know his major.

"So, you live here?"

"Yeah. I have five roommates."

"Five? Ugh."

"So, one of your roommates must be in the frat, then?"

"No. We all are."

"Wait. You're in this service fraternity thing?" The question came out a little more shrill than I'd meant it to. I winced at the sound of my own voice.

"Again, why are you so surprised?" he asked with an awkward laugh as I followed him down the stairs and back into the sweaty crowd.

"I don't know, just ignore me, I guess."

We rounded the corner and found Presley still battling it out against her latest opponent, but Sarah was nowhere to be found. I pushed my way through the crowd and yelled to Presley.

"Where's Sarah?"

"No idea. I've been a little busy," she yelled back, looking annoyed as a ball plopped right into the full cup closest to her hand. The crowd cheered as she chugged. "I'm getting my ass kicked."

"Fine, whatever, I'll find her."

Ben was still scanning the basement when I reached him. "She must have gone outside or something. She's pretty drunk, though, I need to find her."

Ben nodded then gestured for us to keep walking toward the stairs. But it was then that I saw her, leaning against the wall in a dark corner, a tall guy's mouth attached to her neck. Normally, I would walk the other way, not wanting to cock block my roommate, but something didn't feel right when I noticed how forcefully he was pressing her into the concrete wall and how her feet were moving beneath her as if she was trying to slip out of his grasp but lacked the strength to do it.

"Do you know him?" I asked Ben.

"Not sure, we need to get closer."

We walked closer to Sarah and observed them for a minute or two. Sarah could barely keep her eyes open as the guy's hands wandered under her shirt.

"Who is he, Ben?"

"Honestly, I don't know."

"She can barely stand up. She's had way too much to drink, and I don't want her to regret this tomorrow."

Standing tall, Ben shook his head. "Don't worry. I'll be right back. Don't let them out of your sight, but don't say anything okay? Just stay there."

"Fine, but be fast, okay? I don't want him trying to take her somewhere in this house."

Ben walked quickly to the stairs, and his silhouette disappeared in seconds. I watched my roommate, seething and unable to follow Ben's directions. Without hesitation, I stalked toward them and tapped the guy on the shoulder. He was easily a foot taller than me, but I didn't care. I wasn't going to back down.

"Hey!" I yelled.

He turned to me, his hands not moving from Sarah's body. Sarah's eyes perked up and she smiled. "Naooooooooommmmmmi. This is my roommate, um...

um…I forgot your name." A small burp left her lips, and she giggled.

The guy's jaw ticked. "Nice to meet you, roommate. Why don't you get us a beer?"

"I think she's had enough, don't you?"

A hand pressed to the small of my back, and a gruff voice echoed into my ear. "I told you not to do anything."

I turned to see Ben and three other guys standing behind him, their arms crossed in front of their chests.

"Hey, man," Ben said to Sarah's groper. "What pledge class are you?"

"What?" the guy said, looking confused.

"Pledge. Class," Ben repeated. "Which one are you?"

"Fall," he answered with a smirk.

"Fall what?"

"Fall…1994, of course."

"Nice try, smart ass. But if you were actually a member, you'd know why that answer's wrong."

"Huh?"

"We name our pledge classes after people. I'm from the John Lennon pledge class and Sarah, here, is from the Oprah Winfrey class."

"So?"

"So, this is a private party. And it's time for *you* to go."

"Dude, whatever. Fuck off."

Ben's nostrils flared as he stepped closer to the creep, tipping his chin up. I swallowed hard as I watched the other guys stepping closer, almost in unison, backing up Ben. The guy paused, ran his fingers through his hair, assessing the situation. He knew he didn't stand a chance against these four guys who were all equal to his size or larger. It was time for him to admit defeat.

"This party's lame-ass," he said, releasing Sarah and walking toward the stairs. Ben and all of the guys followed close behind.

Pulling Sarah from the wall, I wrapped my arms around her. "You scared the crap out of me."

"Why?" she asked, her eyes glazed over. "He was nice."

"That piece of shit could have dragged you upstairs or something, Sarah. You're practically unconscious. How much have you had to drink?"

"I lost count." Her words were slurred. "Ben killed me in beer pong."

"Yeah, I saw."

Speak of the devil and he shall appear. Although, if I was honest, Ben was currently more of a guardian angel than a devil.

His eyes were concerned but relaxed, and I knew the dirtbag had left the party and was no longer trying to get into my roommate's pants. "How is she?"

"Ripped out of her mind. I should probably get her home."

"I'll walk you."

"No, you don't have to do that. You've done more than enough already, believe me."

He shook his head and walked to the other side of Sarah, placing an arm around her waist to steady her as he finally placed the bottle of water in her hand. "I insist."

"But we live all the way across campus."

"That's okay."

"But it's like, a really long walk."

"I know. It's okay."

"Ben—" I said, suddenly feeling choked up.

"Yeah?"

I stood for a minute, unsure of what to say. "Thank you."

A satisfied smile crossed his lips, and a shot of adrenaline captured my stomach.

"Don't mention it," he said. "Let's get her home."

CHAPTER 6

Ben

aomi, Sarah, and I walked in silence across campus with nothing but the sounds of pebbles crunching under our feet and sirens in the distance. The cool night air whipped against my neck as we entered the almost empty quad where small groups of students walked back to their dorms and apartments after a night of partying.

"You didn't have to do this, you know," Naomi said, her voice soft and unassuming. She glanced my way, tightening her grip on Sarah's arm. Sarah's eyes drooped, but she managed to keep our pace as we began to cross the courtyard of the quad, heading to the freshman dorm area of campus.

"I know," I answered simply. "I wanted to."

"Thanks for all your help back there. That guy gave me the creeps."

"Same."

"And this one," she gestured toward Sarah, "is in *no* state to give her consent."

"She'll thank you tomorrow," I said, offering Naomi a smile of solidarity. "You looked out for her tonight. Everyone should have a roommate like that."

"I guess." She shrugged before kicking a pebble across the wide walkway. It bounced several times before tumbling into the dry grass. "I think it's pretty cool, though. The frat, I mean. I can't believe I didn't know that you were a member. What are the chances?"

"Pretty small campus...and pretty high membership. I guess we were bound to know some of the same people."

"I guess." She looked off into the distance.

"How, um...how is your play going?"

"Pretty good. I love my co-star, he's really talented, and the rest of the cast is pretty great. There are a couple of upperclassmen who aren't so happy that I got the lead, but there isn't much I can do about that, right?"

"You were the right one for the role."

"I like to think so," she said with a warm smile. "Two more months until opening night. I can't believe it's almost here."

"Are you big into Shakespeare?"

She tilted her head to the side and pressed her lips together as she paused in thought. "Not really, no. But, it's a must for the resume, right? I did *Romeo & Juliet* in high school and *A Midsummer Night's Dream* for this youth theater company during the summer. I liked that one, actually."

"Lord, what fools these mortals be," I said, remembering the famous quote. I wasn't much of a Shakespeare fan, but I did love that play. Naomi's eyes lit up.

"Right." She bit down on her lower lip. "Did you do any acting in high school?"

"Nah. I was more of a jock."

"Really?" she said, blinking rapidly and looking impressed for the second time that night. "What'd you play?"

"Football and track."

"Let me guess...running back?"

I laughed. "How'd you know?"

"Track plus football...seems kind of obvious, right?"

"True."

"Plus, you're not some big, beefy guy like *The Fridge*."

"You know Refrigerator Perry?"

"Number seventy-two, baby." She smiled wide. "I grew up only about an hour away. Illinois girl through and through. And a major Bears fan."

"Seriously? I feel like everyone's from out of state. It's cool to know someone else is from here."

"Yeah, I grew up in Wauconda. Ever hear of it?"

"No, sorry."

"It's fine. It's a far north suburb, a sleepy little beach town. My brothers and sisters and I spent our summers at the beach just running around with all the kids from the neighborhood. My mom's friend said it was like the *Lord of the Flies* every summer. Total chaos."

"Yikes."

"She was exaggerating, Ben."

"You sure? Sounds pretty intense if you ask me."

She ignored my teasing. "What about you? Where'd you grow up? Can't be far since you worked over Thanksgiving instead of going home like the rest of us."

"Des Plaines."

"Not far at all—raised on Da Bears?"

"Um, of course. Walter Payton was my idol."

"Ahh, Sweetness. He's so awesome."

"Hey, remember *The Super Bowl Shuffle?*" I asked, and Naomi's eyes lit up. She opened her mouth and shuffled back and forth, snapping her fingers. Sarah groaned. "Ugh, what are you dooooiiiing?"

"I'm shuffling, girl." Naomi waved Sarah away. "She's from Philly. She doesn't get it."

I couldn't help but start to sing. "We are the Bears, Shufflin' Crew…"

Naomi chimed in. "Shufflin' on down, doin' it for you."

We both shuffled back and forth. "Uh-huh. Uh-huh," I said, nodding along.

"Oh, man, I had the *biggest* crush on Jim McMahon. He was so sexy with his 80s shades."

"So, you've always been boy crazy, huh?" I teased, giving her a slow smile.

Naomi stopped walking and placed her free hand on her hip. "Boy crazy? What are we, twelve?"

"Oh, come on! You know you are. The Tom Cruise and Brad Pitt sandwich? And you're nuts about that English guy with the floppy hair."

"Hugh Grant."

"Right."

"I'm telling you...he's going to be a *major* star."

"You think?" I asked playfully, raising one eyebrow. "I don't know. That wedding movie might be a flash in the pan. I don't get the appeal, really."

"I mean," she paused, "he's not some big hotshot runningback-slash-track star or anything, but he's okay."

"Right," I said, recognizing her smooth, flirty tone. And just like every other time that Naomi went into flirtation mode, I was putty in her hands. But for the first time, I didn't resent her for it. In fact, I was lapping it up.

"Do you miss it?" she asked.

"What?" I asked, trying to process my thoughts and not act like a total moron in front of her.

"Football," she said.

"Sometimes," I said, remembering my high school football days. "I miss the excitement of the games. Not having a team at this school was kind of a drawback for me when I was figuring out where to go."

"So, how'd you end up here? I mean, it's my dream school—and I'd guess most people here feel the same way."

"Don't get me wrong, it was mine, too. It's an incredible place and I worked really freaking hard to get in. And I know it's the best school in the Midwest for my major, I just miss some of the standard college town stuff, I guess. You know, going to football games on weekends, tailgating, all that stuff."

"I don't," she said simply.

I did a double take. "Really?"

"Really." She nodded with confidence.

I wasn't sure what to say, so the silence took hold of us

as we exited the quad. Naomi urged Sarah to drink more of her water.

"I'm tiiiiiiired," Sarah said. "Can't I sit down?"

"No, two more blocks to go. Stay with us, Sarah."

"And listen to Naomi, drink your water."

"So..." she paused, "how'd you end up at the store?"

"I started my freshman year...first week of school, actually."

"Oh wow. No wonder."

"What?" I asked, expecting a snarky response. I held my breath as I waited for her answer, hoping this wouldn't erupt into another one of our fights. We'd been around one another since the party without an argument...knowing us, it was probably a personal record. And the shit had to hit the fan eventually...I just didn't want it to happen. Not yet.

She said nothing, so I pressed. "Seriously, no wonder *what?*"

"No wonder you have no tolerance for everyone's bullshit. I'm sure in three years I'll be exactly the same way."

"You think you'll still be working there in three years?" I asked, surprised, thinking Naomi would move on to something else as soon as an opportunity presented itself. She didn't strike me as someone who stuck with things for a long time. She seemed like the type to easily get bored.

And maybe that's why she made me so uneasy.

She shrugged. "I don't know, maybe. The work is easy...and I always know what movies are coming out. And I *guess* my coworkers are pretty great."

"Gee, thanks," I said with a smirk.

"So..." she said, licking her lips and tilting her head to the side. "You know some of *my* celebrity crushes."

"You mean half of Hollywood?"

"Hardly." She scoffed. "What about you?"

"I don't know...I hadn't really thought about it."

"Bullshit."

"I'm serious."

"We look at VHS boxes every day at the store. You watch *all* the new releases, and you have plenty of cinematic opinions."

"What's your point?"

"You've *got* to have a type. Everyone does."

"Okay, okay. Julia Roberts is pretty hot."

She rolled her eyes. "Have you seen how big her mouth is? I have no idea how she made it big. For real."

I shrugged. "There's just something about her. She's beautiful."

"Who else? I'm trying to figure out your type."

I stopped walking, feeling bold. My heart pounded in my chest as I stared at her. The streetlight above us made her eyes glisten ever so slightly. "Why?"

"Why what?"

"Why do you *care* what my type is?"

Naomi pinched her eyebrows together and opened her mouth to speak but then closed it tightly and kept walking.

"Naomi?"

"Oh my God, it's *not* a big deal, Ben. Everyone has a type, I was just curious. *Excuuuse* me."

"What is your problem?" I demanded.

"*My* problem?" She tipped her head forward, placing one hand on her hip. "Why are you getting so freaking upset?"

"Um...the only one getting upset right now is *you*."

"Whatever. Forgive me for trying to make conversation with you. I don't know why you have to act like every little thing is an interrogation."

"You guys are making my head huuurrrrrrt," Sarah said, pressing the heels of her hand into her forehead. "Can't we all just get along?"

"I guess not," Naomi said, picking up her pace and pulling Sarah right along with her. After a couple of minutes of silence, we reached their building. Naomi wouldn't look me in the eye, even though my eyes never left hers.

"You guys okay from here?" I asked.

"Yep," she said, pulling her ID and keyring from her back pocket. "Got it."

"Look," I said, "I'm sorry about all of that. It was stupid, and I didn't mean for it to turn into such a big thing."

Naomi rolled her eyes. "Ben, all I did was ask a *simple* question and you made a federal case out of it."

"I know." I shrugged, feeling the conversation spiraling and trying so hard to hold on to the easier moments, the brief levity we shared. "I'm really sorry."

She said nothing, just nodded and placed her key in the lock.

"I guess I'll see you at work."

I felt defeated, conflicted. Why couldn't things just be

easier between us? Why did we always seem to hit a wall whenever we made a decent amount of headway?

Naomi sighed. "Yeah. See ya."

"Bye, Ben," Sarah said with a yawn.

Disappointment consumed me as I pressed my lips into a thin line and turned to walk the three miles back home. When I'd reached the sidewalk, Naomi called out to me.

"Ben?"

"Yeah?"

"Thanks for walking us."

"No sweat."

I waved and turned around once again. I'd barely taken a step when I heard my name again. Only this time, her voice was earnest.

"Ben?"

I released a breath I didn't even know I was holding. "Yeah?"

"I'm sorry, too." Her smile was genuine, sincere.

It gave me hope. Not a lot.

But it was enough.

CHAPTER 7

Naomi

"Oh my God," I said, stopping dead in my tracks as soon as I heard the familiar sound of the *Home Alone* theme song. I'd just arrived for another shift at the store. It was the Saturday before Christmas, and I'd lost count on how many times I had to hear this dreadful song while working my shifts. Tearing off my winter coat, I glared at the person I knew was responsible for playing this movie yet again.

"Not again, Jasper," I moaned.

"What? It's a modern holiday classic," Jasper replied with a smile that was way too big for my liking. "And it *is* the holidays."

"But you're playing it nonstop! I swear I'm going to have nightmares."

"Nightmares?" he said, waving me away. "Of what? Little Kevin McAllister?"

"Yes! I'd rather watch *Emmett Otter's Jug Band Christmas* than this crap."

"Don't say that word," Jasper said, his eyes wide. "Modern. Holiday. Classic."

"I tried," Emmett said with a noncommittal shrug. "He's already played it three times today...and I can't wait to clock out. Oh, and don't talk shit about *Emmett Otter*. That's a piece of my childhood."

"I know, sorry. But see, Jasper?" I said, pointing at Emmett, who usually tried to stay pretty neutral. "He's probably the biggest John Hughes fan *in* this store, and he's had enough of your *modern holiday classic*."

Jasper stopped scanning videos and glared at me. "*Excuse* me? I don't think so."

I held up my palms. "I mean the biggest John Hughes fan *besides* you."

"You'd better recognize," Jasper said, shaking his head. "No one loves that man's movies like I do. No one."

"And you never let us forget it," Sully said, approaching the desk, rolling his eyes.

"What? He's a genius. Okay, quick...favorite John Hughes movie *ever*. Go." Jasper pointed at Emmett.

"*Ferris Bueller.*"

"Solid choice," Jasper said, shifting his body to point at Sully. "And you?"

"Easy. *National Lampoon's.*"

"But, which one?" I interrupted. "Original, Christmas, or European?"

"Hmmm," Sully said, tapping his chin. "I have to go

with the original. Chevy Chase is in a league of his own in that flick."

"I like the Christmas one," I said, remembering it was on my picks shelf for the holiday season. "That's the one we should be playing right now. Not this nonsense."

"When I clock out, you can change the damn tape. Until then, suck it up," Jasper said.

"What is it with you and this movie?"

He shrugged again. "I don't know. I just love it."

"Blech."

"Naomi, you didn't tell us your favorite John Hughes movie."

"Duh. *The Breakfast Club.*"

"Shocker." Sully shook his head.

"What does that mean?"

"Oh, Lord. You're gonna make me say it, aren't you?"

"Um...yes. Because I have no idea what you're implying."

"You're a total Claire. *That's* what I'm implying."

"What?" My voice was incredulous as I recoiled in shock. There was no part of me that related to that character. She was the snooty prom queen eating sushi in her diamond earrings, looking down on the nerds. I wasn't *anything* like her.

Was I?

"I'm not like *her,*" I said, genuinely insulted. "She's awful."

Emmett chuckled under his breath, and I turned to glare at him, daggers in my eyes.

"You, too, Emmett? Are you guys kidding me?"

"I mean...you *can* be kind of a diva," Emmett said before clenching his teeth.

"I resent that."

"If she's Claire, that would make Ben the Judd Nelson character, wouldn't it? John Bender. Holy shit, Ben... Bender. Coincidence? I think not." Sully looked way too proud of himself.

"Ben is *hardly* a Bender," I said, shaking my head. "If anything, he's an Andrew."

"The jock?" Sully scoffed. "No way!"

"Yes, the jock. He played football and ran track in high school," I corrected him, utilizing the knowledge I'd gained the previous weekend.

"Yeah, but you guys are all...never mind," Emmett said, grabbing some tapes from the bin.

"No, say it."

"I'll take this one, Emmett," Sully said, walking to me and placing an arm around my shoulder. "You see, Ace, there is no sexual tension between Claire and Andrew. But with Bender? There's a shitload."

"What are you trying to say?"

"You're a smart girl. You'll figure it out."

I could feel the heat rush to my cheeks and adrenaline pump through my veins. "You have *no* idea what you're talking about."

"Oh, really?" Sully persisted.

"Yes, really."

So wrapped up in the tension that loomed over the four of us, I didn't even notice that a fifth person had emerged from the back room. My breath caught as I saw her, wondering how much of our conversation she'd heard. We all stopped talking and stared at our newest employee.

"What are you guys talking about?" Jenn asked with one eyebrow raised. "I feel like I just walked into something pretty serious."

We stood for a moment, all glancing at one another. We all knew that Jenn was crazy about Ben, and there was no way we were about to divulge what we were really discussing. She was a nice girl, and no one wanted to hurt her feelings...not even me.

"Not at all." Jasper waved her away. "Just passionate about movies, that's all. Favorite John Hughes movies... your turn, go!" Jasper said, giving Jenn a casual smile before glancing at me quickly to offer a supportive wink as if to say, *I've got you, girl.*

"Hmmm...is he the guy who made E.T.?"

Sully sighed loudly, tilting his head back and throwing his arms out in exasperation. "Who let you work here?"

"That's Spielberg," Emmett said. "Hughes made *Ferris Bueller, The Breakfast Club, Pretty in Pink.*"

"Oh, right. All the movies with Molly Ringwald."

"Right." I tilted my head to the side. "Well, most of them anyway."

Sully pursed his lips, and I knew he wanted to boot Jenn out of the store immediately for not obsessing over movie trivia the way the rest of us did. There was a camaraderie in our over-analysis of movies, directors, characters, and quotes. For a group of people who seemed to have very little in common, when we stepped into the store, the movies that raised us gave us common ground. And because of that, we'd become friends. Good ones.

I guess you could call us *The Breakfast Club.*

And Jenn just didn't fit in. She was there for a paycheck and nothing more. Well, *almost* nothing more.

"What's Ben's favorite?" she asked, her eyes earnest and, if I'm honest, just a little bit pathetic.

"Jenn, come on," I snapped at her. "It doesn't matter what he likes. What do *you* like?"

Jenn looked as if I'd slapped her across the face. "I was *just* curious."

"So, what is it?" Jasper asked; his voice was light as he attempted to break the tension. "Your favorite, I mean."

"Sixteen Candles, I guess," she said, her voice low. "That's John Hughes, right?"

"Yep."

"Congratulations on having an opinion," Sully said, patting Jenn on the back.

"Sully," Jasper warned.

"What? I'm just giving her a hard time, right, Jenn? She knows I'm just kidding around."

"Right," Jenn said. "I'm going to change out my picks."

"Wait," I said, annoyed. "You already have a picks shelf?"

"Yeah, Ben gave me one last week."

"Where have you been, Naomi?" Sully said, nudging my arm. "Old news."

"It's just..." I said, my breathing ragged as I tried to calculate how many weeks Jenn had been working at the store. "He made me wait a really long time, and I had to rearrange the whole *freaking* wall just to get one."

It may have been my imagination, but I swear Jenn's posture changed...like she pulled her shoulders back or something. Like she was proud of herself or that she felt superior all because she got a shelf before I did.

Bitch. I made it possible for you to get one in the first place!

"Well," she said before biting down on her lower lip and flipping her hair behind her shoulder as she walked away, a new spring in her step. "I'll be picking movies if anyone needs me."

Gritting my teeth, I leaned against the counter and looked up at the tv monitor hanging from the ceiling. *Home Alone* was almost over.

Thank God.

"Oh man, here come the waterworks," Sully said, patting Jasper on the back. Jasper stood in awe, watching Kevin's neighbor hug his granddaughter. "Every time, man. Every single time."

"Shut up," Jasper said, clearing his throat and wiping his eyes with the back of his hands before glancing down at his watch. "You can put your stupid jug band Christmas thing on now. I've gotta bounce."

"C'mon, Jasper," I said, "you know we're just giving you hell."

"Yeah, I know. It's all good—my shift ended ten minutes ago, but I wanted to see the end."

"Dude, you've seen it *hundreds* of times."

"Shut it, Sully." Jasper shook his head, the skin beneath his eyes still red from emotion. "Jules and I are going Christmas shopping tonight; it was getting me in the spirit. I haven't bought anything for my family yet."

"Crunch time," Emmett said.

"Exactly. Oh, by the way, Ben will be here in a few minutes. He called earlier to say he's running late."

I held up one hand. "Wait, *Ben's* going to be late?"

A smirk crossed Jasper's face, and I knew he read my mind. "I know, I know. Try not to enjoy it too much, okay?"

"I'll do my best, but I can't make any promises." I matched his smirk with my own.

"I'm sure you can't. See you guys."

A devious smile crossed my face as I bit down on my bottom lip and pondered my attack. Within seconds I had it. Was I diabolical? Maybe. I mean, maybe just a little bit.

"You're up to something," Emmett said, shaking his head.

"Maybe I am," I said, glancing around the store, tempted to hop up and sit on the counter. When I spotted two friends in the horror section, I thought better of it and leaned back into the counter. I lowered my voice. "How many times has he given you shit for being late?"

Emmett smiled. "Honestly?"

"Of course."

"Never. Because I've never been late." He gave me a playful wink.

"Suck up," Sully said. "Ben and I have been around and around on that one."

Holding up my hand, Sully gave me a high five. "Same."

Sully let out a sardonic laugh. "Yeah, we know."

"What is that supposed to mean?"

"You're late more often than anyone."

"What? No way! What about Dutch?"

Sully pursed his lips together as he gave it some thought. "Okay, maybe it's a tie. But seriously, that's not something to be proud of. Dutch is late for every shift. And he's not the brightest bulb in the bunch."

"He got in here, didn't he?" I asked, knowing how difficult it was to get into our school.

Sully shook his head. "Naomi, we go to an art school, of course, he got in. Have you seen that kid's work?"

I hadn't.

"Wait, what does he do?"

"Painter." Emmett jumped in. "The kid's eccentric and probably doesn't know the square root of pi, but he's a genius with a paintbrush."

"I had no idea."

Sully moved closer and gave me a facetious wink. "Like I said earlier, you're a *Claire*."

"And what? Dutch is the *Allison*?"

"Exactly."

"Oh, lord," I said, shaking my head, hating when Sully bested me at my own game. Movie analysis. And I had to admit that he usually did. Sully was the master, which was probably why he was planning to write scripts of his own for a living.

Just then, Ben emerged from the back room. I tilted my head to the side in confusion—why didn't he come through the front door?

"Hey, guys."

"Hey there, Benji Boy," Sully said.

"Bryan," Ben matched Sully's snide tone.

"Sully," Sully reminded him.

"Ben," Ben reminded him right back, and they shared a nod.

"Wait, so...when did you get here?" I asked.

"Oh, I had some work to do in the back room. But wanted to make sure you guys knew I was here."

"Oh, so...did you get here at," I glanced over at the shift calendar. "Five o'clock?"

Ben's posture stiffened. "Yep."

"Really?"

He paused for a second. "Mm-hmm."

"Interesting." I tapped my chin. "Because Jasper just left, and he told us you'd be late."

Ben sighed. "Oh."

"Yep," I said, a devious smile stretching across my face. "So, what's you're excuse?" I asked, totally ready to serve him his own words on a big, shiny platter.

Be better than your excuses, Ben.

But Ben, ever my adversary, took in a deep breath, never breaking eye contact with me, and said, "I don't have one. I'm late. Plain and simple."

I stared at him in awe, not knowing how to respond. Ben shrugged and pressed his lips together. "You guys able to hold down the fort? I need to call corporate."

"You got it, boss," Emmett said.

And I stared at him as he turned and walked back the way he came, my chin still hanging down in disbelief.

Sully patted me on the back. "Better luck next time, Ace."

"Shut up, Sully."

CHAPTER 8

Ben

*a*fter my call to corporate, and almost an hour later, I finally emerged from the back room feeling a little defeated. Heather had a family emergency and was flying back to Maryland for at least a week. And most of the other students would be heading home for the holiday break. Since the store was open 365 days a year, someone had to work both Christmas Eve and Christmas Day. Normally Heather and I shared the bulk of the work with one of us taking the lead each day. We did the same thing with the New Year's holidays. It was exhausting, but the company paid us double time, and it was a great way for me to pad my savings account. Since I was a senior, I knew this was most likely my last Christmas working at the store, but I didn't expect to work both days. Originally, corporate said they'd try to send someone from a neighboring store, but all of the stores were struggling to have enough employees on those days. In other words, I was screwed. Not wanting to make the phone call to my Mom to tell her the news, I decided to check on the staff to make sure all was running smoothly in the store.

"Geez, there you are. We got crazy for a little bit," Emmett said, looking a little frazzled. "We were manning every register and still had a line all the way back to the new releases."

"Snowstorm tomorrow. Everyone's grabbing movies tonight," I said, remembering the forecast. "Why didn't you guys come get me? I would've helped."

"Nah." Naomi waved me away, handing a video to a customer. "Everything's under control. Now we can get caught up before the next wave hits. I think the return box is full."

"But first, you can settle a little wager we have going," Sully said, scratching the tip of his rounded nose.

"Oh yeah? What wager?"

"We have bets on what your favorite John Hughes movie is. Luckily, Jasper already left because I'm sure he already knows."

"What does the winner get?"

"They don't have to clean the bathrooms for a month. The rest of us will pick up the slack."

"Nice." I nodded. "And what are the predictions?"

"Not so fast," Sully said, handing me a Post-It note and pencil. "Jot down your answer, put it in your pocket, and then we'll reveal our guesses."

I shook my head, genuinely amused that they would give a rat's ass about my favorite John Hughes movie, but

I decided to play along. Sully's bets were always entertaining, even when they were slightly irritating. Sully was just one of those people who, despite the fact that he could wear on your patience, always found ways to amuse, to make others laugh, and to keep things interesting. The place wouldn't be the same without him, that was for sure.

Quickly, without even needing to think about it, I jotted down my answer and stuffed the Post-It in my pocket.

"Okay, shoot," I said, nodding to Sully.

"All right. So, first…we have Jenn."

"I thought you'd say *Sixteen Candles*."

Sully blocked his mouth with his hand and lowered his voice. "Mostly because it's the only Hughes movie she knows."

"Sully!" Naomi snapped. "Be nice."

For a second, I was confused that Naomi was coming to Jenn's defense. But then again, it's not that Naomi was a mean girl…she wasn't. She was just opinionated, a little bratty, and terribly honest. But after watching her defend her roommate that weekend, I shouldn't have been surprised that she'd stick up for another coworker, especially since she had no problem going toe-to-toe with Sully. In fact, she was the only woman who worked at Spotlight Video, apart from Heather, of course. Sully didn't intimidate her in the slightest…and I was starting to wonder if anyone did.

"All right, all right. Sorry."

Emmett interrupted, "I actually predicted *Planes,*

Trains and Automobiles. You seem like a John Candy kind of guy."

"That's a good one," I said with a smile. "*Those aren't pillows!*"

Naomi cracked up, placing her hand in front of her mouth as she laughed. Jenn looked confused. I tilted my head to the side. "It's from the movie."

"Gotcha," she said, pointing at me, looking uncomfortable.

"Sully, what did *you* think?"

Sully crossed his arms. "Nope, I'm going last."

"Why?"

"Because I know I'm right."

I rolled my eyes. "Fine, Naomi? What you got?"

"*Uncle Buck,*" Naomi said with a gentle smile. "I'm not sure why, honestly. It just seemed like *you.*"

My heart raced for just a moment when she said that, and I immediately wanted to put Uncle Buck in the player so I could analyze what she meant without having to ask. But knowing I'd look like an idiot, I simply said, "I do love that movie. The giant pancake gets me every time."

"Me, too," Naomi said. "When I was little, I was jealous of whoever got to eat it."

"Probably no one," Sully said sharply. "That was a prop pancake."

"Oh my God, Sully. Shut up," Naomi said, shaking her head.

"Anyway, Ben…I'm confident that your choice was *The Breakfast Club.*"

I closed my eyes and shook my head in disbelief as I

pulled out the Post-It note and held it up for all of them to see.

"Sully! How did you know?" Naomi asked, looking genuinely surprised.

"I know Ben...and the rest of my coworkers, for that matter." And then, Sully winked at Naomi, and her breath caught before she stole a glance at me and looked away. The entire two seconds was incredibly un-Naomi-like, and it left me baffled. I stared at both of them and figured I should break the tension, even if I was the only one feeling it.

"It's John Bender, he's the best part of the whole film. I mean, don't get me wrong—the whole cast is great, but he's one of my favorite characters ever."

"You don't say," Sully said, grinning at Naomi. "Told you, *Claire*."

"Shut up, Sully," Naomi said, her cheeks red. Our eyes met, and then she quickly crouched down to pull movies from the return bin.

"Claire? Is that a new nickname I don't know about?"

"No," Sully said, shaking his head slowly, looking smug. Only I had no idea what he had to be smug about. Guessing the right movie? Not cleaning the bathrooms? Or was it something more? It was sometimes hard to know when Sully was being facetious just for fun or when there really was more to it. Which made it really hard to know when to ignore him and when to actually pay attention to his smart-ass remarks.

"I don't get it," I said.

Sully left the desk and walked past me, his voice low. "Think about it."

"Ignore him," Emmett called from the desk. "He's just gloating because he doesn't have to clean the john…"

"*And* I'm going to have so much fun telling you all to do it," Sully bragged.

"No doubt," Emmett said with an overly fake smile. I had to laugh. Emmett was probably the nicest guy on campus, but no one could push his buttons like Sully.

I patted Emmett on the back as I walked behind the counter and reached for the calendar, scanning the following weekend's shifts.

"You guys all go home for Christmas break, right?" I paused. "Everyone but Jenn?"

They all answered *yes* in unison. I studied the schedule, knowing that it was going to be tight without Heather. Exceptionally tight.

"What's going on?" Emmett asked.

"Heather had a family emergency at home. She flew out of O'Hare this morning."

"Oh no," Jenn said. "Is she all right?"

"Her dad is in the hospital. It doesn't look good."

"Christmas in the hospital?" Naomi asked, her eyes pained. "That's awful."

"Yeah," I said, crossing off all of Heather's scheduled shifts for the rest of the month.

"Oh man," Emmett said, looking over my shoulder. "Who's going to cover for her?"

"Me."

"Wait, on Christmas Day, too? You're already here on Christmas Eve."

"It'll be okay," I said, waving him away and doing my best to hide my disappointment over missing the holidays with my family. "That's why I get paid the big bucks."

"I'll help," Jenn said.

"I can't ask you to do that, Jenn. You're already working Christmas Eve. You deserve time with your family."

"You can call me," Jenn said, looking eager. "I mean, if you need me to come in. Like if you get swamped here."

"Thanks. I appreciate it. I'm going to ask Jasper to come in for a short shift; that might make things more doable. I think his family celebrates on Christmas Eve."

"I'm sorry, man," Emmett said. "I'm on a plane in a few days. Won't be back until January."

Sully nodded. "Same."

"Thanks, guys," I said, noticing that Naomi said nothing, she just stood there staring at me with pity in her eyes. And it pissed me off. I didn't expect her to offer to work, but I also had no interest in her pity. "Really, it's okay."

Just then, a large group of students came in through the front door, breaking the tension that loomed above the desk. "Let's get these movies back on the shelf. Evening rush is about to start."

* * *

AND THE RUSH continued for two straight hours. We took turns covering the registers, scanning in returns, and running movies back to the shelves. Finally, when things slowed down, I listened to Sully pontificate on why there were no famous movies celebrating

Hanukkah...why everything was based around Christmas.

"There have to be some out there," I said, racking my brain for a movie about Hanukkah. "But I can't think of any, can you, Emmett?"

"No, but I just keep hearing Adam Sandler in my head."

"Why?"

"Didn't you watch Saturday Night Live a few weeks ago?" Emmett asked. "The Hanukkah Song? Tell me you watched."

"I missed it," I said. "I was probably here."

"Dude, it was hilarious. He lists all these famous people who are Jewish and probably celebrate Hanukkah. *Put on your yarmulke, here comes Hanukkah!*"

"He's hilarious," said Naomi. "I love him so much."

"Maybe he'll make a Hanukkah movie."

"Adam Sandler? He's a TV comedian, not a movie star," Sully scoffed.

Emmett shrugged. "But he *should* be. He's freaking hilarious. And if anyone would make a Hanukkah movie, it's him. I'm telling you, mark my words."

"Whatever," Sully said. "I just hope he sings that song again. That was a freaking riot."

"I keep forgetting to set my VCR to record it. I need to fix that." Naomi grabbed a pen and wrote on her arm: *TAPE SNL.*

Our eyes met, and she shrugged with a soft smile I wasn't used to. It was almost as if our experience that Saturday at the party had eased the tension between us, even with our argument on the walk to her dorm. It was like she saw me differently or something. I couldn't quite figure it out.

The bell above the door rang, and two guys walked in. Naomi lit up like a Christmas tree and ran around the desk, pouncing on the bigger guy who looked like a freaking Adonis. He had chiseled features and broad shoulders. I wasn't one to be easily intimidated by other guys, but this guy was the exact type I'd always assumed Naomi would end up with. Muscular, extremely confident, and with a hulking presence. Sighing, I tried to look busy, but I couldn't help listening to their conversation.

"You finally came to see my work," she said, playfully pressing on his chest.

That word bothered me...*finally*.

"Yeah, with the snow coming, my roommates and I are going to hunker down, watch a horror marathon."

"Not Christmas movies?" Naomi asked. "It's almost here."

The other guy spoke, "That's what I said. But I was outvoted."

"Are you two the designated movie getters?" Naomi asked, tilting her head to the side and placing her hands on her hips. She was flirting with them both, and it made me want to punch something. Anything.

"Yep," said the big guy, placing his arm around Naomi's petite shoulders and strolling with her down the aisle while the other guy followed behind. Naomi's arm snaked around his waist, and I could feel my blood boil. "Show us to your scariest shit."

"Right this way, guys."

"Ben?" Jenn's voice interrupted my obsessive thoughts,

and I took a breath before turning to face her, pretending like everything was normal. Luckily, I had a decent poker face most of the time. But there was something about Naomi that took me out of my element.

And I resented her for it like nothing else.

"Yeah?" I said, turning to look at Jenn who was studying my face, and I knew she was looking for signs of jealousy. I had no interest in Jenn, despite her obvious interest in me, but she was a nice girl, and I didn't want to hurt her feelings.

"So, um...I organized the children's section. Found this in there, though. I think Dutch's friends struck again." She placed a porno in my hand. I sighed and walked it to the other adult videos that were ready to be re-shelved.

"Thanks, Jenn. I appreciate it."

"Are you okay?" she asked, her tone sounded concerned and hesitant.

"Oh, yeah, just thinking about Christmas Day. My mom will be so pissed. She makes this roast duck every year because it's my favorite thing on the planet. She bought all the ingredients already, and now I have to tell her I won't be home. Like at all. I just don't want to break her heart, ya know?"

"I hear you," Jenn said, nodding. "Like I said, just call me."

"Thanks." I patted her on the shoulder and regretted it immediately as an eager smile crossed her lips.

Damn it.

"You're a good friend, Jenn," I said, and she swallowed hard. She nodded, her eyes growing vacant as she turned and walked to the video bin.

"I'll, uh, just return some of these." She walked away, her head hanging down as she walked to the adult room. And I felt like such a prick. I was trying to let her down easy, but I knew in my gut that I did the opposite. I didn't want to hurt her, but I did just that...and a week before Christmas.

You're such an asshole, Ben.

Before I could spend another minute thinking about how I'd messed up with Jenn, Naomi and the two guys emerged from the horror section. Naomi carried five videos in her arms. She gave me a closed-lipped smile as she brought the tapes to the register and asked for their rental card. The smaller guy handed his to her, and she began to check out the tapes. Once they'd paid, the big guy tapped Naomi's hand with his own. His fingertips danced across her knuckles, and all I could see was red.

He licked his lips and tilted his head to the side. "So... see you Monday? After the storm?"

"Of course," she said and leaned in. "Was there any doubt?"

He placed a kiss on her cheek, and she winked at him, handing him the videos after he walked past the sensors. Once he and his friend left the store, I watched as she stared out the door and watched him walk away, stars in her eyes.

"Who was that?" Sully asked.

She sighed loudly. "His name is Jamal. Isn't he gorgeous?"

"Um...you're asking the wrong guy. Emmett? Ben? Help me out with this."

"He's very impressive," Emmett said with wide eyes. "How tall is he?"

"I don't know," she said with another sigh. And I couldn't take any more of her dreamy stare. Giving her the fakest smile I could muster, I grabbed a stack of videos and made my escape just like Jenn had moments before.

Jenn liked me. And I realized right then and there that I liked Naomi. I really, *really* liked Naomi. But she obviously liked a guy named Jamal, and I'd been kidding myself thinking there was something new between us.

Karma, you are such a fucking bitch.

CHAPTER 9

Naomi

*O*ne more shift.

One more shift and I would be on my way home. My younger brother, Jonathan, had just gotten his license and was excited to pick me up from school that night. My parents only agreed to it because the drive would be an hour long, tops. And my dad was coming, too, to supervise him and make sure we got home safely. Thank God!

One more shift and I would have four blissful weeks at home with my family. Although if I was honest with myself, I was going to miss the store and my coworkers. I'd miss rehearsals, Jamal, and the rest of the cast. The girls who snubbed me after casting were warming up to me, and the looming tension at rehearsals was lessening with each passing week. Jamal lived in Wisconsin, and we'd made plans to rehearse at least twice a week during break so we wouldn't lose our momentum or chemistry. Our director, Mr. Martin, was relieved to know we didn't live too far away from one another. In years past, the leads had sometimes suffered a winter break 'slump' and had to take several days in January to get back in sync with each other. Jamal and I had accepted that challenge, and our new mantra was 'avoid the slump.' And I wasn't exactly torn up about spending so much time with him during break.

It was hard to explain my feelings for Jamal. When I was with him, everything was just...easy. And when we were on stage, our chemistry was off the charts—it was like nothing I'd ever experienced with another student. If I was honest with myself, that chemistry dwindled some-what when the curtain went down as an amiable detach-ment seemed to possess Jamal once the audience was gone. But he was still gorgeous, still brilliant, and still someone whom I loved to be around. So, I hadn't ruled out the possibility of something happening between us. Not yet, anyway.

Marley pulled me from my daydream as she walked to the front desk and stuffed her coat and purse underneath. I snickered, knowing how much it drove Ben crazy when we did that. I'd worked at Spotlight Video for two months and I'd yet to even open my locker in the back room. He liked to remind me of that from time to time.

Oh, Buzzkill.

As if she read my mind, Marley shrugged. "I know Ben wants us to use the lockers, but I'm lazy."

"I totally get it."

Marley reached down and grabbed her things, a pensive look on her face. "Maybe I should...today at least."

"What do you mean?" I asked. "What's going on?"

"Didn't you hear...about Ben having to work Christmas Eve *and* Christmas Day?"

"Well, yeah, but I figured someone else would fill in. Jasper or maybe Jenn. She seemed pretty eager the other day."

"I guess he doesn't want to make anyone else work both days."

"Oh."

"I know." Marley shook her head. "I'm working Christmas Eve, but I think the poor guy's going to be here all by himself on Christmas Day.

"That sucks," I said before taking a sip of my Snapple, feeling guilt stir in my belly. I hadn't felt a lot of sympathy for Ben on Saturday night when I'd heard the news. I honestly thought corporate would figure something out. But now, it was only a couple of days before Christmas Eve. If corporate hadn't figured it out by now, they weren't going to. And Ben was going to be spending his entire holiday at the store—alone. My heart ached for him.

"Jenn told me his mom makes this incredible roast duck every year, and she was so upset that he wouldn't be able to make it, she stuffed it back in the freezer. I guess they're going to celebrate some other time, but she's so upset she doesn't even want to plan anything."

"That's sad," I said, genuinely feeling uneasy.

"It's just the two of them. Ben's dad left when he was little, and his mom's family lives in New Hampshire."

"Wow."

"Yeah," Marley said with a sigh, "so, I think I should put my stuff back there. For today, at least."

"Good idea," I said, eyeing my own peacoat and purse that I'd stuffed under the counter. But using my locker wouldn't be enough. My mind wanted to do something bigger for Ben. A present? Maybe a card that I could leave on his desk before heading home that night? I had to think of something. Something good.

The bell above the door brought me back to reality. I turned to greet our latest customer, but instead, Dutch strolled in with a couple of friends and a strange-looking ice cream bar in his mouth. It was all green with red candies that looked like eyeballs.

"What are you eating?" I asked, kind of grossed out.

"What, this?" Dutch pulled the bar from his mouth and grinned, his lips and tongue green from the dye. "It's a Teenage Mutant Ninja Turtle ice cream bar."

"Ew."

"Dude, they're so good. Although I still like the Flintstone Push-Ups better," said his friend with hair that spilled down his back. It was snarly with knots, and I had to resist the urge to grab the hairbrush from my purse and brush it for him.

"Oh yeah. *Bedrock Berry*, baby!" Dutch said, nodding as he gave his friend a high five.

"Yabba Dabba Dooooo," his friend said before licking his popsicle stick and tossing it over the counter and into the trash.

"You're lucky you didn't miss that shot," I said, narrowing my eyes. "This isn't your dorm room."

"Sorry," his friend said with a dismissive shrug as he walked straight back to the porn room. Rolling my eyes, I turned my attention back to Dutch, who was standing in front of me with his half-eaten ninja turtle. The purple mask was running into the green, and it was grossing me out in a big way.

"What are the eyeballs on that thing?" I asked, scrunching my nose and taking a sip of my drink.

"Gumballs," Dutch said before biting one of the red gumballs off of the ice cream and chomping on it with his mouth wide open.

"Gross."

"Don't knock it 'til you try it, *Ace*."

"Don't you start calling me that, too," I warned. "Sully is already more than enough."

"Hey, Dutch," Marley said as she walked back to the counter, holding a stack of papers. "I didn't know you were working today."

"I'm not. My roommate and I are just grabbing some porn."

"Ew," Marley said, clenching her teeth.

"Like I just said to Naomi, don't knock it 'til you *try* it," Dutch said, wiggling both eyebrows before turning to meet his friend amongst the small sea of adult videos. Marley shuddered and walked to the phone.

"Calling the late people again?" I asked with a laugh. "You know I'm not bailing you out this time."

"Ugh, I know. I don't know why Ben makes me do this all the time," she said, looking at the list. "At least *half* of these are porn. Why can't porn and punctuality go together?"

I laughed. "Just do what I do."

"And what's that?"

"I don't even mention the name of the movie when I call, I just tell them how many videos are late. They know what movies they rented; why do I need to spell it out for them?"

"But Ben says I need to be specific."

"Well, Ben's not here, is he?"

"Hmph," Marley said, "I guess I'll try that."

Marley took a deep breath and made her first call as I laughed to myself while emptying out the return bin. Dutch came running back to the desk, something small in his hand.

"I need the phone," he said, out of breath. He tapped his pager against the countertop as Marley held up her finger to shush him and then pointed to the phone.

"She's calling customers," I said. "You have to wait."

"I caaaaan't," Dutch said, his eyes wide. I'd never seen Dutch stressed about anything, but something had him all worked up.

"And why do you have a pager? Do you have a little side business?" I asked, pretending to hold an imaginary joint to my lips.

"What—drugs?"

"Obviously."

"No, I have a dealer for that," he waved me away. "And really, you don't have to sell drugs to have one of these. You sound like that girl from *The Real World,* which is very ironic right now."

"Wait, who?"

"I forget her name...the innocent one from the first season. Southern accent, from Alabama, I think."

"Oh, Julie, right?"

"Exactly."

As soon as I remembered her name, I remembered the scene where she asked her roommate, Heather B, if she sold drugs simply because she had a pager. And I immediately felt like a jerk.

"Sorry, Dutch. It's just...you know, you *are* kind of a 'Dead' head."

"Oh, I totally am. But I don't *sell* anything. My parents would string me up by my fingernails."

"Really?" I asked, surprised. "I always pictured you having a laidback family."

"Not at all," he shook his head. "They're majorly conservative."

"Interesting."

"Marley, are you almost done?" he asked, tapping his hands against the counter.

"Go find a pay phone."

"There's no time for that!" he whined.

"Why not?" I crossed my arms and leaned back into the counter.

"It could be them...about my audition tape."

"I don't know what you're talking about. What audition tape?"

"*The Real World.*"

"You auditioned for *The Real World*?"

"Hell yeah! They're casting for London. London, man! A semester across the freaking ocean." He smiled wide. "Hello, Gov-nah."

I didn't have the heart to tell him how awful his British accent was.

"And you think they're *paging* you?" I asked in disbelief.

"Right. That's why I need the phone, Marrleeeeeeey."

"You think *MTV* is *paging* you." I said it again, emphasizing the word even more.

He looked genuinely confused as he ran his hand through his greasy curls. The smell of patchouli wafted to me. "Well, I mean...I gave them my pager number."

Rolling my eyes and shaking my head, I waited for Marley to hang up the phone before encouraging her to take a break from her calls.

"Why can't you find a pay phone?" Marley asked. "I need to get these done before Ben gets here. I have, like, ten minutes."

"I'll be quick."

"With MTV?" I egged him on. "You'll be quick?"

"That's what I said," Dutch said, grabbing and turning the phone to face him, punching in the number on his pager. He paused, and we all stood in silence. I was about 99 percent certain that MTV didn't page their prospective cast members, but stranger things had probably happened. And Dutch was nothing if not entertaining. I could imagine him being one hell of a cast member on that show. He'd be the guy they begged to take a damn shower or stop smoking pot in the common areas.

"Yeah, hey this is Dutch. I got a page." He was quiet as he listened. "Um, no. Wrong number, dude."

He slammed the phone down, his brow knitted in disappointment. He swallowed hard as he pressed his hands into the counter. I wasn't used to seeing Dutch so emotionally invested in something. He really wanted this.

"Sorry, Dutch."

"Yeah, sorry, Dutch."

"There's still time to be cast, right? Don't rule anything out. One wrong number doesn't mean anything," Marley said, walking around the counter and patting him on the shoulder, trying to give him the most reassuring words she could.

"Exactly," I echoed, smiling and nodding as enthusiastically as possible.

He sighed and gave us a genuine, relaxed Dutch smile, and I could tell he was shaking it off. "True."

Just then, Ben walked through the door, carrying a slice of pizza in a little individual-sized box. He gave us all a polite smile. "Hey, guys."

Marley looked panicked as she scurried back to the desk, wanting to hide the late video list from Ben. Knowing what she was up to, I stepped to the side, pulling the list behind me, hoping that if it was out of sight, it was out of mind. Marley looked relieved as she rounded the corner and saw what I'd done.

"No meatball sub today?" Marley asked. Everyone at Spotlight knew that Ben was crazy about the meatball subs from the pizza place next door.

"They're out," he said with a shrug. "This'll do. I'm going to snarf this down really quick, and I'll be up to help out. Dutch, did you clock in?"

"Nah, man, just renting something with my friends. I leave tomorrow for break."

"Safe flight, man," Ben said with a nod.

"Poor guy can't catch a break," I said under my breath as Ben walked out of sight.

"I know," Marley said. "They don't even stay open on Christmas, so he can't even get dinner there."

"Geez, does anything stay open besides us?"

"Hardly anyone on campus. Corporate should really think it through. We aren't like regular towns. Campus towns shut down...and that's coming from a townie. I've lived here my entire life, and I've never rented a video on Christmas." She shook her head and shrugged. "But they want to be fair to all the other stores."

"Corporate B.S.," I said, "Give me a second."

Walking to the picks wall, I started to brainstorm all of the things that I knew about Ben. Aside from his love of meatball sandwiches covered in mozzarella cheese and super crispy French fries...what exactly did I know? He liked to help others—or at least I assumed so since he was in APO with Sarah and the other do-gooders. He lived with five roommates in a dilapidated house and kicked ass in beer pong. He wanted to work in special effects and loved *The Breakfast Club* and the Bears. But I wanted to know more, and I was hoping that by looking at his picks shelf, I'd be able to figure out my big holiday gesture and start to put my plan into motion.

But so far, I had nothing. Bubkis. Nada.

When I reached the picks shelf, I smiled at his choices:

The Princess Bride: the funniest fairy tale ever...and Wesley was hot. Damn hot.

An Interview with the Vampire: interesting.

The Breakfast Club: very interesting.

Uncle Buck: very, *very* interesting.

117

Home Alone: <eye roll>

And the absolute kicker: *Emmett Otter's Jug Band Christmas.* Had Jasper told him about our Christmas movie debate on Saturday? If not, it was a really strange coincidence. I wondered if Jasper and Ben talked about me…

My mind was racing, and suddenly, I wanted to put a hole in a washtub to make sure Ben had a nice Christmas…just like Emmett Otter did for his sweet mom. But I still had nothing solid in my mind. I raced to the counter to look at Ben's shifts, writing them down quickly on my wrist. I had time to figure this out. I was bound and determined to make sure that Ben's holiday was a happy one.

And then it came to me. In a flash, I knew *exactly* what to do.

"You look like you're up to something," Marley said.

"How very right you are," I said, wiggling my eyebrows. The bell over the door rang, and I turned to see my dad and brother walk in, their cheeks bright red from the winter chill. "Hey!" I yelled, running to greet them. "You guys are early."

"This one has a lead foot," my dad said, tilting his head toward my brother. "Just like his sister. You ready to go, kiddo?"

"Yeah, I just need to grab my stuff." I paused, giving my dad the sweetest smile that I could, and asked, "Do you think I could borrow your car on Christmas Day?"

CHAPTER 10

Ben

Snow flurries danced outside the window of the store. It was Christmas morning—just before noon—and I'd yet to see one customer, as predicted. The night before, Marley had left me with her mom's specialty: apple pie with raisins. My stomach growled as the pie called to me from the countertop. Knowing that no one else was able to work today, I needed to eat my meals at the counter, which would normally be a royal pain in the ass. Eating at the counter always made me feel like an animal at the zoo, on display for customers to watch. But since I was pretty sure I wouldn't see any customers for at least a few more hours, I didn't really care.

I'd decided to watch a marathon of all of my favorite Christmas movies. I'd started with *Santa Claus is Coming to Town*, my favorite stop-motion Christmas special. And feeling nostalgic, I'd followed it up with and thoroughly enjoyed the little mouse who broke the clock in *'Twas the Night Before Christmas*. As the credits rolled, I walked to our holiday section to pick a new movie. With a smile, I glossed over *Home Alone*, knowing that if Naomi was with me, she'd be rolling her eyes.

I hoped she was having a nice Christmas with her family.

Thinking of Naomi, I grabbed *National Lampoon's Christmas Vacation*, knowing it was her favorite. It was hard to be in a bad mood while watching Clark Griswold do just about anything. I'd just popped the movie into the player when the bell above the door rang. The VCR and receiver blocked my view of the door, so I stepped to the side just as she rounded the corner. Our eyes locked, and I felt my breath catch as I took in the sight of her. Navy blue peacoat, a plaid scarf, and her blonde hair pulled back into a high bun on the top of her head. She looked a little disheveled, with hardly any make-up on her face, but I'd honestly never thought she'd looked more beautiful.

"Merry Christmas," Naomi said, holding a pizza box.

"Merry Christmas," I replied with a smile. "What are you doing here?"

"Well," she said, reaching inside her bag and pulling out an elf hat. "I was sent here by the North Pole."

"Oh really?" I asked, amused to see her in the bright green and red cap with fake pointy ears that hung in front of her own. "I didn't know they made pizza at the North Pole."

"It's not a pizza," she said, cocking her head to the side. "I just needed the box."

Good lord, she's gorgeous. Almost too gorgeous.

"Huh," I said, not sure what else to say. I knew she'd done something she was awfully proud of, but if there wasn't a pizza inside that box, then I had no idea what there was.

"So, a friend of mine works for *Rosati's,* and I told him I needed the biggest box he had."

"Oh yeah?" I said, narrowing my eyes, trying to smell what was inside the box without being obvious.

"Should we end the suspense?" she asked, bouncing just a bit on her toes.

"Please," I said, soaking in her excitement.

Naomi walked to me and held out the box. "Go ahead."

A sweet, vanilla scent wafted toward me as she stood beaming with the cardboard box. Slowly, enjoying every second of this still mysterious gesture, I opened the box, revealing two enormous pancakes.

The smell of buttermilk and melted butter tickled my senses, and my stomach roared as I stared at the golden-brown cakes. "You brought me pancakes?"

She nodded. "*Uncle Buck* style. I know they weren't big enough to need a shovel to flip them. But my little brother works at the diner in town, and his boss let me in early to use their flat top. Jonathan and I needed two *huge* spatulas to flip these suckers, so I think that counts."

"It definitely does," I said, nodding. "I can't believe you did this."

"But wait. There's more," she said in her best game show host voice, releasing her backpack from one shoulder and whipping it around to rest against her chest. With a swift move of the zipper, she pulled out a jug of maple syrup, but interestingly enough, I smelled the rich scent of marinara sauce. She handed me the jug, and I glanced at the bottle. One hundred percent real maple syrup.

"The real stuff, huh?" I'd only ever had pancake syrup, not real maple syrup. I wondered what it would taste like.

"My parents are syrup snobs." She shrugged. "I would offer to warm these in the microwave, but that might be a challenge. A big one."

"Yeah, I doubt they'd fit. Cold pancakes are my favorite."

"They shouldn't be too bad. I wrapped the box in a big fleece blanket from our couch. I bet it smells amazing now."

"Naomi, I don't know what to say. Why did you do all this?"

She paused for a second, her bright blue eyes warm and kind. "Because it's Christmas. Just because you have to work, doesn't mean you should resign yourself to a shitty holiday, right?"

"Right."

Naomi glanced up at the TV when she heard the familiar tune of the Christmas Vacation song. *It's that time...Christmas time is here.* She smiled in appreciation and passed me a set of silverware and a napkin from her bag.

"Okay, so you get started on your pancakes, and I'll show you what else I brought."

"I smell pizza or something. Is that weird?" I asked.

"Could it be the box?" I leaned in and sniffed the cardboard box in my hands. Nothing.

"Nope," Naomi said with a grin. "It's your lunch...or maybe your dinner. We'll see how much of those pancakes you finish."

I sat cross-legged on top of the counter and placed the box on my lap. Carefully, I drizzled syrup over a small section of the pancakes, digging my fork into the soft, golden cakes. The sweet taste of sugar and maple enveloped my senses as I chewed.

"Wow," I said. "You're a good cook."

"Just pancakes." She laughed. "My dad taught me when I was really little. My math isn't the greatest, though, so I'm relieved they turned out okay. I've never made a batch this big before."

"They're amazing. And the real syrup is...wow. You may have spoiled me for the regular stuff."

"I know, right? It's expensive, but it's worth it."

I nodded, taking another bite as she reached into her bag and pulled out a large paper bag. "I happen to know that Rosati's makes the best meatball marinara sandwich. Even better than next door, I promise. And they put, like, a half a pound of cheese on top."

"I thought I smelled that."

"Yeah, sorry—pancakes and marinara don't exactly go well together."

"Are you kidding me? Don't apologize. This is awesome, I can't wait to eat it...all of it." I took another bite of the rich cake, topped perfectly in sticky, sweet syrup.

Her smile drifted from her face, and she knitted her

brow. "I know it's not the roast duck that your mom usually makes, but if you have to be here today, I wanted you to have something delicious…or a couple of delicious things. I don't know—maybe it'll make the day suck a little less."

"Today doesn't suck."

Naomi's eyes lit up. "It doesn't?"

"Not anymore."

Her cheeks turned a beautiful shade of pink. "Good. I'm going to put this in the fridge in back. I was going to get you fries, too, but they would be horrible in the microwave. So…" She dug back into the bag. "I got you chips instead and a two-liter of root beer. I know it's your favorite. Oh, and a bag of grapes that my mom insisted I bring. She doesn't want you just eating 'junk.'" Naomi used air quotes for that last word, which made me laugh.

"Your mom sent me fruit?"

You told your family about me.

"Well, yeah." Naomi shrugged one shoulder. "I tried to convince her to let me work all day with you, but Margaret Parker takes her traditions very seriously. I have to be back by two o'clock."

"Wait, you're going to work, too?" I was so pleasantly surprised. Naomi wasn't exactly the first to volunteer for extra hours or shifts. I was blown away.

"For a little while. So, I'm thinking that, if you want, you can go to the back room to eat your pancakes. Take a little break or something."

For a second, I was tempted to do just that. But my desire to be near Naomi was stronger than my possible embarrassment about eating in front of customers.

Besides, there were no customers anyway, so I ignored her suggestion.

"Are you hungry?" I asked her, holding out the pizza box. She waved me away.

"Already ate. Those are all yours."

"There's no way I can finish. This is like two pounds of pancakes."

"Felt like three to me," she said with a wink as she walked to the return bin. The empty return bin.

"No returns, huh?" Naomi asked before pressing her palms into the countertop and hopping up, facing me, as she crossed her legs.

"Nope, it's been dead all day. I'm thinking it'll be like that until tonight when people get bored."

"We always end up watching a movie after dinner. We turn off all the lights so we just have the glow of the Christmas tree. Oh, and now the lights from my mom's Christmas village, too. She's crazy about her little village."

"What is that?" I asked, genuinely curious. When I thought of Christmas villages, I thought of real towns all decorated for the holiday, but somehow, I knew the Parker family couldn't fit an entire town in their living room.

"It's this set of little ceramic buildings with Christmas decorations and lights, sometimes music. My mom picked the one that's actually based on Bedford Falls, you know, from *It's a Wonderful Life*. All the buildings are from that little town. She told my dad it's all she wanted for Christmas, so he bought every single building, every figurine, everything."

"That's really nice. I've never seen that movie."

"Seriously?" Naomi recoils. She looks at me like I have three heads. "How could you have never seen that movie? It's the ultimate Christmas classic."

I shrugged. "No idea…maybe my mom doesn't like it. I don't know. We always watched the network specials. Rudolph, that kind of stuff."

"So, you haven't seen *A Miracle on 34th Street* either?"

"Nope."

"Oh, Ben. You need to be schooled."

I chuckled as Naomi hopped off the counter and hustled to the Christmas movie shelves. "Damn it. They're all out. If I didn't live so far away, I'd run home and get it. You need to see it, Ben. I'm so serious."

"Okay, okay. Since you brought me all this delicious food, I'll watch your movie once a copy comes back. I promise."

"I'm telling you. You won't regret it. It's one of the few movies that actually makes me cry."

"I have no idea what it's about. Although now I know it takes place in Bedford Falls."

"There's this guy, George Bailey, and he's at a really low point in his life. Suicidal."

"Wow, sounds like a real heart warmer."

She held up one finger. "I'm not done. Anyway, George wonders what the world would be like without him. He's all ready to end everything, and then this angel comes to earth. His name is Clarence, and he helps George see just how blessed he really is. So, George comes to appreciate his wife, his family…everything. It's really powerful, actually. Like I said, it's a classic."

"Is it on your picks shelf?"

She pauses. "No, but it should be. I'm going to fix that right now."

"Naomi, it's Christmas Day."

"So what? That movie's a classic no matter what day it is. I'm moving it to my shelf."

"Do what you've got to do," I said before taking another huge bite of delicious pancakes and glancing at my watch. I had eighty-five minutes with Naomi, and I wanted to savor them all.

"So," she said, walking back to the counter with a devious but playful expression on her face. "I really like your current picks."

"Oh?" I asked, with no idea where she was going with that.

"Yep," she said. "A lot, actually."

Still clueless, I bit down on my lower lip, trying to figure out what she was thinking, but I came up empty. Looking amused, Naomi shook her head and hopped back onto the counter, only this time she sat on the same side of the registers as me.

It was nice.

"So, how'd you know about the duck?" I asked. I remembered telling Jenn about the traditional Christmas meal my mom and I shared every year, but that was it. And I couldn't imagine Jenn and Naomi had gotten chummy in just a few days. But stranger things had happened.

"Marley." Naomi pressed her lips into a thin line. "She felt bad...and so do I. Is your mom still upset?"

I nodded. "More than I thought she'd be. It's just the two of us, though, so I get it."

"That must've been lonely. I have five brothers and sisters."

"Whoa. Six kids?"

"Yep. Total chaos, but I don't know any other way."

"I guess not."

"But it would be heavenly to have my own room. What's that like?"

"I mean…" I paused. "Quiet, I guess."

"I don't know what quiet's like," she laughed, reaching over to dip her finger into a pool of maple syrup off to the side of the pancakes. I watched as she wrapped her lips around her finger, and I had to shift in my seat.

She has no idea the power she has over me. None at all.

She licked her lips when she noticed me staring, looking sheepish for possibly the first time. "Oh, sorry. Does that gross you out? My dad hates when I do that."

"Oh, no. It's all good."

"Phew," she said, wiping her forehead with the back of her hand dramatically.

"So, you want to be a movie star, huh?"

She shook her head, dipping her finger back into the pool of syrup. "Of course, that's the dream, right? But really, when it comes down to it, I just want to be a serious actress—to be taken seriously for my talent, you know?"

"Yeah."

"And you? Do you dream of being one of the top special effects people in Hollywood?"

"No, I just want to make a living doing what I love. If I can support myself, and one day, a family, I'll be happy."

She paused for a second, her eyes still soft. "Wow. You're really mature, Ben."

I shrugged. "In a few months, I'll be on my own. Officially. I think that's just sinking in. You, on the other hand, have plenty of time to get there."

"Part of me thinks I never will. Like I'll be forever chasing the dream. My mom always says that about me...I get so wrapped up in the dreams, in the castles I envision in the air, that I miss out on what's around me."

"So, your mom is basically Ferris Bueller, huh? You've got to stop and look around every once in a while, or you could miss out on life?" I teased.

"Yeah," Naomi said with a wide smile. "Yeah, I guess she *is*. Who knew?"

My stomach was so full, I placed the box on the higher countertop and patted my stomach. "I'm stuffed. I don't think I could eat another bite."

"You did some major damage on those. Good work."

"I do what I can," I said. And an awkward pause hung between us. "Hey, thank you...for the pancakes, for being here. For everything."

"There's nowhere else I'd rather be."

And even though I knew we were at work. And even though I knew I was forbidden to get involved with any of my subordinates at the store, I didn't care. I found myself slowly leaning toward her, and she let out a breath and matched my movements. This was it. I was going to kiss Naomi, and if she kissed me back, I was going to tell her how I felt about her. That I couldn't stop thinking about her, that her showing up on Christmas Day turned my worst holiday into the best, and that I wanted to do whatever I could to be with her, even if it meant keeping us a secret to the rest of the staff at Spotlight. I wanted to tell her everything.

Our lips were only inches apart, and I could feel my heart pounding furiously within my chest.

Naomi swallowed hard. "Ben," she whispered, her breath ragged.

"Yeah?"

She opened her mouth to speak, but as soon as she did, the bell above the door rang, and we were startled away from each other. A mom and two small kids covered in flurries walked through the door. "Merry Christmas," the mom said, looking a little guilty, like she knew she'd interrupted something.

"Merry Christmas," Naomi and I said in unison as we both hopped down from the counter. Naomi cleared her throat and walked closer to the customers. "Looks like it's really coming down out there."

"Yeah," the mom said. "It's not letting up anytime soon."

Naomi turned back to me, avoiding eye contact, her cheeks red with embarrassment. "I, uh...my mom would kill me if I got stuck in the snow. Especially today. Is it okay with you if I head out a little early?"

"Of course," I said, trying to sound as casual and unbothered as possible, even though her wanting to bail after we almost kissed was tearing me apart. I wanted her to stay. Desperately. "Hey, thanks for everything."

"Of course," she said, putting her coat back on and taking off the elf hat, stuffing it into her coat pocket. "Merry Christmas, Ben."

"Merry Christmas."

Once she'd left, I stood for a moment, trying to figure out what went wrong. I knew in my gut that she was leaning into me just as much as I was leaning toward her. So, what was it? Did she just get caught up in the moment? Was she really not interested in me like that? Did she feel obligated since it was Christmas? My brain was swimming in possibilities.

"I love your employee picks wall," the customer called from the corner of the store. "Ben's picks are some of my favorites."

Her mention of my picks brought me back to Naomi's comments about my picks and the sly, knowing look on her face. My curiosity getting the best of me, I rushed as casually as possible to the corner. The customer gave me a cordial smile as I offered her a polite nod, studying the movies on the shelf.

And then it hit me. Every movie I'd chosen was a favorite of Naomi's or something she and I had discussed while working in the store. But when I'd picked them, I had no idea. None at all.

She was under my skin even more than I'd realized.

And after today, she knew it, too.

She knew it, and she'd run away.

Fuck.

CHAPTER 11

Naomi

Snow flurries melted the second they hit the windshield as I clutched the steering wheel with white knuckles. It was coming down pretty hard, but that wasn't the reason I left the store. And even though I was almost home, my heart was pounding just as furiously as it did an hour ago when Ben almost kissed me. When *I* almost kissed *him* back.

Almost.

My brain was just as twisted up as the winding roads of my neighborhood. And as I turned into my driveway and pulled into the garage, I knew I needed one certain person to help me make some sense of my thoughts.

My sister, Samantha.

Samantha was a senior in high school that year. A total math and physics nerd, we had almost nothing in common. While I was in a school for the performing arts, Sam dreamed of going to The University of Illinois to study engineering. In fact, she was waiting on her acceptance letter. Not patiently, I might add.

While I loved anything with chocolate or caramel, Sam preferred vanilla and strawberry. While I preferred baby doll dresses and chokers, Sam preferred ripped jeans and flannels. I was crazy about poetic singers like Tori Amos and Lisa Loeb, while Sam was blasting Hootie & the Blowfish and Toad the Wet Sprocket. And, unfortunately, during winter break, we had to share a stereo.

But that was an easy price for me to pay because no matter our differences, Sam was the one I relied on, the one I missed the most when I was away at school, the one who helped me find my way when I royally screwed up. Which was often.

Sam was curled up on the couch, her arms tucked under a fluffy pillow. I could hear *A Christmas Story* coming from the TV. When I walked through the door holding the fleece blanket I'd used to keep Ben's pancakes warm, she jumped to her feet. "How did it go? Did he like the pancakes?"

My brother, Jonathan, popped his head out of the kitchen. "Did we get the ingredients right?"

"He said they were delicious," I said, distracted.

"What's wrong?" Sam asked, raising one eyebrow and placing her hands on her hips. "You look weird."

"Gee, thanks." I swallowed hard, tossing the blanket to the couch.

"Come on," she said, grabbing my hand and pulling me down the hall to our bedroom. She closed the door behind us and perched herself on the edge of her bed, facing me. "Spill it."

"I don't know what happened."

"What do you mean?"

"I mean...everything was good," I said, pacing the room, dodging piles of dirty clothes, CDs, and Sam's textbooks. "Until it wasn't."

"Nay, I'm going to need more information than that."

"He loved the pancakes and the sandwich, thanked me a bunch of times. Everything was fine, we were hanging out, and then..."

"What?" Sam asked gently.

"He almost kissed me."

"Whoa," she said. "I didn't think Ben had it in him."

"I know." I swallowed hard once more. "One minute he's *Buzzkill Ben* and the next minute, he's leaning in to kiss me when we're sitting on the freaking counter talking about our careers, our dreams..." My words drifted off, and I let out a huge sigh.

"Aww, like *Sixteen Candles*."

"No," I snapped at her. "Nothing like that."

Even though it was everything like that. Minus the birthday cake.

"Did you kiss him back?"

"No. A customer came in, and we jumped off the counter, then I got the hell out of there. I blamed the snow."

Samantha's eyes grew wide. "Wait, you just *left*?"

I threw my arms out to the sides in exasperation. "Well, I didn't know what the hell to do. I panicked, Sam!"

Sam rose to her feet and crossed the room to me,

rubbing my arms with her hands to calm me down. "Okay, okay, sorry."

Closing my eyes tight, I took a deep breath and shook my head. "I didn't know what to do."

"Did you want to kiss him?"

I paused, placed a hand on my forehead, and nodded. "Yes."

"So, then, why the panic? I mean, don't get me wrong, I have a freaking panic attack any time a guy asks me on a date, but you? No way. Guys have never been your problem."

"I know, right?" I walked away from her, pacing the room once more. When I stubbed my toe on her binder, I snapped, "Jesus, Samantha, will you pick up your shit?"

I was trying to distract her by getting Sam wrapped up in an argument over our room and stopping our conversation about Ben. A feeling of panic and dread was taking me over again. And it was a feeling I didn't recognize or understand. I mean…it was *just* Ben.

Just. Ben.

So, why was I freaking out?

"I'm not going to let you pull me into a fight. Now tell me why you left that store."

"I don't know, I—I mean, it's Ben. Buzzkill Freaking Ben."

"And? You told me he's gorgeous."

"He is. But he's also stubborn and rigid, and he always finds ways to piss me off. Like, always. I've never argued with anyone this much—at least, not with someone who didn't live in this house."

Samantha snickered.

"I know Mom and Dad bicker all the time, but that's after, like, twenty years of marriage. Not just a few months of knowing each other. He just makes it so hard all the time."

"Or *you* make it hard. You're making it hard right now."

"Sam."

"Naomi," she mocked me. "I'm serious. You're not exactly the easiest person to get along with, you know."

"Oh my God, if one more person calls me a *'Claire'* I'm going to lose it."

"A Claire?"

"You know, Molly Ringwald in *The Breakfast Club*."

"Well…" She wrinkled her nose.

"Samantha Rose Parker," I said with a sneer as my blood pressure soared.

"I mean, take away the sushi and fancy clothes, and they kind of have a point."

"She's a rich bitch."

"She's not a bitch, she's just…popular. You're popular, big sis. And I know that because I know what it's like to be Naomi Parker's little sister. I know what it's like in that shadow, and that's okay. I'm fine with it because I do my own thing. But, yeah, you may not have been the prom queen, but things have never come especially hard for you."

"Nice," I said, shaking my head.

"And don't forget that deep down, Claire's a decent person—she's just too wrapped up in what other people think about her."

"You think I'm like that?"

"I mean...you're ready to turn Ben down because of him being a buzzkill or whatever."

"That's not it. It's the bickering. We fight *all* the time."

"So did Claire and Bender, but they had a happy ending."

"Right...until Monday morning when she probably ignored him in the hallway."

"But you wouldn't do that," she said with a smile.

"Wouldn't I?" I asked with a shrug, sitting on my bed. "Maybe I *am* a *Claire*."

Samantha plopped down next to me and placed her head on my shoulder. "I just think you like someone you don't think you're supposed to like. And that, big sister, is *so* high school."

I sighed. "It's not that, honestly. Like I said, it's the constant arguments. We're always getting on each other's nerves. Anything can be twisted up into a fight."

"So...maybe it's how the two of you flirt."

"No, because we've had that, too. And it's nice. Like really nice. He's just...always surprising me, keeping me on my toes...and not always in a good way. It's absolutely unnerving."

She patted me on the thigh. "You've never shied away from a challenge before."

Another face popped into my head. A ridiculously handsome face that I thought would be at the forefront of my mind on Christmas Day. Not Ben.

"And then, you know, there's Jamal."

"Ah, right...Othello."

"Yeah. I'm supposed to see him in a few days."

"Maybe that's it," Sam said. "Maybe this isn't even about Ben. Maybe you really want Jamal."

Doubt crept into my brain. "Maybe. I'm so confused."

"Maybe you're flipping out because you feel bad for leading Ben on or something."

"I don't know...maybe?"

"You do still like Jamal, right?"

"Yeah, I mean I think so. I've told you he's beautiful and talented and charismatic and basically everything I've *ever* wanted in a guy. But..."

"But?"

"But it's easy. Sometimes too easy."

Samantha rolled her eyes. "Okay, Goldilocks, which is it? Do you want someone who's too easy or too difficult?"

I knitted my brow and glared at her, crossing my arms. "Maybe I want someone who's *just right.*"

She looked me dead in the eye. "That doesn't exist."

"This coming from you—the queen of romantic comedies," I scoffed. My sister was obsessed with rom-coms. While I got swept up in the occasional romance, my sister lived and breathed them. Next to our tiny TV/VCR combo that sat on the edge of her dresser, was a stack of VHS tapes. Every single one rom-com. And here she was telling me that true love, a true match, didn't exist.

"That's just the movies, Nay. No one's perfect."

"You're a real piece of work, you know that?"

"Don't go there," she said, rolling her eyes. "I'm trying to help you."

"Or make me feel stupid."

"Whatever. You got that damn pizza box, you got

Jonathan's manager to let us in at the butt crack of dawn today, you dragged me to the diner in my PJs—"

"You said you were happy to help me!"

"Ugh," she scoffed. "I was. That's not the point. The point is—why did you *do* it?"

"To give Ben a nice Christmas."

"Why?" Her eyes were serious, like they were boring into my very soul.

"What do you mean why? It's Christmas!"

"Because you *like* him."

"No, I don't."

She ignored me and continued, "You like him a *lot,* and that scares the absolute shit out of you, doesn't it?"

That feeling of dread filled my chest once again, and tears welled in my eyes as I looked at my sister in contrition. "Yes."

"Why?"

"I don't know. No one has ever...gotten under my skin like him. It's like, somehow, I know he could hurt me like no one else has. And that's the worst feeling ever."

"I disagree."

"Oh, spare me, Dr. Seaver," I said, knowing my sister was going to bust out the best sage advice she'd learned from the dad on freaking *Growing Pains.* I always hated that show, but when we were younger, Sam was crazy for Kirk Cameron and covered her side of the room with posters from Teen Beat magazine. To me, he just looked like a curly-haired doofus.

"No, hear me out," she said, her voice calming just like that pain in the ass, Alan Thicke.

Damn you, Alan Thicke.

I sighed loudly for dramatic effect.

"And the Oscar goes to..." Samantha said, patting my leg again.

"Shut it," I said, but this time, I put my head on her shoulder, relaxing into the comfort of her care and concern.

"If life was easy, what would be the point?" Sam asked, her voice gentle and kind.

"So, you think I should go for it?"

"I think you should consider it. What do you have to lose?"

"My dignity? Maybe my job? I need this job, Sam. If things didn't work out, you know I'd have to quit. He's the assistant manager, I'm on his turf."

"So, you'd find another job. There have to be a million places you can work on campus."

I shook my head vigorously. "You don't get it. This place is different. I love it there—the people are total weirdos who obsess over movies and pour over quotes and..."

"And they're just like you."

"Yes. Only with a little less fashion sense," I said with a laugh.

"Okay, Claire."

"Ugh. I hate that so much."

"You know I'm only teasing. You've found your people, and you don't want to jeopardize that," she said knowingly. And it was then the final piece of the puzzle clicked into place. I released a breath I didn't even know I was holding deep within my lungs.

"Right," I said with a nod.

"I think we've found the problem."

"Yeah, maybe."

"So, what you have to decide is…is he worth it? Is he worth the risk?"

"I don't know."

"That's what you have to figure out."

"Yeah, I think you're right."

"And no matter what, you gave him a nice Christmas. You did a really nice thing, big sister. Claire would never have done what you did today, especially not while wearing an elf hat."

"Hey, I love that elf hat."

"So do I. But Claire wouldn't. That's the difference between you and her. She doesn't have your heart. Your great big heart."

"You think so?"

"I know so."

We sat in silence for a moment, and then I placed my hand on top of hers. "I shouldn't have left him like that. He probably thinks I didn't want to kiss him."

"Probably."

"Shit."

"Yeah," she said, squeezing my hand. "But you can fix it. I have faith in you."

"I wish I could say the same."

CHAPTER 12

Ben

*E*ven though I hadn't had much of a Christmas holiday, it still bummed me out to take down the holiday decorations at the store. There was something about taking down the garland and mistletoe that always felt like closing the door on a happy time of year only to welcome the rest of the dismal, bitterly cold winter.

Or maybe it was my own bitterness that was casting a pall on my entire attitude at the store. Everyone had returned from break, and the store was as busy as ever with people spending even more time indoors and needing to pass the winter nights. Although I was happy to be busy and to see Dutch, Emmett, and the rest of the employees, being near Naomi again was…a challenge.

I put myself out there.

And she clearly didn't feel the same about me.

And so, I'd spent the last few weeks building a mental armor around myself, preparing for her return. I knew I had to be indifferent, evasive, blank...I had to let Naomi know that I wasn't pining away from her like some silly, lovestruck puppy. There was no way in hell that I would put myself out there again. It was clear to me that her Christmas gesture was just a friendly one and that she had her sights set on someone else. And despite my sour attitude about 'the kiss,' I did appreciate everything that she did that day. I know her heart was in the right place. It just wasn't with me the way that my heart was with her. And it was really hard not to be embarrassed by that.

"Hey," she'd said when she walked through the door, her pale cheeks a bright shade of pink from the gusts of wind that poured through the streets of Evanston that afternoon.

"Hey," I said, only making brief eye contact.

"Happy New Year," she said with a soft smile.

"Yeah, 1995. Hard to believe it."

"The 90s are going by so much faster than the 80s, don't you think?" Naomi said, pulling her scarf from around her neck, her eyes bright and eager for conversation. But I wasn't going to be pulled in like that scarf. I was going to keep my armor intact. And even though I agreed with her wholeheartedly and normally, I'd tell her that childhood makes those early years go by slowly, and as we get older, busier, we realize how much faster time flies by. But instead, I just shrugged.

"I guess." I grabbed the calendar from its spot on the bulletin board. "Hey, can you take another shift on

Sunday morning? Heather's still in Maryland and won't be back until Monday."

"Of course," Naomi said. "I have rehearsal at three. Will that be a problem?"

"Nope. You'll be done by two. Thanks." Without meeting her eyes, I scribbled her name next to the empty shift on Sunday morning, grateful that our shifts would only overlap for thirty minutes that day.

I needed space from her, and I needed it badly.

"Ben, about Christmas—" Naomi began, and I turned to face her, quickly cutting her off with a fake smile and a wave of my hand.

"The sandwich was just as good as the pancakes. Thanks again." I placed the calendar back on its hook and walked around to the return bin as casually and dismissively as humanly possible without coming across as a dick.

Because no matter how bitter I was that she didn't feel the same for me, she didn't deserve to be treated like garbage. She'd done a nice thing and couldn't help how she felt.

"Oh," Naomi said, looking a little stunned by my demeanor. She swallowed hard and ran her fingers through her hair. "Well, you're welcome. It's just that—"

"The store was pretty dead the rest of the day, and Jenn and Jasper showed up to help later on." I looked up to see Jasper approaching the desk. "Speak of the devil."

"Naomi, welcome back, girl," Jasper said, giving Naomi a high five. Her eyes looked pained as she appeared to shrug off our interaction.

"Great to see you, Jasper. How was your Christmas?"

Jasper clutched his belly. "Other than gaining five pounds from my mom's cooking? Pretty great. I slept like twelve hours a night and took my little cousins to Lincolnwood to see all the lights."

The town of Lincolnwood was famous for having the best Christmas lights in all of Northern Illinois. Elaborate, beautiful light displays that people came from all over the state to visit. My mom and I had gone every year after our Christmas dinner. This was the first year that I couldn't go.

"Aww, I've always wanted to do that," Naomi said. "But there's so many of us, my parents never had the patience."

"Ben goes every year."

"You do?" Naomi asked.

"Most of the time," I said. "My mom loves it."

"Dude, did you see the house with the Christmas tree that looked like it went all the way from the first floor and up through the roof?" Jasper asked.

I nodded. "One of my favorite houses. It looks so realistic."

"Do you think the lights are still up now?" Naomi asked, looking optimistic. "Maybe I can convince Sarah to go."

Why not Jamal?

"Nah, they've probably been down for a week or two now. Next year," Jasper said.

"Right."

"Hey, did you guys see the new Jim Carrey movie?" Jasper asked just as Sully walked through the door, giving us a nod as he took off his hat and gloves, looking like a human icicle.

145

"*Dumb & Dumber?*" Sully asked with a smile. "That shit was hilarious."

"I haven't seen it," I admitted.

"Neither have I," Naomi echoed.

"*Our pets' heads are falling off!*" Sully yelled as he ripped off his coat. Jasper threw his head back in laughter, clapping his hands in front of him. "Classic, man."

"Ben, you've gotta see it, man. So freaking funny."

"I'll put it on my list."

"And take Ace with you," Sully said, nodding toward Naomi. "You *both* need to see this flick. I'm so serious."

Naomi and I locked eyes and quickly went back to our work, ignoring one another.

"Ohhh-kay," Sully said before stuffing his coat under the counter.

"See anything good over break, Ace?"

"My sister and I went to see *Legends of the Fall*. It was pretty amazing."

"Brad Pitt, right?" Jasper asked, and I shook my head, closing my eyes and smiling ironically.

"What?" Naomi asked.

"You and your Brad Pitt obsession."

"Oh, Ace, c'mon. Brad Pitt, really?" Sully asked, looking disappointed. "The guy's a hack. No one will remember his name in five years."

"You're wrong, Sully. He's going to have a long career."

"Looks fade."

"He happens to be an *incredible* actor," Naomi said.

"So, his looks have nothing to do with his appeal?" Jasper asked, looking genuinely curious.

"I didn't say that. I *said* he was talented."

"And hot," Sully said. "Come on, all the girls think so."

"Well," Naomi paused. "Have you seen the man? He's perfection. But he's more than just a pretty face. Go see the movie, and then we'll discuss it."

"Whatever," Sully said, not backing down. "I wouldn't waste my money."

"This coming from the man who thinks Jim Carrey is the second coming."

"No. But he makes me laugh so hard I feel like I'm going to hurl, so yeah—I'll take Jim Carrey any day over your pretty boy."

Naomi rolled her eyes. "And this is why you're a writer, not an actor."

"Maybe," Sully said. "But I know talent when I see it. And I'm sorry, Ace, but your man Brad is just that...a pretty boy who probably screwed a talent agent."

"Watch it, Sully," I warned. "Customers in the store."

"Oh my God," Naomi said, looking offended. "Is that what you'll say when I get my first big break? That I slept with someone to get there?"

"That depends."

"On what?"

"On whether or not you would *do* that?" Sully asked, crossing his arms and raising one eyebrow.

Naomi's chin hit the floor as she stared at him indignantly.

"What did you just say?"

"It's a simple question. Would you sleep with someone if it meant the role of a lifetime...that you could become a household name. Would you?" Sully pressed.

"I'm not going to dignify that with a response."

"So, you're refusing to answer the question?" I asked, intrigued.

"No." She shook her head vehemently. "I'm too annoyed to answer it. And you should all know me better than that." She paused. "Especially you."

Her eyes pierced my own, and I felt like the wind was knocked out of me. She was referring to our conversation before our almost kiss—I knew she wanted to be respected for her talent, to be a serious actress. I knew it all. And yet, I'd played into Sully's teasing, falling into it like a crutch.

It was a shitty thing to do, and I knew it.

We both did.

"Okay," Jasper said, attempting to slice through the thick tension that loomed over the desk. "I think it's safe to say that Naomi, here, is going to be a respectable woman of the industry."

"Thank you, Jasper. At least *someone* knows me," Naomi said before grabbing a stack of tapes and storming off.

"What was that about?" Jasper asked, lowering his voice and leaning in closer. "I thought daggers were going to fly out of her eyes and stab you right in the face."

"Yeah, you noticed that, huh?"

"Uh, it's kind of hard to *miss* it," Sully said, his tone condescending and a little bit irritated.

"Shut up, Sully." I shook my head. "You started the whole thing."

"Riiiiiight," Sully said. "Keep telling yourself that."

"Ignore him. You guys will figure it out," Jasper said. The phone rang and he grabbed it on its first ring. "Spotlight Video. Oh hey. Yeah, just a second." He put his hand over the mouthpiece. "Ben, it's Jenn. She says it's important."

"I'll take it in the back."

"Oooh, phone calls with Jenn with two Ns in the back room? Sounds serious," Sully teased just as Naomi rounded the corner of an aisle, still holding the stack of videos in her hands. She stopped dead in her tracks and stared at me for a moment before continuing on her way.

"Thanks a lot, Sully," I said, shaking my head. "Remind me again why I haven't written you up?"

"Because you love me."

"Sure, that's it," I said, my words acerbic as I left the desk and headed to the back room. Just as I was approaching the door, Naomi rounded another corner, and we both froze. One of the videotapes fell from her grasp, and I crouched down to pick it up.

"Here," I said, holding it out for her. Her eyes were cold, impassive.

"Thanks."

"Naomi, I—"

"Don't you have a call to get to? Don't keep Jenn waiting."

I couldn't read her expression. Was she jealous? Or still upset that I didn't have her back with Sully. It was impossible to tell.

"Right," I said with a nod before walking to the back office and closing the door behind me.

"Hey, Jenn," I said. "What's up?"

"Ben, hey."

The line got quiet. "Everything okay?" I asked.

MELISSA BROWN

"Yeah, yeah, I just…well, I was wondering if you would be my date for my cousin's wedding in a couple weeks. February 11."

Right before Valentine's Day. Ugh.

"Oh…," I said, stalling a little bit. "You could have just asked me tomorrow here at work."

"I know, this just…well, it felt easier," she said, her voice cracking against her will. "Just in case, well…you know."

"Oh." I paused. I knew I didn't feel anything for Jenn. She was a sweet girl with an obvious crush and terrible taste in movies. We had almost nothing in common. But I knew I'd already hurt her at the store and didn't want to do it again. Plus, if I was honest with myself, a tiny part of me—okay, maybe not such a tiny part—wanted to let Naomi know that I wasn't about to wait around for her. And so, without thinking it through, I blurted out, "Sure. I'll be your date."

"You will?" Jenn asked, her voice hopeful and light, and I felt just the opposite, wondering if I should have just her let down easy. Would I be leading her on somehow? That was the last thing I wanted to do.

"Oh my god. Thanks so much!" she said.

"Sure," I said, still unsure if I'd done the right thing. "I'll make sure neither of us is on the schedule that night."

"Great. Awesome, thanks."

"See you tomorrow, Jenn," I said, rushing to get off the phone, feeling awkward.

"Yeah, see you then."

Hanging up the phone, I pressed my elbows into the desk and sank my forehead into my palms, wondering how the hell this was all going to go. Since meeting Naomi, I'd barely looked at another girl—even when I had no idea how crazy I *actually* was about her. But now she'd made it pretty clear that nothing was going to happen with us. And things were tenser than they'd ever been... which was really saying something.

I doubted that anything real would develop between Jenn and me, but I owed it to myself and her to, at least, give it a try. And so, right then and there, I decided to do just that. To go into this wedding date with an open mind. And, I guess, an open heart...if that was possible.

Out with the old and in with the new as my mom always liked to say.

Easier said than done, Ma. Easier said than done.

CHAPTER 13

Naomi

"*M*arley," I huffed, looking up at the television screen and seeing the all-too-familiar face of Nicolas Cage staring back at me. "You're turning into Jasper."

Marley furrowed her brow in confusion. "What do you mean?"

"Remember Christmas...Jasper and *Home Alone*? That's you with this movie."

And it was true. Marley had become infatuated with *It Could Happen to You*, a sweet romantic comedy with Mr. Cage and Bridget Fonda. The plot goes like this: A cop doesn't have money to tip a waitress, so he offers to split the winnings if his lottery ticket pays out. And it does. Big time.

"What?" Marley asked, faking surprise while shaking

her head. "It's only been out a few weeks, so I haven't played it *that* much. I think you're exaggerating just a little."

"I don't think so. Every shift you work, you play it, right?"

Marley wrinkled her dainty, little nose. "Maybe."

"Exactly."

"C'mon, it's based on a true story. I mean, how cool is that?"

"Very." I nodded. "And I actually liked the movie the first five times you played it. But now, I just cringe whenever Rosie Perez speaks. And, honestly, sometimes when Nic Cage does, too."

"Bite your tongue, Naomi!" Marley was crazy about Nicolas Cage. Ever since she'd watched *Moonstruck* with her mom, she was hooked. I personally thought he had crazy eyes, but that was just me. Everyone else I knew seemed to love the guy.

I shrugged dismissively. "Sorry, just keeping it real."

"I'm glad you finally said it. She's driving me crazy with this thing," Dutch said, clenching his teeth and walking to the counter. "But she brought me brownies, so my hands are tied."

"A brownie muzzle, huh?" I teased, staring at Dutch's mouth. "You missed a spot," I said, pointing to the brownie crumb stuck to the corner of his mouth.

"I'm saving it for later," he said with a wink before hoisting himself up on the counter. His ratty Phish t-shirt was starting to fray right along with his equally tattered gray corduroys.

"Oh, Dutch, what are we gonna do with you?"

"I need some sugar," Dutch said, patting his belly. "Feed me Valentine's candy and find me a woman."

"Oooh, Dutch wants a girlfriend?"

"Hell yeah. I've been putting out the Damone vibe and everything."

"The what?" Marley asked.

"Don't even tell me you haven't seen *Fast Times*," I said, in shock.

"*Fast Times*?"

"*Fast Times at Ridgemont High?*" I asked incredulously. "It's a teenage rite of passage, Mar."

"Haven't seen it." She shrugged.

"But you've watched this cheese-fest dozens of times," Dutch said with a laugh.

"I'm not bringing you brownies tomorrow," Marley said, tilting her head up and poking out her chin in irritation.

"Fine." Dutch shrugged. "Then *you* can put the porn back on the shelves. Boo-ya, baby!"

Marley pressed her eyes tight. She was trapped.

"Ugh, okay, I take it back." She put her arms up in surrender. "Tease me all you want, but I wasn't allowed to watch rated R movies growing up, so there's a lot of stuff I haven't seen."

"You're in college now," Dutch said, not letting her off the hook.

"But she lives at home," I reminded him. "Her parents are still a factor here."

"Don't you have any friends?" Dutch pressed.

"Ouch," Marley said, recoiling. "You've been spending too much time with Sully. You're getting kind of rude."

"Sorry, my bad. But, for real, you need to see this movie." Dutch turned to me. "Watch it with her in your dorm room. Then her parents don't have to know."

I smiled at Marley. "You have an open invitation, my friend."

"Thanks," she said. "But enlighten me, Dutch. What's so special about *Fast Times*?"

"The question is, what *isn't* so special about it? Sean Penn is the best. He plays Jeff Spicoli—best character in the movie—"

"Gee, I wonder why," I said, rolling my eyes. Then I grabbed a VHS tape and tapped it against my head. "*That was my skull. I'm so wasted!*"

Dutch cracked up, but Marley looked confused. "The character's a total stoner."

"And he's *awesome*," Dutch said with enthusiasm. "And Mike Damone is this cool cat...well, he's pretty cool, I guess. He puts out this vibe, you know, to the ladies."

"*Whatever happens, your toes are still tappin',*" I said with a shake of my head.

"Exactly! That's what I've been doing.... So far, no dice. I've started asking out customers even though Heather told me to knock it off. What *she* doesn't know won't hurt *me*, right?"

"There have to be some stoner chicks you hang out with," I said. Dutch was a good-looking kid, despite the greasy hair and patchouli stench. "Are you putting out the vibe to them?"

"Nah, they're my friends. That's weird."

"Why?" Marley asked. "Friendship can turn into more if you want it to."

Dutch bit down on his lower lip, looking guilty.

"What?" I asked. "What are you not telling us?"

"Here's the thing…and you're not allowed to call me a dick, okay?"

"Ohhh-kay," Marley and I said in unison.

"The girls…you know, that are like me…I'm not into them…physically."

"You're not attracted to people like yourself?" Marley asked, raising both eyebrows.

"So, what is it?" I asked, playful sarcasm in every word. "The baggy clothes? The dreadlocks? The sweet smell of patchouli?"

Dutch rolled his eyes. "I just like…cute girls. Preppy, I guess you could say."

"Seriously?" I asked, looking at Marley and back to Dutch.

"Why is that so weird? Opposites attract. You know that better than anyone, Hollywood." Dutch narrowed his eyes, and my stomach flipped.

"What is that supposed to mean?"

"You know what it means."

"Um, guys…what are you talking about?"

"Nothing," I snapped before turning to glare at Dutch. "He's just being ridiculous. And don't give me another nickname. I have too many as it is."

"Fine, whatever. I'm just saying, I need your help finding a girl."

"A preppy girl," I corrected him.

"Yes. A preppy girl." He looked at Marley. "Any takers?"

Marley's cheeks turned crimson. "I…I, uh…uh."

"I think you have your answer, Dutch."

"Fine, whatever. I knew it was a long shot. So, help me out. Seriously."

"Fine. I'll see what I can do."

"What about your roommate?" Dutch asked. "She's hot."

"Sarah?"

"Yeah. The blonde with the dark eyes, right?" Dutch wiggled both eyebrows.

"That's her." I shrugged. "I guess I don't really know her type."

"Soooo," Dutch said, reaching for the phone. "Call her up and get her down here. I'll give it my best shot, and we'll see what happens. Maybe she'll let me take her out for Valentine's Day."

"A first date on Valentine's Day? Are you high?"

"Not currently," he said with a wink, and I couldn't help but laugh.

"She has plans already."

"A date?" Marley asked.

"Nah, we're going to The Bitterness Bash over at The Pour House."

"Bitterness Bash?" Marley repeated.

"It's a party for single people. Drink specials, fish-bowls, all that stuff. And no dates allowed."

"But you're a freshman," Marley said, confused. "The bar age is nineteen. Are you nineteen already?"

"I have a fake," I said casually. "Girl looks almost nothing like me, but it works every time. I could probably get one for you if you wanted to go with us, Mar."

"Um...nah, I'll probably just stay in."

"My offer still stands," Dutch said, winking at Marley.

"Tempting," Marley said sarcastically. "But no."

"Can't blame me for trying," Dutch said, hopping off the counter and glancing at the calendar. "Ben should be here soon, maybe he can hook me up."

"Oh, yeah because Ben is such a matchmaker." Marley laughed.

Dutch shrugged. "You never know. I'm keeping my options open...and I'm still willing to take you out."

"Dutch, she said no."

"I'm just saying, she could change her mind. Ben's finally giving Jenn a shot. Stranger things have happened."

"Wait, what?" I asked, my stomach dropping to my knees.

Ben and Jenn? First, he blows me off, and now he's dating Jenn?

"They're going to a wedding together this weekend. He's her plus one."

Marley glanced at me and back to Ben. And for a second, I was mortified that even Marley picked up on the tension between Ben and me. "He's probably just being nice. He doesn't like Jenn."

Dutch shrugged. "Not according to Sully."

"Oh, like Sully knows anything about anything," I scoffed.

"We'll see," Dutch said. "We'll see."

"Yeah," I said, seething but doing my very best to conceal it. "I guess we will. I'm gonna put some tapes back."

As I walked the store, I did my best to breathe deeply, to shake off the idea of Ben and Jenn actually dating. But all I could do was picture them together at the wedding.

Him holding her in his arms as they swayed on the dance floor. Her throwing her head back in laughter as he took her in with his attentive eyes.

I. Wanted. To. Scream.

I needed to find a way to channel my anger, my jealousy, my rage. I wasn't angry with Ben but with myself. I'd had an opportunity, and I was too afraid to take it. And now Jenn was reaping the rewards of my less than stellar choice.

Without thinking, I placed the last tape on the shelf and sauntered back to the counter, doing my best to appear aloof and unbothered. Marley and Dutch stared at me with apprehension in their eyes, but I ignored them, projecting as much confidence as I could possibly muster. Grabbing the phone, I dialed the one person I thought could help me through this.

He answered right away.

"Hey, Jamal. It's Naomi."

"Hey, wassup? How are you doing, girl?" His voice was gravely and deep, and if I wasn't so wrapped up in wanting to make Ben jealous, I'd actually be genuinely enticed.

"Good, good. But I could use a little rehearsal...how about you?"

"Tonight?"

"Yeah. I'm at the store, but my shift ends in an hour. Maybe you could pick me up? We can go to my dorm or something."

"Yeah," he said, his voice as smooth as silk. "Yeah, why not? The show is coming up soon, and I could always use a little more time with my Desdemona."

I giggled. "I'll see you soon, Othello."

Hanging up the phone and all-too-satisfied with my ability to distract myself, I crossed my arms and leaned into the countertop.

"You're evil," Dutch said before shaking his head and leaving the counter.

"What?" I asked, my voice incredulous.

"Don't make me say it," Dutch said, glancing at Marley. Stopping dead in my tracks, I dropped the conversation and walked to the return bin to scan in videos.

But Dutch's words haunted me.

Was I evil?

Was I a terrible person?

Either way, Ben would be walking through that door in just a few minutes, and Jamal would be close behind him. And even if it was the wrong thing to do, for me, it was the only way that I could cope with the idea of Ben and Jenn together at a wedding.

For better or for worse.

Jamal arrived right on schedule and according to plan. Ben was standing at the counter when Jamal sauntered through the door. Even bundled up in a puffy winter coat, hat, and scarf, Jamal still managed to look cool. I wasn't exactly sure how he pulled that off, but somehow, he looked just as hot in a parka as he did in his Othello costume. His eyes lit up when he saw me and, with a quick side glance, I saw Ben's jaw tick.

That's right, Ben. You're not the only one with options.

Another person, however, entered the store just moments behind him...and this was not according to my plan. Just the opposite, in fact.

Jenn.

Her thin lips curved up into a curt smile before she beelined to the counter where Ben stood. He offered her a warmer smile than I was used to. Something was different between them. Whether it was just the broken ice of a date to a wedding or something much more, I had to use every ounce of strength within me to stop myself from sneering in her direction. With a deep breath, I focused on Jamal instead.

He pulled off his hat as I approached, giving me a hug as he wrapped his strong arm around my waist.

"Almost ready?" he asked, and I turned to Ben, who was watching us.

"Yeah, almost. I just have to clock out."

"Cool."

"I'll be right back," I said, giving him an overindulgent smile before heading to the back room to punch the time clock. What I didn't realize was that Jenn was right behind me.

"Hey, Naomi," she said, her voice cheery and annoying.

"Hey."

"How's it going?" she asked, sitting on the corner of Heather's desk as I searched for my timecard, flustered. It was gone. "Hey, have you seen my timecard? It's not here. It's always right here in the fourth slot down, but it's missing."

"No idea. I just came in to pick up my paycheck." She shook her head and made a silly face like she'd forgotten something. "Oh, and to give Ben directions to my apartment."

Oh, give me a break, Jenn. I'm so on to you.

"That's nice," I said dismissively. I wasn't about to give her the satisfaction of knowing that under my hard-as-nails exterior, I was crushed into little pathetic bits at the thought of Ben driving to her apartment...of buzzing her door...of bringing her flowers. It was all too much to handle as I was finally understanding the depths of my feelings for Ben.

Unfortunately, I was just a little too late.

"I need to find my time card," I said, looking under Heather's desk. "Someone's waiting for me."

"Yeah, I saw. He's pretty hot."

"Yep," I said, my voice clipped as I continued to look through the back room for my missing card. After several minutes of searching, I walked to the front desk. "Has anyone seen my timecard?"

"Nope," Ben said, not even looking up from the movies he was scanning.

"No, I haven't been back there," said Marley.

"Dutch?" I asked. He was handing a customer their change but gave me a shifty smile. I tilted my head slightly. "Dutch. What did you do?"

"I don't know what you're talking about."

"This isn't funny. My shift is over, I want to go now."

"Then punch out," he said with a shrug. "I don't know where your timecard is."

"I think you do."

"You think I took your timecard?"

"Yep."

"Why?"

Because you want to punish me for asking Jamal to come here. Because you're just as loyal to Ben as he is to you. Because you want to teach me some sort of lesson.

"Because, you—I...um," I said, unable to say any of the thoughts scurrying through my head, knowing Ben was only a few feet away. I couldn't let him know that he was the reason I called Jamal to pick me up. Dutch had me frozen, stuck.

"See? You can't even think of a reason," he said, hopping over the half-wall and strutting toward the back room. He was way too proud of himself and his little prank. "I'll help you find it."

"Sure you will," I said under my breath as I followed him to the back room.

He climbed onto Heather's desk, his feet resting on her chair.

"I thought you were going to help me look."

"I lied," he said with a shrug.

"Dutch, what the hell? I thought we were friends."

"We are. But you went too far. You know how he feels about you, and you're trying to hurt him. Why?"

"I'm not trying to hurt anyone."

"You're lying."

"And I do *not* know how he feels about me."

"Another lie."

"You said yourself he's taking Jenn to a wedding. For all I know, they're probably dating now."

"Yeah, right." He rolled his eyes. "You're really reaching, Naomi. Either shit or get off the pot."

"Excuse me?"

"He likes you, we *all* know he does. So, if you want him, great. I think you two would actually be a pretty rad couple. But if not? Stop parading your theater dude in front of him. It's really uncool of you, and I'm getting sick of it. We all are."

"Oh...you *all* are? So, you've discussed me with everyone else?"

"Pretty much," he said with a goofy, yet diabolical grin. It seemed I had underestimated our resident stoner...and in a big way. There was much more to Dutch than movie quotes, Grateful Dead shirts, and corduroy. He had a heart, and he was determined to shield his friend with it.

"Well, you're all wrong. Ben doesn't like me, and that's that. Now, do you know where my timecard is?"

With a sigh, Dutch reached down to open the top drawer of Heather's desk and pulled out my timecard. Without leaving the desk, he stretched out his arm for me to retrieve the piece of card stock.

"Oh look, I found it," he said, his words full of disdain as he glared at me. This was not the Dutch I was used to. Apparently, he'd grown a pair, and if I wasn't so annoyed with him, I'd be impressed.

"Dutch, c'mon, don't be like this. We're supposed to be friends."

"We *are* friends—the kind of friends who tell each other when they're screwing up. Feel free to reciprocate at any time. I can take it."

"You sure about that? Because I'm not going to hold back."

"Be my guest," he said, extending his open palm, encouraging me to speak my piece.

I shrugged. "Fine. You don't have a chance with Marley, so stop trying to wear her down, you're only making things more awkward between you. You're not her type."

Dutch nodded, closing his eyes. "Fine. Consider it dropped."

"Just like that?'

"Just like that," he said with a shrug before running his fingers through his loose curls. "Now *you* think about everything *I* said."

I paused, looking down at my timecard. "Fine. Whatever. I will."

"Great. Keep on truckin', Hollywood."

"Ugh," I said, plunging my card into the noisy, rusted time clock. "You're too much today."

"I love it when you talk dirty to me," he said with a wink, hopping off the desk and walking back to the main area of the store.

After taking a second to compose myself, I walked back to the counter. Jamal was waiting quietly, reading the back of a video box. Jenn was leaning against the counter, tilting her ass to the side as she talked to Ben and Marley. When I approached, Ben stood up straight, clearing his throat and looking at Marley, Dutch, and me.

"Hey, guys, did you hang the new posters Heather left in the back? I don't see them."

"Ohhhhh," Marley said, clenching her teeth.

"Pretty sure Naomi was supposed to do that," Dutch said with a nonchalant stretch of his arms. "Maybe you'd better clock back in, Hollywood."

I rolled my eyes. "That's dumb. You two are still here for a few more hours."

"It's fine. Dutch and I will do it," Ben said before glancing at Jamal and back to me. "You go ahead, Naomi."

No jealousy, no attempt to get me to stay.

It seemed my plan had backfired in a major way. I was so confident that Jamal would ruffle Ben's feathers, but the only person whose feathers were ruffled was me. First by Jenn, then by Dutch. As Mike Myers's Coffee Talk character on SNL always said, I was completely *verklempt*. And not in a good way.

Swallowing hard, I waved goodbye to Ben and the others, noticing the pity in Marley's eyes as I took Jamal by the hand and led him out of the store. I didn't even look back to see if Ben noticed.

Obviously, it didn't matter anymore.

He was over it and moving on.

And I had no one to blame but myself.

CHAPTER 14

Ben

"*W*ant another slice of cake? Kaley's not going to eat hers," Jenn asked, offering me a little rectangle of chocolate cake and buttercream. We were seated at a large table, surrounded by some of her first cousins who were pounding shots and taking pictures of each other with the disposable cameras left in the center of the tables.

I put my hand on my full belly. "No, I'm good, I think."

We'd enjoyed a pleasant enough dinner with plenty of cocktails. I was grateful that we were staying the night in the hotel where the wedding was being held. I was in no shape to drive. Luckily, Jenn's parents had no intention of allowing us to share a room, so they'd booked me a room of my own. I was really hoping this would keep the night from getting too awkward.

"Want to dance?" she asked. Not wanting to be a total dud of a date and knowing those cocktails would keep me nice and relaxed, I nodded, and we left the table and walked to the dance floor. As soon as our feet met the solid floor, a new song began, and I could not have picked a more awkward song for us to dance to.

"I'll Make Love to You" by Boyz II Men.

If I was a religious guy, I'd think God was pranking me. Or at least having a laugh at my expense.

Ignoring the lyrics of the song but swaying to the beat, I kept my hand on Jenn's hip. Even though she was in heels, she still looked up to meet my eye line.

"Did you hear R.E.M. is coming to campus this spring?"

"Really?" I asked in disbelief. Despite their popularity, they'd never had a show since I'd been a student at Lurie's. "I need to get tickets. They're my favorite band."

"Mine, too," Jenn said.

Surprised, I smiled. "I didn't know that."

Jenn shrugged, a tipsy and bold smile crossing her lips. "There's a lot you don't know about me."

I nodded, a little impressed with tipsy Jenn...although it may have just been the alcohol coursing through my own veins that was calling the shots.

"I'm starting to see that," I flirted back. "Soo, what else?"

"Um..." she said, looking up at the crystal chandelier above our heads. "I love football, especially the Bears."

"Same." I smiled. "Baseball team?"

"The Cubs, of course." She shook her head, waving me away.

"Same."

Maybe we have more in common than I thought.

"But, wait, aren't you from Michigan?"

"Well, yeah, but I've been going to school *here* for a couple of years." She looked at me like I was a little dumb for even asking, so I decided to drop it.

"Okay, where do you stand on Brad Pitt?"

She wrinkled her nose. "He should've gone into modeling. Not acting."

"That's what *I'm* saying," I said, my eyes wide.

"I hate *The Real World*. Those people annoy the crap out of me."

"Jenn, seriously? It's like you're reaching into my brain right now," I said, aghast...and pleasantly surprised. "I can't stand that shit. The whole concept of TV shows that follow real people around is just stupid. People are never going to be 100 percent themselves on camera, it's just impossible."

"Right." Jenn nodded, her fingernail gently skimming the skin of my neck, just above my collar. The feel of her touch was foreign but not completely unwelcome, thanks to the drinks I'd had. "I agree completely."

"What if they start making more shows like that? Can you imagine?"

"Nah," Jenn said. "I don't see that happening. I think that's why people love it so much. It can never be duplicated. Thank *God*."

"Cats or dogs?" I asked her, narrowing my eyes. Thinking this was way too good to be true. How could I have not seen this sooner? Jenn and I were so alike. Had I been so consumed by Naomi that I'd ignored the perfect girl all along?

Jenn hesitated for just a second, then answered my 'cats vs dogs' question, but her answer sounded more like a question itself.

"Dogs?"

"Hell yeah," I said, thinking of my dog, Newman, named after my favorite minor character on *Seinfeld*. "Sometimes I miss my dog more than I miss my mom. But don't ever tell her that. I'd be dead. Do you have any pets?"

"Two cats. Well, my parents have two cats."

"But you love dogs?"

"Yep," she said, swallowing hard, looking up into my eyes, the lights of the chandelier shined on her tan skin. For a second, I wanted to push the hair from her face and kiss her. But something inside me said to wait. Not yet. I just wasn't sure how things were going to go between us.

"Where do you stand on *Seinfeld*?" Jenn asked, raising her eyebrows in curiosity.

"It's my favorite show, hands down. I named my dog after Newman. He's a pain in the ass, just like the character," I said with a laugh.

"Have you seen that new show that's on Thursdays? About the friends who live in New York? The one girl runs out on her wedding, I think."

"I've seen a couple of episodes. It's pretty funny. I like the Chandler guy."

"Yeah, he's pretty great."

"*The last dentist caved, and now they're all recommending Trident?*" I said in my best Chandler Bing voice. No idea how I remembered that line, especially since I think it was the first episode that I watched...but then again, maybe that's why I remembered it. It made an impact.

"Not sure how long it'll last, though," Jenn said with a cynical shrug of one shoulder as we continued to sway on the dance floor. To a new song that wasn't about having sex...*thank God.*

"What do you mean?" I asked, thinking that show had an incredible amount of potential.

Jenn shrugged. "I just don't think it can compete with *Seinfeld*. I mean, that's the funniest show on TV right now."

"True, but same network, same night. So, I bet they're safe. Even if only for a little while."

"True." She nodded. "I love this song."

I hadn't been paying much attention to the song playing in the background, but once Jenn brought my attention to it, I had to force myself not to cringe.

Celine Dion.

I don't think there was anyone in the world who annoyed me more than Celine Dion...except maybe Michael Bolton. Both of their voices just hit this pitch that grated on my nerves, yet millions of people around the world worshipped them. I didn't get it. I also didn't know the name of the song we were hearing, but it was something about Celine being someone's lady and him being her man. Blah, blah, blah. I couldn't stand it.

But I decided not to pull a Sully and get all judgmental on Jenn. I knew how annoying it could be to have someone judge your favorite things—even your guilty pleasures, which I had to assume this song was for Jenn.

There was no other explanation for an R.E.M. fan to love a song like this. Not one.

I gave her a weak smile as we danced. "Don't you love it?" she asked as she leaned in to nestle her head just beneath my neck, her arm wrapping tightly around me.

"Um," I said, swallowing hard. "It's okay I guess."

She tensed beneath me. "What? You don't like it?"

"We don't have to like *all* the same stuff, Jenn." I grimaced. "How boring would that be?"

"Yeah, I guess."

Celine was quickly replaced by Ace of Base, and Jenn pulled away from our embrace. "I need another drink."

"After you," I said, placing my hand on the small of her back and guiding her through the crowd to the small bar in the corner of the banquet room. The bartender handed a bottle of Zima to Jenn who guzzled down half the bottle in seconds.

"Thirsty, huh?" I asked before popping my lime wedge into my bottle of Corona and taking a swig. The citrus quenched my thirst, but I took another sip anyway. Jenn tilted her head back and finished her drink, placing it on the bar and asking for another.

"Whoa, slow down there."

"I have a really good tolerance." She waved me away, but her slightly slurred words told another story. "Really, I'm fine. Finish your beer, let's dance!"

Minutes later, we were back in the center of the banquet hall, dancing in unison to all the traditional wedding songs: "YMCA", "Shout", "The Chicken Dance". When she was dancing and not trying so hard, Jenn was actually sweet, fun. I was enjoying myself with her more than I'd ever expected, and I found myself getting wrapped up in the energy and excitement of the room. So when the next ballad began and she threw her arms around my neck, leaning her head on my chest, I went with it, pulling her close, wishing that my feelings matched hers.

Could I have more feelings for Jenn? Did we just need more time to get to know each other? Did I just need to get Naomi out of my head to get some closure and move on? Jenn *was* cute...very cute, actually, and I'd be lying to myself if I didn't admit that I found her simplicity attractive. No fights, no bickering, no tension you could split with a knife. She liked me, and it was obvious.

But I also knew I couldn't force myself to be invested in someone. So, could I be invested...genuinely invested in Jenn?

Even though my life would have been a thousand times easier if the answer was yes, the trouble was I knew how she would be once the alcohol left her system and she was back to regular Jenn. Not that she was an awful person or anything like that—but she was just a little too much, a little too eager, a little *too* simple.

"Let's go upstairs," Jenn said, her hand gliding down my back.

"And miss the bouquet and everything?" I asked, feeling apprehensive to be alone with Jenn, knowing I was going to disappoint her. And I had no idea how tipsy Jenn would handle rejection.

"Yep," she said, taking me by the hand and leading me to the lobby. Once we stepped into the elevator, I could see just how unsteady she was on her feet as she held on to the rail, leaning in to catch her balance.

"Are you okay?" I asked.

"Peachy keen, jelly bean," she said, tilting her head to the side and licking her lips. "I've never been better."

Oh boy.

"I think you've had a few too many."

Jenn nodded and a hiccup left her lips. "Probably."

"Let's get you to bed," I said as the elevator door opened and we began the long walk to the room Jenn was staying in.

"I like the sound of that, Ben...Ben...Benny in my beddie." She threw her head back in laughter and almost lost her footing. Quickly, I secured the small of her back with my hand.

"Easy there, tiger."

When we got to her room, she dug inside her tiny handbag and pulled out the key card. Over and over, she attempted to place it in its slot but failed.

"Let me," I said, placing my hand over hers and flipping it around so that the arrow pointed the proper way. The lock opened in seconds.

"You're so smart," she said with a loopy smile.

As we entered the room, she kicked off her shoes, then turned around, her eyes hungry—like she wanted to devour me. My dick stirred as she stalked towards me and wrapped her arms around my waist, her hand squeezing my ass.

Hey. She may not have been my type, but I was still a guy.

"Hey, hey," I said, grabbing her hand gently. "You've had a lot to drink. I think you need to rest."

"That's the last thing I want," she said, leaning in to kiss my neck. "I want you, Ben. I've always wanted you."

"I know. But I'm not going to take advantage of you."

"Advantage? You're just as drunk as I am," she said with another hiccup.

Hardly.

"Come on," I said, guiding her toward the bed and pulling back the covers. "Lie down, Jenn."

"Noooooo," she whined, pulling on the lapels of my jacket.

"Trust me, if we're ever going to do this...it shouldn't start like this, okay? Just lie down, Jenn, please."

Her eyes widened in vulnerability, and she nodded.

"But...you're hard. I felt it," she said, and I sighed. I'd hoped she hadn't noticed.

"Don't worry about that."

"But...won't you get blue balls?" she asked, reaching to cup my dick. Her touch made me sigh again, only this time because I knew I was turning down something my body wanted badly.

"I'll be fine," I said, pulling her hand away and placing my hands on her hips, guiding her to sit down and then lay down on the bed. Finally, she submitted and laid her head on the pillow. Covering her with the blankets, I sat down next to her, brushing her hair from her eyes.

"You're a good guy," she said, her eyes closing.

"Thanks."

"Please give me another chance."

"What do you mean?"

A tear rolled down her cheek. "I know I'm screwing this up."

"You're not screwing anything up, Jenn." I wiped her tear away with my hand. "Just rest now. Everything's going to be okay."

Giving her the warmest smile I could, I smoothed her hair down and kissed her forehead. She sighed beneath my touch, and I knew she was going to be fine.

Within seconds, I could hear Jenn's breathing get heavier as she drifted off to sleep, and I quietly filled up a glass of water and put it on the nightstand before making my way to my own room.

I walked down the quiet hallway, wishing I could be as crazy for Jenn as she was for me. Wishing I hadn't thought about Naomi at least two dozen times that night.

Wishing that I didn't want what I couldn't have.

CHAPTER 15

Naomi

Valentine's Day, 1995

*E*ver since the fifth grade, I'd been part of a couple on Valentine's Day.

No joke.

When I was ten, Tommy Gunderson and I were in a passionate note-passing love affair, and he brought me a pink carnation that his mother had gotten from the gas station a block from our school. I gave him a bag of candy hearts that I'd gone through the night before, picking out the perfect ones to give him. And then, when he popped several of them into his mouth without even reading the sentiment, I knew it would never last. I wanted someone who noticed the details. Someone who paid attention. Even at age ten, I knew what I wanted.

And since age ten, I'd always had a boyfriend on the most romantic holiday of the year.

That is…until this year.

This year, I was as single as could be. Aside from our intense stage chemistry, nothing had developed between Jamal and me. I couldn't figure out exactly how I felt, and so I was a little relieved that he wasn't actively pursuing a relationship with me. I wondered if he was just waiting for our play to be over so that we didn't have to risk a breakup while still having to portray lovers on the stage. But would that be enough time for me to figure out what I wanted? Things with Ben were more awkward than ever as we'd gotten to the point where we were hardly speaking. I knew he had gone to a wedding with Jenn over the weekend and, from what I could observe at the store, things between them seemed pretty normal. I couldn't quite decide if they were officially dating or still just friends and coworkers. And the last thing in the world I was going to do was ask my coworkers. I'd be a sitting duck…exposed for them to tease, ridicule, and remind me that I'd already had my chance with him.

And so, when Sully asked us all what our plans were for that night, I said nothing. Minding my own business, I grabbed a stack of tapes from the return box and wandered the store, keeping my ears wide open to see what Ben's answer would be. And, if I'm honest, Jenn's answer, too.

Damn it.

"I'm here until closing. I'll probably go home and pass out," Ben said, and I sighed in relief.

"Riveting," Sully said. "And you, Jenn? What are you up to?"

"Well, I work until ten o'clock, but I don't know... nothing planned really." I wasn't facing the counter, so I was free to roll my eyes. I knew Jenn was hoping Ben would ask her to stay until closing. She was so predictable it made me ill.

"And you?" I heard Sully ask Jasper.

"Jules and I are getting a cookie cake and watching movies."

"What are you watching?" Sully pressed.

"She told me to bring home three of the most romantic movies I could find. Then she'll pick which order we watch them. Or, I should say, which ones she *allows* us to watch."

"Aww, that's cute," Jenn said, and I rolled my eyes again. Lately, everything that girl said made my skin crawl. I was fully embracing the green-eyed monster inside of me.

Not my proudest moments.

"So, what'd you pick?" Ben asked. "I'm not sure you two have the same taste."

"Exactly, hence my disclaimer," Jasper said with a chuckle.

I stopped in my tracks, wondering what movies Ben found romantic. Part of me wanted to cross the store and see what was currently on his picks shelf. Would it be more movies that I liked or that we discussed? Or would it be a Jenn-influenced shelf?

Okay, Naomi. You've officially lost it.

"End the suspense, man. What do you consider romantic?"

"I'm still narrowing things down, but here's my top six."

"Six? Why not five?" Sully asked.

"Because I couldn't decide. You guys can weigh in."

"Done. Lay 'em on me," Sully said, and I could hear a lightness to his tone that I'd never heard before. It piqued my curiosity, and I found myself inching back toward the group, wondering what had come over him. This wasn't the Sully I knew. Not really.

"*Sleepless in Seattle.*"

"I love that movie," Jenn said.

Insert eyeball roll here.

I wasn't much of a Meg Ryan fan...although *When Harry Met Sally* was one of my very favorite films. She was a little annoying in *Sleepless in Seattle*...a little flighty, a little...I don't know. Something. And lately, it seemed like she was in every freaking romantic comedy. Everywhere you turned, there was America's sweetheart...in the theater, on our new release wall. It was just too much. Tom Hanks, on the other hand, was sweet and endearing. I didn't think I'd ever get tired of seeing him on the screen. He was the everyman that a woman could easily fall in love with. His laugh was infectious, and his eyes were soulful. Killer combination for an average-looking guy. But I digress...

"What else?" I called from the aisles, and I heard Sully laugh right along with Jasper. They liked that I was participating from afar.

"*Ghost.*"

"Solid choice," Sully said. "With a supernatural twist. I approve."

"Plus, you know, Patrick Swayze is hot," Jenn added, and everyone ignored her. No one watched that movie to ogle Patrick Swayze. That's what *Dirty Dancing* was for. *Ghost* was about true love, about the afterlife, about so much more.

I know...I really need to work on forming opinions of my own, don't I?

"*Coming to America*," Jasper continued.

"Wait, what?" Jenn asked. "The one with Eddie Murphy? I don't remember that being romantic."

"No," Ben argued. He paused for a second before continuing. "It is, actually. This prince who can have anyone he wants flies across the world to find his wife instead of just marrying a hot, obedient woman who will do whatever he wants."

"Exactly," Jasper agreed. "He doesn't want obedience, he wants love."

"What a fool," Sully said with a snicker.

"Sully!" I scolded, rounding a corner and giving him the stink eye. He may have seemed more cheerful, but he was still a pain in my ass. And that's why I loved the crap out of him.

"It's unconventional but still... romantic," I said as I rounded a corner and came closer to the desk, still not fully ready to be near all of them for the entire conversation. I liked having the freedom to walk away when Jenn irritated me. For an actress, I didn't have much of a poker face in real life.

I was working on it, though.

"I kid, I kid," Sully said. Again, not sounding like his usual, bitter self. "What are the last two?"

"*When Harry Met Sally.*"

"My favorite," I called out. "Harry is, like, the best character ever."

"Waiter," Ben said, and although I couldn't see him, I could hear he was clenching his teeth, just like Harry did in the movie.

"There is too much pepper on my paprikash!" we said in unison, using our best Harry clenched-teeth voices. And as I rounded another corner, I placed a hand on a shelf and bit down on my lip wishing I could go back to Christmas Day and kiss him. Kiss him hard.

"I don't get it," Jenn said, and Sully cracked up.

"You had to be there," Jasper said dismissively and, for a second, I wanted to kiss him, too. "The last two are older. Jules loves old movies—she loves mocking the clothes and the hair while she secretly melts into a puddle of romantic mush. I figure we'll watch a couple new ones and finish with a bang."

"Ugh, I hate old movies," Sully said. "Snoozefest."

Ben recoiled. "Considering you write scripts, that's a little short-sighted, don't you think?"

"How come?"

"You're obviously saying that only modern writers have what it takes to write a decent story. I'm just surprised."

"No, I just can't stand the slow pace of old movies. They're boring."

"Maybe someone will say that about *your* stuff in thirty years," Ben added, and Sully rolled his eyes as I finally made my way back to the counter. "I sincerely *hope* not. But, anyway, Jasper, tell us about these old movies that I know will make me want to barf."

"Shut up, Sully," I said, shaking my head before gesturing for Jasper to continue. I had a soft spot for old movies. My mom, Samantha, and I had curled up on the sofa over break and watched over a dozen of them. From Clark Gable to Robert Redford, I was hooked on vintage movies and the dashing leading men who played their roles in such a classy way. Not to mention the gorgeous, elegant movie starlets. I was in awe of them. Heck, I wanted to *be* them. And so, I wanted to know what Jasper's picks were. I could think of at least five movies that would fit the bill.

"Okay, first...*Ice Castles*." Jasper's eyes widened with pride, hoping we would agree with his first choice.

And I did. Big time.

"Aww," I said, placing my hand over my heart. "That movie kills me."

"We forgot about the flowers," Ben said in a soft voice. Our eyes locked, and my eyes widened. That was my favorite line in the movie...and Ben had said it. I was speechless. And that wasn't easy to accomplish.

"Never seen it. Sounds lame," Sully said as Ben and I continued to stare at one another. A slow smile formed on his handsome face, and I had to grip the counter to get my bearings. You hear those songs where they say they feel weak in the knees. And I did. In that exact moment, I was weak.

For the first time in my life.

"Okay, last one…drumroll please," Jasper said, "because it's a good one.

The room was silent.

"Thanks a lot, guys," Jasper said, shaking his head.

"Just tell us already," Sully said. "End the suspense, Jasper. For real."

"Fine, fine, fine. *The Way We Were*. Redford, Streisand…total magic."

"Wait, wait, wait," I said, recoiling. "You think that's a romance? That movie is gut-wrenching. I cried for an hour after the credits rolled."

"It's not *that* bad," Ben said.

"It's definitely not romantic," I argued. "The guy… what's his name? Hubbell? He's too much of a wimp to be with Katie and they end up apart. How is that romantic? It's depressing. One hundred and ten percent."

"Tell us how you really feel, Ace."

I whipped my head around, feeling all fired up. "Have you seen it, Sully?"

"Nope. And by the sounds of it, I don't want to."

"Good, then you don't get a say in this. Jasper, I'm vetoing that choice."

"Just because it has a bittersweet ending, doesn't mean it isn't romantic. They spent many years together. They were happy," Ben argued, his eyes challenging me.

"Yeah, until Hubbell spoiled it. He couldn't hack it with the girl who challenged him. He had to go for the simple girl instead." Without meaning to, I glanced at Jenn, and the room went silent.

Ben crossed his arms in front of his chest. "Maybe

Katie was just a little too much…maybe she pushed too hard and for no reason at all."

"No reason?" I asked, glaring at him. My knees were no longer weak. No. They were strong as oak, and I was ready to duke it out no matter the outcome. "She fought for what she believed in. She was passionate. Hubbell was weak. He wanted everything to come easy to him."

"No, he didn't."

"Yes, he did," I snapped. I could feel my nose flaring. Ben's blue eyes felt like ice as he sneered at me. This wasn't about a movie anymore. It was personal. Jenn was his simple girl, and I knew I was the Katie he couldn't handle.

Or did I have it all wrong?

Maybe *I* was the *real* Hubbell…maybe I was the one who didn't fight for what I wanted. Ben put himself out there. He was going to kiss me, and I ran. He wasn't the Hubbell. *I was.* My world was spinning, but I did my best to appear strong, indignant, steadfast. My pride wouldn't allow me to give in.

"Okay, okay, I'm putting that one back," Jasper said. "Go to your corners, guys."

"Um…now I actually want to see this flick," Sully said. "Anything that can get these two arguing is something I want to see."

"What is that supposed to mean?"

"Usually, you like all the same movies. *Pepper in my paprikash?* What the hell is that? I've seen that movie twice, and I have no idea what you're saying."

Ben cracked a smile, and I couldn't help but follow right behind, my lips curling against my will. He turned to

Jasper before looking back at me. "*When Harry Met Sally.* That gets my vote."

"Mine, too," I said softly, tilting my head to the side. "Or *Ice Castles.*"

"Or both," Jasper said. "Thanks, guys."

Out of the corner of my eye, I could see Jenn glaring at me, not even trying to hide her disdain anymore. Not intimidated in the slightest, I hopped up on the counter and glanced at the clock. Five more minutes and I could clock out.

Thank God. I need to get the hell out of here, or I'll lose my freaking mind.

"You're off in a few minutes," Jasper said, glancing at the shift calendar. "Where are you headed on Cupid's special day?"

"The Bitterness Bash."

"At the Pour House?" Sully asked.

"Yep."

"Nice," Sully said before biting down on his lower lip. "I went to that last year. Good times."

Silence fell over the five of us as Sully pressed his lips together and nodded, looking...happy.

"So...isn't anyone going to ask me what *I'm* doing tonight? Or are you all too wrapped up in your movie quotes to ask dear old Sully what he's doing on Valentine's Day?"

We all paused, looking at one another. Sully was the last person I expected to have plans that night...*and* to want to tell us about them. Something was definitely going on.

"Fine, Sully, what are you doing tonight?" Ben asked.

"I have a date." Sully nodded proudly, his eyes were bright and a little bit dreamy, like he was under that familiar spell of new love. That time when everything is perfect. The sun is always shining, the birds are singing. And you just feel like you can take on the world. The whole damn world.

Sully smiled widely. "Her name's Wendy. We met in script writing class. She writes horror. And I mean like scary, messed up shit."

"Yikes."

"Yeah, man, I know," Sully said, looking enchanted. "I think I'm in love."

"Horror?" I asked. "Wow. That's kind of awesome."

"I'm telling you, this girl's the bomb," Sully said. Normally that was a phrase that I'd never expect to come out of his mouth. For the first time since I'd known him, I noticed his eyes were bright, his smile was wide, and he wasn't his normal, cynical self.

Sully really was in love.

He must have noticed that I was staring at him because he looked from side to side with raised eyebrows. "What?"

"Nothing, it's just…I've never seen you like this."

"Oh man, don't start, Ace—"

"No, no. It's all good, Sully. I'm happy for you—like *very* happy for you. For real."

He blushed. Sully's cheeks actually blushed.

Who are you, and what have you done with my misanthropic coworker?

"Thanks."

"So…where are you taking her?" I pressed, taking full advantage of his openness and excitement. My lonely heart wanted details—to live a little vicariously through Sully's excitement. "And tell me quickly before I have to clock out."

"I haven't decided yet."

"Wait, what? Sully, it's Valentine's Day...you don't get the luxury of being spontaneous on Valentine's Day. You need a reservation, like, *anywhere* you go."

"She's right," Jasper said through clenched teeth.

"What?" Sully asked, looking panicked. He placed one hand on his forehead. "Well, help me, damnit. I'm supposed to meet her at her dorm in an hour. I can't screw this up."

"Okay, okay." Jasper stepped in. "Here's what you do."

"I'm listening."

"When do you clock out?"

"Half an hour."

"Okay, and how far does she live?"

"Ten minutes tops."

"Perfect. Okay...the bakery three doors down has the most amazing cookie cakes. I picked ours up before my shift and they had tons left. They have balloons, too. Everything you need. Stop there on your way to her place and find a lounge to sit in."

"Dude. This girl is into horror movies, Dungeons & Dragons, and Magic the Freaking Gathering. I can't bring her a goddamn cookie cake."

Jasper stood, stunned. "Okay, then..."

"So, how about this," Ben said, drumming his fingers against the counter. "Grab a pizza from next door, stop at your place, get all your gaming stuff and a blanket. Set up a picnic in her room, and play all your magic games or whatever. We can send you with a couple of horror movies, too."

"Now that's what I'm talking about!" Sully said, and his face lit up. "Thank you, Ben. I've got to pick something really gross. Something that'll really freak her out."

"I do not understand you at all," Jasper said, shaking his head slowly.

"No one does…except maybe Wendy. We'll see."

"So, when do we get to meet this 'horror goddess'?" I asked, genuinely interested in meeting the woman who'd flipped a switch on Sully. In my opinion, if she was capable of that, she was capable of greatness.

"Hmm, not sure," Sully said with a shrug. "I'm not going to parade her through the store, so if that's what you're thinking…don't."

"I didn't say anything like that."

Jasper hopped off the counter in excitement. "There's an APO party on Saturday at Ben's house. Bring her."

"I've never gone to one of your parties," Sully said, looking suspicious. "Not exactly my thing."

"What is there not to like, Sully? Beer pong, quarters, music—"

"And," Ben said, tilting his head forward, "free beer."

"The man makes a solid point," Sully said with a nod. "I'll ask her, but I make no guarantees."

"Fine with me."

"Sounds fun," Jenn said. "Are we all going?"

Ben glanced at Jenn and then back to me. "Um, sure. I live there, so I guess I can invite as many people as I want. So, you're all invited."

I pressed my lips together in a thin line. Tempted but

unsure. I really wanted to meet this infamous Wendy the Horror Chick. And if I was honest with myself, I was feeling like it could give me another chance with Ben. He was different at the last party—relaxed, protective of both Sarah and me, and a damn good beer pong player. He impressed me that night. And I think that's the night that my feelings for him jumped to another level—I just couldn't see it, or him, clearly enough.

"Ace?" Sully asked. "You going?"

"Maybe," I said with a smile. "I'll ask Sarah. That reminds me, I'd better head out. She's waiting for me at the bar."

Jenn perked up and gave me a condescending smile. "See ya!"

Resisting the urge to bare my teeth and hiss at her, I ran to the back room to clock out and make my way out the door.

It was time to get drunk.

Very, very drunk.

Thank God.

* * *

THREE-AND-A-HALF HOURS LATER, that's exactly what I was.

Drunkety-drunk-drunk-drunk. Oh boy, was I drunk.

After splitting an electric blue fishbowl cocktail concoction and guzzling down way too much booze, Sarah and a guy from our dorm had their tongues down each other's throats, and I was stuck entertaining his handsy, annoying roommate. With every story and joke that he told, he placed his hand on my thigh. And each time, I grabbed that hand and placed it back on the table. By the fourth time, I glared at him.

"Dude. I don't even know your name. You're not getting in my pants."

"Isn't that what tonight is all about?" he asked. "Hooking up? I mean, it's the Bitterness Bash. Relax already." He placed his hand on my thigh for, at least, the tenth time that night. And I shook my head, removing it once again.

"Never going to happen, Cletus. Keep walking."

"Cletus? My name's Kurt."

"I don't care what your name is. Walk away."

Kurt drained the rest of his beer, slammed the bottle on the table, and walked away. I was pretty sure he called me a bitch under his breath. Whatever.

Join the club, asshole.

"Wow," a familiar voice said from behind my chair. I turned to face the gorgeous Jamal, who stood with his arms crossed and one eyebrow raised. "Here I was thinking you needed rescuing. I should've known you could handle that dick all by yourself."

"Damn straight," I said, hopping up from my chair only to lose my footing and trip into Jamal's arms. "Shit!"

Jamal cracked up, steadying me with his strong hand. "You're a clumsy one, aren't you?"

"Not usually. You bring it out in me, I think."

"Not on the stage but definitely when I see you on campus," he said with a chuckle. "Well, I guess I'll take that as a compliment. What are you doing here?"

"I came with my roommate. We're both single at the

moment." I turned to look at Sarah who was still sucking face with what's-his-name. With a liquor-infused giggle, I corrected myself. "We *were* both single anyway. What about you?"

"Same. All the guys from my apartment are free agents right now, so here we are."

"It's good to see you," I said. "I mean, we see each other every single day, but you know what I mean—off the stage."

"I do. Can I buy you a drink? Or should I cut you off?"

I hopped back into my chair and tapped Kurt's now empty seat. "Take a load off. We can get another fishbowl."

"I don't think that's the best idea. Those things will knock you on your ass, and you're already halfway there."

"Yeah, probably," I said. "So, let me ask you something."

"Sure."

"Is *The Way We Were* a romance?"

"The Way We What? I don't know what you're talking about."

"It's a movie. Barbra Streisand, Robert Redford…"

He looked at me with blank eyes, clearly not following. "You've never seen it, have you?"

"Nope."

"*Ice Castles?*"

"Definitely not."

I wrinkled my nose. "You want to be an actor, right?"

"Yes." He paused. "What are you getting at?"

"An actor who doesn't watch movies. That's…peculiar."

"I never said I don't watch movies. I do. You know I do, I've seen you at the video store."

"Good point." I nodded, licking my lips. "What's the most romantic movie you've ever seen, then? Tell me."

"Give me a second to think about that," he said before taking a sip of his drink. "*Jason's Lyric*. It's not just a romance, it's so much more than that. It's about family, loyalty, loss. But I think it's romantic. Have you seen it?"

"No, but I've seen the tape in the store. It came out last year, right?"

"Hmm, for an actress, you haven't seen many movies, have you?" he teased with a wink. "I'm just playin'. You should see it, though. Broaden your horizons a little bit."

"Maybe I will." I tilted my chin forward.

Jamal stepped closer to me, running his fingers through my hair. His dark eyes peered into mine. He smelled like the men's counter at Marshall Fields. Manly. Sexy. Irresistible.

"We could rent it now. Go back to your place." His voice was smooth as silk.

I swallowed hard before glancing at my watch. "Store closed five minutes ago."

"You have connections, don't you?"

And then I remembered my connection...Ben. I'd wanted to make him jealous in the past, but now...now I didn't want that. I didn't want to rub salt in the wound that was our almost-kiss. I didn't want him to think there was more between Jamal and me than there actually was. Although, what was between us was becoming clear—at least on Jamal's end. From the register of his voice to the feel of his fingers dancing in my hair, it was undeniable that he was ready to take our relationship to a new place...even if only for one night.

"I'm hungry," I said. "And I just realized I never ate dinner."

"Naomi, you're tiny, and you've had a lot to drink. You need some food in your stomach, girl."

"There's a pizza place near the store. It's open for one more hour. We could grab a few slices and go back to my dorm. I have a few movies in my room. Interested?"

"You know I am," he said before patting his stomach. "And I can always eat."

"Let's go then." I walked to Sarah and tapped her new friend on the shoulder. "We're heading back to the dorm. I expect you to deliver her to me in one piece."

"I'm fine, Naomi. You had way more tonight than I did." And I honestly believed her. For once, Sarah was right. While my speech was slightly slurred and I was having trouble focusing my eyes, she looked almost sober. She leaned in close. "I want to go home with him."

"Are you sure?"

"Um, yeah. And he lives in our building. It's fine, I promise."

"Okay." Then I looked back at the guy who was eyeing her like a piece of meat. "What's your room number?"

"304."

"Got it," I said before pointing to my eyes and then to his. "I'm watching you."

Sarah laughed dismissively, then glared playfully at Jamal. "I could say the same to you."

"We're going to get some pizza and hang out in the room."

"Put a sock on the door," she said with a wink. And I winked right back, although something in the pit of my stomach was telling me that's not what I wanted. And yet, the alcohol coursing through my veins directed my every move. Giving Sarah a pat on the shoulder, I grabbed Jamal with the other hand.

"Let's go get some pizza."

* * *

"WHY DOES this taste so good after midnight?" I asked, taking my first bite of pizza, all bundled up in my coat, hat, and scarf. The wind chilled my already frozen fingertips, but I didn't care. The pizza was worth a little frostbite. My arm was linked with Jamal's as we made our way down Green Street, a few blocks from my dorm.

"Maybe you're one of those Gremlin things. Maybe I shouldn't feed you after midnight." Jamal made an overly exaggerated scared face, his eyes wide, his mouth stretched open. Then he leaned in and pretended to dramatically bite me on the neck. His ice-cold nose made contact with my skin, and I shivered but smiled wide. Giggling, I pushed him playfully on the arm as we walked toward Spotlight Video. The outside sign was dark, but soft light glowed from inside the store. I glanced at my watch, surprised that anyone would still be in the store. I was sure Ben had already left to take the deposit to the bank before going home for the night and had just forgotten to turn the lights off. I shrugged off my curiosity and brought my attention back to the amazing taste of the pizza I'd had dozens of times before.

"I'm serious—it tastes *so* much better than any other time of day. Why is that?"

"It's the alcohol. Trust me," Jamal said. "We probably shouldn't eat too much of this, or we won't fit in our costumes next week."

"Ugh, don't remind me. I hate those corsets. And I can't believe it's almost tech week. This year is flying by already."

Tech week was the week before the official Othello performances. All cast members, all crew, and all musical pit members were required to be at rehearsals every night. I'd received ten guest tickets for each night of the performance. I'd reserved the first night for my family and a few close friends. Saturday was for my coworkers. Of course, I wanted Sully, Emmett, Marley, and Jasper to come...but if I was really honest with myself, really tuned in to my own intentions, I'd have to admit that the one I really wanted to attend was Ben. I'd be dropping the tickets off at the store as soon as Mr. Martin made them available to all of us.

"Are you excited?"

"Beyond," I said with a sigh. "And a little relieved."

"Your first university performance, it's a big deal, Naomi."

"It is," I said with a nod.

Jamal took a bite of his pizza and the steam drifted into the frigid night air. "Thank God you live close by."

"I normally take the bus."

"What—three or four blocks?"

I shrugged. "I'm lazy. And they come every ten minutes. Annnnnnd, if you hadn't noticed, it's the middle of winter. Chicago winter nonetheless."

He waved me away. "You don't know anything about

winter until you've been to Northern Wisconsin. My grandmother lives way up there, and I'm telling you, this is balmy."

"Remind me never to go to northern Wisconsin," I said with a shiver.

We both went back to eating our pizza slices, walking quietly as the sounds of buses and car horns surrounded us. My mind kept drifting back to the lights at the store.

Was Ben inside the store?

Had I inadvertently paraded Jamal in front of him?

And why couldn't I stop thinking about Ben and focus on the gorgeous man walking beside me?

Why? Why? Why?

Just as I'd popped the final bite into my mouth, we approached my dorm. Jamal took my hand in his, and I stopped in my tracks. The pizza was sobering me up, and I finally knew what I wanted. I was only able to think of one person, and it wasn't the person whose hand I was holding. As he leaned in to kiss me, I pulled my head back in haste.

Surprising even myself.

Ben.

I wanted Ben.

"Wait," I said, closing my eyes tight. "Maybe we should slow down."

Jamal let go of my hand, placing both hands out in front of him in surrender. "What's wrong?"

"I, uh...I think I need to just...get some sleep. Alone."

"Are you serious?" Jamal asked, a genuine look of shock on his face. "But I thought—"

"I know. I'm so sorry for leading you on."

He tilted his head back and looked up at the dark, cloudy sky. "I was afraid of this."

"Afraid of what?"

"This. Exactly this."

"I don't understand." I was waiting for him to call me a tease. It wouldn't have been the first time I'd changed my mind once I'd sobered up, but it was always with someone I barely knew. Never someone like Jamal. I cared about Jamal—if nothing else, I considered him a friend. But he was more than that. He was my partner on the stage. My rock. My Othello.

"The play's in, like, two weeks. You're panicking, aren't you? That we'll kill the chemistry. Because I've thought about that, too. You *know* I have."

"No, I just—"

"That's why I wasn't going to make a move until *after.*" He stepped closer. "But you look *so* hot tonight. So unbelievably fine, I couldn't help myself."

"You always look hot. Always," I echoed his sentiment.

"So, then what's the problem? If we both want this, then what's the harm? We've already cracked open Pandora's Box. Might as well just open it all the way."

"I can't," I said, shaking my head. "I just…I changed my mind."

"Why?"

"It's complicated."

"Fuck," he said, shaking his head. "I knew this would happen. Months of work down the drain."

"This is my fault, I know that. I should never have invited you back here. This is all on me."

"Right." He gritted his teeth, not looking at me. "Way to let a guy down easy."

"Are you pissed?"

"No." he shook his head, pressing a hand to his forehead. "Well, yeah, maybe I *am*. This performance is everything to me, and now it's screwed up...and for what? Nothing."

"It means everything to me, too, you know!" I snapped, a little too defensively.

He nodded slowly in recognition but still angry and still not looking me in the eye. The lack of alcohol in our systems was putting a wet blanket over everything, and now we were both clawing to get out from under it...just in different ways.

"Let's just pretend this never happened, all right? Can we do that?"

He furrowed his brow but said nothing.

"Come on, Jamal. *Nothing* happened."

"No. I guess it *didn't*," he said, his nostrils flaring. My heart sank into my gut.

"Can't we just go back to the way we were before? Friends in real life and partners on the stage—Othello and Desdemona giving one hell of a performance? We can still be amazing up there; I *know* we can."

"Yeah, well, I mean it's not like we have a choice. Casting is set in stone, isn't it?" he said, an acerbic laugh leaving his lips. His jaw ticked as he breathed in. "God, I feel like a fool."

"Don't, please."

"A straight-up fool," he said, glaring at me.

"Jamal, you're one of my favorite people. I mean that. And honestly, I've had a crush on you for *months*."

"What? You what?"

I shrugged. "It's true."

"Then what the hell?" He shook his head, looking confused, frazzled.

I sighed, scrunching my frozen forehead. "It's hard to explain."

"I don't get you, Naomi. I really don't."

"I just…I think my heart is somewhere else—w*ith* someone else. And I didn't realize that until today. And my head was all cloudy, and you looked so good, and you smelled so good, and I…I got lost in the moment…lost in the haze. I'm sorry."

"So why were you at the bar tonight? If you know who you want, why aren't you *with* him? Why were you at the Bitterness Bash? And why were you wasting my time?"

"Jamal—"

"I'll see you tomorrow."

"Please don't be pissed."

He paused and shook his head. "Please don't be a tease."

I gasped.

"Oh wait," he smirked and raised both eyebrows. "Too late."

"Jamal!"

He walked away, holding up one hand as a flippant goodbye. I stood, speechless, and watched him disappear into the night. Finally, I pulled my key from my purse and walked into my building, wondering what else in my life I could possibly screw up.

CHAPTER 16

Ben

J was going to miss these parties. I really was.

It was hard to believe that my senior year was more than halfway done, and soon I'd be interviewing for jobs—careers at *actual* production companies, theme parks, and special effect studios. Suddenly it was becoming all too real, and as excited as I was to begin my career and to use everything that I'd learned in school, I wasn't exactly ready to be a full-fledged adult. Was that weird? I wasn't sure. I liked to tell myself that all of us felt it to a degree and that the bittersweet feeling that I had was just an indicator of what a great experience my years at Lurie University had been. I was going to miss it.

I would miss it all.

Luckily, it was still only February, and our fraternity was having another party at my house. The best part about hosting these parties was that our frat organized a clean-up crew who came the next morning to clean the house from top-to-bottom. Our pledges and members got extra service hours, and my participation was optional. Of course, I always helped, but it was nice to know that if I needed to sleep one off, I could do just that while my house was cleaned. In fact, my roommates and I loved when we hosted APO parties because our house was at its cleanest in the days that followed. It was a win-win for everyone involved.

"Yo! What up, home skillet?" my roommate, Jeff, said, joining me at the keg as I scanned the crowd in our basement. I passed him a fresh beer.

"Here you go, man."

"More people from your work are here."

"What do you mean *more?*" I asked, surprised. I hadn't seen any of the Spotlight Video people at the party yet, and I had mixed feelings about that. "Well, yeah, that kid with the ponytail, some skinny kid, and a creepy girl."

"Creepy?"

"You know...goth or whatever."

"Sounds like Emmett, Sully, and his new girlfriend. But you said more. Who else is already here?" I asked, feeling my blood pump fiercely through my veins.

Maybe Naomi was here.

And I had mixed feelings about that, too.

No matter what had or hadn't happened between us, I was still drawn to her like a freaking magnet. I wanted her desperately, but after seeing her walk past the store with that guy, Jamal, and especially after seeing him nuzzle her neck while she smiled, everything finally made sense. She hadn't kissed me back because she was with him. As my mom would say, she was already spoken for. Why she felt the need to tell everyone at the store that she was going to The Bitterness Bash instead of just telling us the truth, I had no idea. Maybe she was trying to spare my feelings in her own way. Either way, I was a masochist because I was still dying to see her, even though I knew I didn't stand a chance. I knew I needed to get over Naomi Parker, but that probably wouldn't happen until I left Spotlight Video and moved on with my life.

Until then, I was crazy about her despite my better judgment.

"Yeah, a girl with a nose ring showed up with some stoner dude a little bit ago. Jenn, I think Jasper said her name was. And I can't remember his name. Something weird."

"Dutch."

"Yeah, maybe."

"She was asking for you, too. Is she your girlfriend?"

"No, I wouldn't say that. But we went to a wedding together last weekend. I probably shouldn't have agreed to go, looking back on it." I took a sip of my beer.

"Why is that? She's cute."

"Just not for me. We don't click, you know?"

Jeff looked to the side, then turned his body toward me, leaning in. "Brace yourself, buddy. Here she comes."

"Thanks," I said, shaking my head and preparing another beer.

"Hey," Jenn said, walking up to the keg. "Thanks for inviting me."

"No sweat," I said with a weak smile. I didn't want to

be rude to her, but I just wasn't feeling it. I knew that I had to be completely honest with her or I'd start to feel like a dick for leading her on. There was no doubt that hope still lived in her eyes when we spoke. Jenn wasn't giving up.

"Beer?" I asked her, and she nodded, grabbing the cup and downing it in seconds.

"Easy, killer. The night is young."

"Yes," she said, raising her eyebrows. "It is."

Awkward.

"So, where's Dutch? You came together, right?"

"Well, I mean, not *together*-together. Our shifts ended at the same time, so we walked over. But there's nothing going on between us or anything."

"I didn't think there was," I said, giving her a kind, but hopefully not misleading, smile. "Where is he?"

"Not sure. He was talking to Naomi in the kitchen I think."

Naomi.

I swallowed hard at the realization that she'd actually come to the party. As pathetic as it was, I was thrilled she decided to come. I could only hope that she'd arrived alone...and not with Jamal in tow. I did my best to harness my enthusiasm, not to be too obvious in front of Jenn, but by the look on her face, I was definitely failing miserably. Luckily, Jasper approached before I could dig myself into too big of a hole.

"Yo!" Jasper said, approaching with his hand raised, ready for a high five. Of course, I obliged and then offered him a beer. He nodded as he took the cup from me. "Thanks, man. Great crowd tonight. What's up, Jenn?"

Jenn, looking irritated, gave Jasper a curt smile before handing me her empty cup. "Nothing much."

Clearly, she thought Jasper was cock-blocking her. Ignoring her foul attitude, I passed the cup back to her, filled to the brim.

Jenn took two more large gulps of beer, and Jasper and I shared an uncomfortable glance. It was obvious that neither of us was in the mood to handle Jenn. "Ben, I heard you're great at beer pong. Wanna play?"

"Dude, did someone say beer pong?" I heard the familiar voice say as Dutch wrapped his arms around Jasper and Jenn. Jenn shifted uncomfortably then looked down at her feet. Her face was panicked as she bent down to grab a piece of paper.

"What's that?" Jasper asked.

"Nothing," Jenn said, shoving it into her front pocket. "I just dropped something."

"What's up, Dutch?" I said, pouring him a beer, having no idea why Jenn was acting so strangely. "I have to man the keg for a little longer. But I have a feeling you've just found an opponent, right, Dutch?"

Jenn's shoulders sagged, and she pressed her lips into a thin line, obviously disappointed.

Dutch, on the other hand, looked anything but disappointed. "I'm all over it. Prepare to suffer, Jenn with two Ns."

"Are you ever going to stop calling me that?" Jenn asked, her brows knitted.

"Not anytime soon," Dutch answered as they walked away. "Just go with it."

Jasper refilled his beer and nudged me in the arm as

TLC's "Creep" blasted in the background. "So, what's going on with you two? That was awkward as hell."

"Ya think? I keep trying to let her down easy, but she just isn't picking up my signals."

"Maybe you have to be more obvious."

"Probably, yeah."

We both took another sip of beer, trying to shake off the uncomfortable feeling that Jenn left in her wake.

"Naomi's here," Jasper said.

"I heard." I took another sip.

"So…" Jasper leaned his head forward.

"So, what?"

"Try again, man."

"No dice." I shook my head, gritting my teeth. "I think she's seeing someone."

"Who?"

"That guy, Jamal. You know the one that keeps coming to the store."

"Oh yeah, *her Othello*," Jasper said in a sing-songy tone, clearly imitating Naomi's dramatic nature. I didn't laugh. I was too preoccupied with the fact that this Jamal guy was such an important fixture in her life. Someone she saw even more often than she saw me. And not only that, someone who shared her passion for the dramatic, her fervor for the stage.

How could I *ever* compete with that?

"Wait." I paused. "*That's* the guy who's playing Othello?"

"Yep."

"How am I supposed to compete with *him*, man? They're together every single day. They probably have to make out for the freaking show! And have you seen the guy? Shit!"

"All right, man, calm down."

"She makes me crazy, Jasper. I just...I don't know what to do."

Jasper shook his head. "From my vantage point, I'd bet money that she's into you. And I'm not just saying that because we're friends. She's different with you, Ben. Hard to explain, but it's obvious—to me, at least."

"I don't know, man."

"And what she did for you on Christmas? I *definitely* think she's into you. No doubt."

"Well, then what about him? I literally just saw them on Valentine's Day all snuggled up together as they walked in front of the store."

He shrugged. "Oh. Good point. You know...maybe she likes you both. Maybe she's trying to figure it out."

"And what? I'm just supposed to wait for her to decide? I graduate in three months, man. I don't have time to wait around."

"Then don't. Life is short. You should go for it—at least find out where her head is at. If you strike out, just get really hammered and pretend you don't remember anything."

"Wow. Brilliant plan."

"Come on. You'll always regret it if you don't. Trust me."

"I already did. I tried to kiss her, and she ran out the door. That girl preferred driving in a snowstorm to being with me."

Jasper laughed, shaking his head. "I'm sure there was

more to it than that." His posture changed, and his muscles went rigid. "Now play it cool. She's heading this way."

A few of my fellow fraternity members shifted, and I saw Naomi, Marley, and Sarah walking toward us. Naomi lit up, pointing at Marley with both of her hands. "Look who I brought with me!"

"Oh my God, would you stop announcing it to everyone?" Marley said, tucking her brown hair behind her ear, her cheeks turning bright red. "I *do* go to parties!"

"Sometimes," Naomi said, rolling her eyes. "Anyway, she's here. Yay to APO for getting this girl out of the house." She turned back to Marley. "Sorry, I'm kidding. You know I love you."

"Welcome, Marley," Jasper said as I pumped the keg. "Sully's here, too."

"Why do you think we're here?" Naomi said, only looking at Jasper, not yet making eye contact with me. "I mean, no offense. Your parties are great, but Sully has a freaking girlfriend. We *have* to meet her."

"No offense taken," I said with a half smile as I handed her a beer. We locked eyes, and she bit down on her lower lip just a tiny bit, almost looking a little bit shy—if that was even possible. I'd never seen Naomi even attempt shyness. It wasn't in her DNA.

"Thanks," she said, and for just a second, I wondered if Jasper might be right about the two of us. Maybe she felt what I felt.

She has a boyfriend, dumbass. It's all in your head.

"So, where are they?" Marley asked, scanning the crowd and snapping me from my thoughts.

"Right behind you," a voice said from behind Marley, and she jumped a bit in surprise. The rest of us laughed as we tried not to crane our necks too hard to see the girl standing behind him.

"Sully!" Marley said, playfully slapping his shoulder. "Where did you come from?"

Sully ignored her question, smiling widely as he stepped to the side and pulled the infamous Wendy's hand so that she could see us all. "This...is Wendy. She's a sophomore like me, she writes horror, and she's the smartest girl I've ever met. Oh, and you guys know Emmett. He's here, too."

Emmett gave us all a wave, shaking his head and rolling his eyes.

Wendy grinned. "Wow. That was quite the introduction. It's nice to meet you guys. Bryan talks about you all the time, so it'll be good to put faces to the names."

I paused for a moment, waiting for Sully to get annoyed. But it didn't happen. She'd called Sully by his first name...and he hadn't corrected her. He didn't even bat an eye.

He really was crazy about this girl.

As Sully introduced us all, I studied her, and I could tell everyone else was doing the exact same thing. Wendy was petite with jet black hair that fell to her shoulders, pale porcelain skin, and really dark eye make-up. A bandana was wrapped around her head, and she looked almost like a 1950s pin-up girl. In fact, if I had to choose the ideal girlfriend for Sully based purely on superficial physical features, Wendy would be the exact girl that I would choose. She was dressed almost all in black, just like Sully, with big, clunky combat boots and large silver hoop earrings.

With a look of pride on his face, Sully placed his arm around Wendy's shoulders. "So...now you've all met her. You can see she actually exists."

"We never thought she didn't, Sully," Marley argued, but the rest of us stayed silent. I had to admit the thought had crossed my mind. Not that Sully was gross or anything, he just had such a distinct, strong personality that it was hard to imagine him as part of an actual couple. He stood out so much as an individual, and because of that, it was hard to see him in a different way. But he looked happy. Really happy.

"So, Bryan says this fraternity volunteers and stuff?" Wendy asked.

"Yep," Jasper said. "We're always open to having new pledges if you're interested."

"Maybe," she said as I held out a beer. She smiled and took it from my hand with a gracious nod. I liked her already. "Oh, and I suppose I should probably thank you guys for the Valentine's Day plan. It was pretty rad."

"So, you liked that, huh?" Jasper asked, looking surprised. "D & D and pizza?"

Wendy smiled at Sully, then nodded. "It was the best."

"I'm shocked he gave us credit," I teased, knowing Sully could have kept all the accolades for himself.

"Oh yeah, he went on and on about all of you guys— why do you think I came tonight? I had to see what all the fuss was about."

"Same," said Marley before giving Sully a wink.

"Parties aren't normally her thing. But she's sucking it

up…for me." Sully looked all too proud of himself as he pulled Wendy in and gave her a kiss on the top of her head. Her pale cheeks turned red.

"That's true love," said Emmett. "So, *Bryan…*"

Sully shook his head, his eyes indignant. "Nope. Only Wendy and my mother are allowed to call me that. You know this."

"Okay, okay. Sorry." Emmett put his hands up in surrender. "*Sully—*"

"That's better."

"Are you sleeping at our place tonight? Your bed's been made for, like, six days straight. I think that's a record. I've never seen your half of the room so clean before."

Wendy's hand was wrapped around Sully's waist. She pulled him closer and winked at Emmett. "Don't wait up."

"You heard the woman," Sully said with a laugh. "So, you know, feel free to bring someone home tonight if you want. Live it up, get crazy…just stay on your side of the room and don't touch my shit. I'll be back eventually."

"I wasn't… I mean that's not…" Emmett said, looking flustered. He ran his fingers through his hair, shaking his head. "Never mind."

"An-y-way," Naomi said, saving Emmett from his obvious embarrassment. "Guys, you all remember that Othello is next weekend, right? Saturday, seven-thirty. I'm going to leave the tickets at the store tomorrow." She scanned the circle, then her eyes landed on me. "I expect you *all* to be there."

"I think I'm working Saturday night," Marley said as two hands wrapped around my eyes and a familiar voice whispered into my ear. "Guess who."

Jenn. And she wreaked of beer.

"I take it Dutch kicked your butt in beer pong?" I asked as she placed one hand on my ass and the other on my free hand.

"Maaaaaybe. Come, dance with me. I love this song."

"I'm not really—"

"Come onnnn," Jenn said, pulling me aggressively. If I pulled away, it would be more than just a little awkward.

My eyes darted to Naomi who looked...impassive, unaffected, bored. And it pissed me off. Just seconds ago, I thought she was hinting that she specifically wanted me to come to her show. And now...it was like she didn't care at all. So I let Jenn lead me to the dance floor. After throwing her hands around my neck, she pulled me close, and I placed my hands gently on each of her hips, making sure not to hold her too closely or too intimately. She was way too tipsy to have a serious conversation, so I decided to suck it up, dance just one dance, and then head back to the group.

"Your eyes look like ice," she slurred. "So blue."

"I've heard that before."

"Ben..." she said, her eyes glassy as she stared up into mine.

Shit. You're forcing me to say it, aren't you, Jenn?

"I think I want to join your fraternity."

Oh, God. Please don't. I can't keep doing this.

"Really?" I asked, feigning interest. "Unfortunately, you'll have to wait until fall. Pledge class has already gotten started, so it's too late to join this semester."

"Well, that won't work."

"Why not?"

"Because *you* graduate this semester."

"That's right, I do."

"That's stinky." She made an overly dramatic pouty-face. And it was then that I realized I had no idea what year Jenn was. Sophomore? Junior? I had no clue.

"You know," I said, clearing my throat. "Heather was pretty clear about the policies at the store. I'm not supposed to date any of the associates."

Jenn shook her head. "What she doesn't know won't hurt her, right?"

I opened my mouth to speak just as Jenn lost her footing. I scooped her up with my arm and helped steady her on her feet. "Whoa. Maybe we should get you some water."

"I'm not drunk."

"I didn't say you were, but you should pace yourself. It's not even midnight yet. Come on, let's go back to the guys."

"No, I want to dance some more," Jenn said, pulling on my hand, trying to force me back to the dance floor.

"Maybe later," I said, starting to get annoyed and feeling ready to be honest with her if she pushed any further. I managed to bring her back to our circle of coworkers. "Hey guys, I'm going to get Jenn some water."

"A little drunk, are we?" Sully teased.

"Maybe a little," Jenn said, looking around the circle until her eyes landed on Naomi. "Not nearly drunk enough to handle Naomi, though. Can I get another beer?"

"What did you just say?" Naomi demanded.

"I said I'm not drunk enough to handle you and your

attitude."

"Oh really?" Naomi's hands flew to her hips, and she glared at Jenn and then at me. "Well, then, let me fix that for you."

Jenn threw her head back in laughter, and I stared at her, shocked at how rude she was being. I knew Naomi wasn't her favorite person, but this was a new low. Naomi stormed off. Marley and Sarah followed right behind. Everyone else looked uncomfortable, like they had no idea what to say.

Join the club, guys.

"What the hell, Jenn?" Jasper said, one eyebrow raised high before taking a sip and wiping the foam from his upper lip. "That was really uncool."

"Oh relax," Jenn said, waving Jasper away.

"Come on, let's get you some water—"

"No! I'm sick of putting up with her. She's a total bitch, and you all just let her walk all over you."

"All right, that's enough!" I felt like I was going to explode. My hands balled into fists at my sides. "Maybe you haven't figured this out yet, but we don't rag on the people we work with. Period."

"Oh," Jenn said, "well then. I guess you told me."

"Anything you want to say to Naomi, say it to her face."

"Ugh! It'll always be about her, won't it?" she deadpanned.

"What are you talking about?"

"You know what, Ben? I'm so sick of this. I'm out." She took that piece of paper out of her front pocket and ripped it in half. It floated down to the floor as she stormed away. Everyone stared at me. Dutch crouched down, and his eyes widened as he read the paper.

"Dude. You've got to read this." He passed the paper to Sully, who held it out for himself and Wendy to read. They both grimaced.

"What is it?"

"Shit. This girl could teach Stalker 101," Wendy said.

"What do you mean?"

"Ben, this whole paper is about you. Your favorite songs, favorite movies, favorite foods. It's like she's been taking notes the entire time she's worked at Spotlight."

"What?" I said, still shocked as I grabbed the two pieces of paper and held them together. Sure enough, it was an ongoing list about…me. Different pen colors were used, various dates listed in harsh scribbles. Jenn didn't just have a crush on me. She was *studying* me.

In a rage, I stormed after her. Did I have a right to be angry with her? Probably not. But I'd spent so much time trying to spare her feelings while she was perfectly content to manipulate mine.

"What the fuck, Jenn?" I yelled just as I reached the side door of the house. Jenn was halfway across the frozen yard. She turned to face me, crossing her arms and tilting her head.

"What?" she asked, throwing her arms out to her sides.

I waved the papers. "What the hell is this?"

She clenched her jaw, taking in a deep breath. "I don't know."

"Bullshit."

"I wanted you to like me, okay?"

"So, you took *notes*?" I asked, reading the paper aloud.

"Favorite Band: REM. Favorite song: "Losing My Religion". Favorite color: navy blue. Favorite TV show: *Seinfeld*. Favorite Food: meatball sub from next door with extra mozzarella?"

"I was paying attention."

"Um, I think it's a little more than that."

"No, it's not!" she yelled back. "I just thought that if we had a few things in common, maybe…"

"Wait, so you pretended to like R.E.M.? *Seinfeld*? What else?"

"Just forget it."

"No, I can't!"

"Well, maybe if you weren't so obsessed with Naomi, I wouldn't have had to make that list or pretend to like things I can't stand. Maybe you would have actually noticed me if not for her."

"Leave Naomi out of this."

"I can't—she's the reason I never had a chance with you. We had a spark, Ben. You know we did."

"No. We didn't! Look, I tried to like you, okay? Maybe that was shitty, but I was trying to notice you, trying to give you a chance. But, this?" I held up the papers again. "This is crazy!"

"I'm not crazy!" she snapped, and a tear slipped down her cheek. "You know, it's bad enough that you lead me on—"

"Lead you *on*?" I yelled in disbelief.

"You heard me. You lead me on for *months,* and now you want to turn things around and make me feel like some kind of stalker. Well, that's *not* going to happen."

"I *never* lead you on!"

"The hell you didn't!" She crossed her arms again, looking up at the dull winter sky. "She *doesn't* like you, Ben! She never did! And it's so obvious, so ridiculously pathetic."

"Don't you think that's a little harsh?"

"No, I don't. I know exactly how pitiful you look. And so do they," she said, looking past me, and I knew she was talking about our coworkers. "None of those assholes have the *guts* to tell you the truth. They all watch you make a fool of yourself, and they say nothing! She's never going to go for you, Ben!"

I felt like I was underwater, sinking into an abyss with a weight strapped to my leg, pulling me down, down, down. Could it be true? Could all of my coworkers be biting their tongues, watching me make an ass out of myself these past months—fighting with Naomi, flirting with Naomi, pining for Naomi...while secretly, or collectively, thinking I was pathetic? The thought of that made me physically sick.

"Tell Heather I quit," Jenn said, wiping her eyes. "I hope I never see any of you *ever* again. Especially you."

I watched as she stormed away. Speechless.

Jenn had finally rendered me completely speechless.

Slowly, I made my way back into the house. Marley and Emmett were talking to Dutch, and I could see Sully and Wendy making out on the dance floor. But Naomi was gone.

"Hey, Ben," Marley said. "Everything okay?"

"Sorry about Jenn, man," Dutch added. "That chick is batshit, huh?"

I shook my head, not wanting to give my honest

answer. "Where's Naomi?"

"I don't know," Dutch said with a dismissive shrug. "I think I saw her talking to some guy by the keg."

"Some guy? Who?"

Dutch's eyes softened, and he lowered his voice, leaning in close. "Sorry, man, I think it's one of your roommates. But I'm sure she's fine; Sarah was with her."

"I'll be back."

I had to know who Naomi was talking to. Wandering the party, I scanned the room until I saw them. She was leaning back against the wall, and Jeff, my roommate, had one hand on the wall just above her shoulder. She was smiling and so was he. Dozens of questions bounced around my brain like an old-fashioned pinball machine.

And one question lingered like no other...was Jenn right about everything? Was I a total fool who had no chance with her? Had she been trying to show me that for months? Did Naomi see me the way I saw Jenn? The thought made me cringe.

For just a moment, I thought about stalking towards them, of pulling her away and demanding to finally know the truth—to know where we stood, to know what the hell I was to her. I wanted to punch a hole in the wall. I wanted to break Jeff's face.

And then it finally hit me.

I was done.

Done making a fool of myself.

Done wasting any more time on someone who didn't give two shits about me.

I was completely done with Naomi Parker.

I had to be.

CHAPTER 17

Naomi

*I*t's funny how you can look forward to something for months, years even...and then something happens, and your world is turned on its axis. Totally. And everything changes. Suddenly, instead of wishing the days away to get to that moment, you wish you could stop time. Go back. Wait a while. Get things back to normal so that what you were looking forward to will still resemble what you'd built up in your mind. Instead of being one gigantic mess.

Jamal and I hadn't spoken off the stage since Valentine's Day. Sure, we'd had marathon rehearsals with the rest of the cast, but as soon as our director yelled *cut* we retreated to our separate areas, not even looking one another in the eye. And the play suffered because of it. The chemistry we'd spent months cultivating was almost completely gone. In its wake was a stilted pair of actors who were struggling to find their new dynamic, their new normal. And there wasn't nearly enough time to fix it. Or at least, that's how it felt.

It was finally opening night of Othello, the night I'd looked forward to, planned my entire school year around, and I wanted nothing to do with it. I wanted to pretend it wasn't happening at all, but that was impossible. Our costume director, Lisa, had just squeezed me into my corset and was helping me into my white gown for the opening act when there was a knock on my dressing room door.

"Who is it?" I asked.

"It's Samantha."

"One sec," I called before looking at Lisa. "It's my sister. Are we almost done? I'd love to talk to her for a minute if there's time."

"Yes, but," Lisa said, straightening her glasses and looking at her watch, "Marie will be in shortly with make-up."

"I'll be ready, I promise."

"All right," she said, smoothing out a few wrinkles in the gown before making her way to the door. "Break a leg, Desdemona."

"Thanks," I said, feigning enthusiasm, but as soon as the door opened all the way and Samantha and my eyes locked, there was no way to hide my sadness. Sam's smile settled into her sweet face just as a wrinkle formed between her eyebrows.

"What's going on?"

She always knew when something was up. Always.

"I'm a mess."

Samantha closed the door and walked to me, hugging me gently and carefully as not to get anything on my costume. "You certainly don't *look* it. This dress looks amazing on you," she said. "Nerves?"

"Of course, but...there's more to it."

"Do you have time to spill?"

"If I don't, I feel like I'm going to lose it."

"Okay, talk fast."

"Remember Jamal?"

"How could I forget him?"

My words came tumbling out rapid-fire. "Well, there was...a misunderstanding. I guess I lead him on, and he got really pissed off when I said I didn't like him like that. And I can't really blame him because I invited him back to my room after we'd had a few drinks, but the choice should have been mine no matter what. And now it's totally killing our chemistry, and I kinda want to blame him...even though I don't. I'm so confused. All I know is that tonight's the night. And I feel screwed. Like we flushed it all down the toilet."

Samantha looked at me, stunned, like she was still trying to wrap her head around all the information I'd dropped on her.

I clenched my teeth. "Did any of that make sense?"

"Sure, but one thing doesn't make sense to me."

"A *lot* doesn't make sense to me."

"You have a thing for Jamal, so I don't really get why you told him that you don't."

I shook my head, resisting the urge to rub my fingers between the delicate layers of the dress skirt to work out some of the crazy, nervous energy coursing through my body. If I destroyed the fabric, I'd be in deep shit. "I *did* have a thing for Jamal, but I finally figured out who I want…and it's not him."

Sam tilted her head to the side, looking mischievous. "Ben, right?"

I nodded. "Right."

"I knew it!" she said, her eyes bright like she'd just solved the puzzle on *Wheel of Fortune.*

I turned away, pacing the room. "Ugh, don't even get me started on *that* mess. Basically, I'm self-destructing over here. How are you?"

Sam laughed, shook her head, and followed me across the room, taking my hands in hers. "Listen. Put all of your personal stuff to the side. Now is your time to do what you do best."

"Oh yeah, and what is that?" I asked her.

"Shine," she said with a simple shake of her head. "Shine, big sister."

Holding back tears, I pulled Sam in for another hug. "What would I do without you?"

"You'd figure it out. You're a smart girl even when you don't believe it."

"I don't think I'll ever be as smart as you."

"Well, that's a given," Sam said with a wink. "But, if I had a fraction of the talent you have, I'd be applying to this school, too. You were born for the stage, Naomi."

"Thank you. I wish I felt that way right now."

"Look, it sucks that you and Jamal aren't really getting along, but when you're on that stage, you aren't Naomi anymore…you're Desdemona. *Be* Desdemona."

I thought of Ben, knowing that he wouldn't the tension between Jamal and me to distract from my mission on that stage. To give a damn good performance. And letting anything else stand in the way of that would only be giving myself an out, an excuse not to do my absolute best.

"Be better than my excuses," I said softly, my eyes looking off into space.

"Uhhh." Sam looked confused. "I didn't say that."

"No," I said, shaking my head as my eyes welled with tears. "I know you didn't. It's just...never mind. Thank you for coming back here. I didn't realize how much I needed this."

"Thank God you haven't gotten all made up yet," Sam said with a laugh, wiping a tear from my cheek with the back of her sleeve. "Your director would kill me."

"Yeah, probably."

There was another knock at the door. "That must be make-up."

"I'll get back to Mom and Dad. Knock 'em dead, Nay."

"Thanks, Sam," I said, walking to the make-up chair in front of the mirror when I heard Sam's voice speaking to the person on the other side of the door.

"Oh, hey. Knock 'em dead."

Why would she say that to Marie? Unless she wasn't talking to Marie.

I turned to face the door and saw Jamal, and for a second, my breath caught in my chest and all of the negative feelings I'd had for him over the past couple of weeks flew right out the window. I just wanted to get our chemistry back. I wanted to be us again. I wanted to let go of my excuses.

"Hey, um...you got a minute?" he asked, looking slightly sheepish.

"Sure," I said, gesturing for him to close the door. He wasn't dressed in his costume yet, but instead was wearing a gray Lurie U sweatshirt and dark jeans. He looked as gorgeous as ever.

"Listen, this isn't easy for me to say, but hear me out, all right?"

"All right."

"I'm sorry about Valentine's Day. I was an asshole."

"What?" I asked, surprised. I really didn't ever expect to get an apology from Jamal since I was all too aware of how badly I had screwed up that night by inviting him back to my room when I didn't know what I wanted. No matter how tipsy I was, it was the wrong decision, and I knew it. But, at the same time...didn't I have a right to change my mind?

As if he could read my mind, Jamal continued, "You had *every* right to change your mind that night. We'd both had a lot to drink, and it was not cool for me to get all pissed off at you."

"Wow," I said, wide-eyed. "I don't know what to say."

"Say you'll forgive me. Please."

"Of course, Jamal," I said through tears. "And I'm sorry, too. Really, I am. We should have kept things as they were. Perfect."

"God, I've missed this," Jamal said, moving his hand in the space between us, "we've been off. So off."

"I know we have."

"I hate it."

"I hate it, too."

"Outside your dorm, you said you knew we could be great again. Do you still think so?"

"Of course." I nodded through my tears. "We've both worked so hard. It was breaking my heart to think we'd never be us again. You're one of my best friends, Jamal. I need you."

"You're *the* most talented person I've ever shared the stage with, and I mean that...sincerely. I don't want to have any regrets about this show, this performance, our friendship. Anything."

"Me neither."

"But I can't do it without you..." He tilted his head to the side, looking a little embarrassed. "Obviously."

"I know what you meant."

"Good," Jamal said, taking my hands in his. "Then, Desdemona?"

"Yes, Othello?"

Yes, we were total cheeseballs.

"Would you join me on the stage in like...." He glanced at the clock above my dressing table. "Twenty minutes? We have some making up to do."

I threw my head back in laughter and relief before wrapping my arms around Jamal and pulling him close. "Absolutely, I will."

He sighed loudly. "Thank God."

"Hey," I asked, feeling a little daring now that we were getting back to being ourselves. The tension was lifting and my naturally inquisitive nature was rearing its head.

"What?"

"Did you apologize just because it's opening night?"

He pulled away from our hug, shrugging his shoulders. "Well, I mean...if not now, when? If I waited, we'd both regret it, right?"

I nodded. "Right."

We hugged again just as Marie knocked on the door. "Time for make-up, Naomi."

"I'd better get all suited up," Jamal said. "See you out there."

"Yeah," I said, biting down on my lip, finally feeling the fire build within me once again. And after weeks of dreading the stage, dreading this performance, I was all in —completely ready to knock that audience dead.

"Ready?" Marie asked as she closed the door. Taking a deep breath, I brushed the wisps of hair from my forehead.

"Let's do it."

* * *

I DIDN'T THINK that the cast could possibly do any better than opening night. But, as the curtain closed, I knew we'd done just that. As my dad liked to say, we'd hit it *out of the ballpark*. Every line was delivered flawlessly, every emotion spilled off the stage and danced through the audience. The applause roared on the other side of the curtain as Jamal grabbed me by the waist and twirled me around the stage before setting me down quickly and taking my hand. Our friend, Chris, who played Iago, took my other hand as the curtain raised once again. We walked downstage and took a dramatic bow, throwing our hands up in solidarity as we rose back to stand tall.

I knew my coworkers were in the audience, namely Ben. And I had already decided that I was going to ask them all to stay for the cast party. I was going to drink a few cocktails and tell Ben how I felt, get everything out in the open, tell him that my heart belonged to him...and only him. And that not kissing him on Christmas was the biggest regret of my life.

I'd tell him everything.

Excitement danced through every cell of my body as I scanned the crowd, looking for the Spotlight crew. Just as I thought I spied Emmett's warm, innocent smile, I felt myself being pulled backstage by the rest of the cast and the curtain closed. With a deep breath, I hugged my castmates and grabbed a bottle of water from one of the crew members.

"Great job, everyone. You did it!" Mr. Martin said with the widest smile I'd ever seen on the man. He wasn't one to show great enthusiasm or positive emotion—my theory was that his unimpressed attitude pushed us to do our absolute best, to always strive for new personal best performances, to always push for his approval. And from the looks of him, we'd finally gotten it.

And that felt damn good.

"Go greet your friends and family, change back into your regular clothes, and meet back here. Food and beverages will be coming shortly, so bring your appetites." Mr. Martin gave us a wave before joining the stage manager and patting him on the back.

Chris and Jamal shook hands. "Nice job, man. That was awesome."

"Agreed."

"My parents are here tonight. Naomi, you want to come meet them?" Jamal asked, and I nodded.

"I'd love to."

Hand in hand, Jamal and I followed the cast into the long hallway that ran along the length of the mammoth auditorium. Jamal's parents were standing near the front, his mom, a strikingly beautiful woman with her hair pinned back and a plaid scarf around her neck, was holding a bouquet of flowers. Jamal embraced each parent as they congratulated him on a job well done.

"We're so proud of you," his mom said, holding him so tight. And it made me reminisce about the night before when my mom had said those exact words to me. Those words made me feel like I could do anything on that stage. Absolutely anything.

"Mom, Dad. This is my Desdemona…Naomi Parker. Naomi, these are my parents," Jamal said with a look of pride on his chiseled face.

"It's wonderful to meet you, young lady. You dazzled us up there last night. We told Jamal we had to meet you," his father said with a nod. His mother handed the flowers to me.

"These are for you."

"For me?" I asked, looking to Jamal and then back to her.

"Of course," she said. "You were magnificent. The two of you up there…" She paused. Her eyes welled with tears. "It was like magic. I've never been so proud of my boy."

"Thank you," I said in awe, especially with the roller-coaster Jamal and I had been on together both on and off the stage. For a moment, I wondered if his parents knew about that. "Thank you so much."

"Naomi," a voice called from down the hallway. It was Emmett.

"If you'll excuse me, I'm going to say hi to my work friends. They all came to support me tonight."

"Of course," his mother said. "So good to meet you."

"You as well." I squeezed Jamal's hand, so relieved and thrilled that we'd found our chemistry once again. One that had no strings attached, no pressure...just friendship, loyalty, and the stage. "See you later?"

"Of course," he said with a nod before looking back to his parents. I scanned the hallway until my gaze landed on Emmett. Hustling down the hall, I couldn't wait to see them all. Especially Ben.

Only one problem.

He wasn't there.

Emmett was there. And so were Sully and Wendy, Dutch, Jasper, and Marley. But no Ben.

Ben didn't come to my show.

My heart sank to the floor, and I attempted to hide my absolute disappointment as they all greeted me.

"Impressive, Ace," Sully said with a grin. "For real."

"You were really incredible up there," Jasper said.

I cleared my throat. Knowing that if I didn't say anything, I'd work myself up so badly that I'd throw up. I did my best to seem casual, but I knew I wasn't fooling anyone. "Where, um...so, where's Ben?"

"Oh, um, he...took my shift tonight so that I could come. He knew how badly I wanted to see you perform."

"Oh," I said with a faked smile and a nod. The last thing I wanted to do was to make Marley feel guilty for attending the performance, but my heart was lying on the ground, crushed by the thought of Ben preferring work to seeing me on stage—he preferred putting in hours at Spotlight to supporting me, to cheering me on.

I was so wrong about him.

Clearing my throat, I rubbed Marley's arm. "Well, I'm so glad you came."

"Hey," said Sully. "It was his loss because you were awesome. And you know I don't say that word lightly, Ace."

"He's right," Wendy said, "Really, you blew us all away. Bryan was bragging to the guy next to him."

"You were?"

Sully pressed his lips together, and his cheeks flushed. He shook his head and shrugged. "I mean, I may have mentioned that we work together. I don't really remember."

"Stop it, Bryan. You're proud of her, it's okay to say it out loud."

"All right, all right. Anyway, want to get a beer with us?" Jasper asked.

"There's a cast party that's starting soon. You're all welcome to stay. Our director ordered way too much food last night, and I'm sure he'll probably do the same thing again."

"Sounds great," Emmett said.

"I just need to get changed," I said, gesturing to my gown.

"Of course," said Marley. "Take your time. Need any help?"

"No, I've got it." I gave them a weak smile. "Just follow the hallway to the backstage area, I'll see you guys in a bit."

Forlorn and feeling like a shadow of myself, I made my way back to my dressing room. And with each step I took, my sadness transformed into anger. Where the hell did Ben get off? Even if things didn't work out romantically between us, we were still, at the very least, supposed to be *friends*. He knew how many hours, weeks, months I'd worked on this performance. He knew how important it was to me...and he didn't show up.

And suddenly, I didn't want to waste another minute without giving him a piece of my mind. Without even thinking of the weather that awaited me outside, I stormed out the side door of the auditorium, knowing it was going to be a cold four blocks to Spotlight, but I didn't care. I didn't give two shits about how cold my hands were or the fact that my face felt like an icicle. I didn't even care that snow was falling all around me or that between the snow and the frigid temperatures, my hair was freezing up and frostbite was slowly forming on my ears. Nothing mattered, nothing at all but my anger, my fury, and my heart that had been ripped to shreds. Nothing but telling Ben Watson that he could go to Hell.

And if I didn't storm down to that store and do just that, then I'd regret it for the rest of my life. And I'm not a woman who planned to live in my regrets.

CHAPTER 18

Ben

The second I told Marley that I would take her shift so that she could go to Naomi's play, I regretted it. Terribly. I had just seen Naomi talking to my roommate, leaning back into the basement wall and smiling like he'd said something brilliant or hilarious. And, in anger, and knowing I had to get over her, I'd walked right over to Marley and offered to take her shift so that she could go with everyone. A few days later, I changed my mind. I felt like an asshole for wanting to bail. I wanted to be there to support Naomi, but Marley couldn't stop talking about *Othello* and how excited she was to see it. I couldn't ask her to take her shift back. Knowing Marley, she would do it because she was such a sweet girl. But it wasn't right. I wanted to ask someone else to cover, but with Jenn quitting, Heather and I were the only two left who weren't already going to see the play. And for a Saturday night, only having two people working was already pushing it.

I had to live with my decision. But I wasn't happy with myself.

At the very least, Naomi and I were friends, and I knew how hard she had worked. I felt like such a dick for bailing on her. And I'd been too much of a coward to give her a heads-up. But the thing was, I knew this weekend would be a whirlwind for her. She'd have dozens of people coming up to her after the play, praising her for her performance. Would she really notice if I wasn't one of them?

Time would tell on that.

Our next shift together wasn't for a few days, so if she was irritated, she'd probably be over it by then...at least a little bit.

Who am I kidding? This is Naomi. She'll rub it in my face for months.

That's if she gives a damn...and the jury's still out on that.

"Hey, Ben," Heather, who had just taken a call from the back room, said as she approached the desk. "I hate to do this to you, but I have to make a few calls."

"Sure, everything okay?"

"Not really. My dad has the flu and can't take my mom to her dialysis appointment tomorrow. I have to find someone else who can do it, or I'll be on the next plane. Again."

"I'm sorry," I said, gritting my teeth and not really knowing what else to say.

"It's fine, I just feel bad abandoning you on a Saturday night."

"We're in a lull right now anyway. It's probably the perfect time, actually," I lied as I stared at the overflowing return box.

There was no one currently in the store, so I could get caught up on scanning and placing tapes back on the shelves. We had a couple of hours before our late Saturday night rush began.

"Thanks, I appreciate it. Not sure what I'd do without you holding this place together."

"No worries. Just make your calls. This place will still be standing when you finish."

Heather smiled and returned to the back room, and I focused my attention on the return box. I was scanning tapes into the system when it happened.

Naomi.

She plowed through the door with a furious, pink, frostbitten face, a snow-covered medieval dress, and a random bouquet of flowers in her ghostly white hand. She slammed the flowers on the front desk, gave me a death stare, and walked away.

"Naomi? What the hell?"

She ignored me as she charged forward; snow flurries fell from her dress onto the floor and were absorbed into the carpet. I called her name again, but she said nothing. I could hear her teeth chattering and her lungs heaving as she paced the aisles.

"Is that your costume? Where's your coat? It's freezing outside."

Once again, she said nothing. Quickly, knowing she

must have been frozen solid, I ran to the back room and grabbed my coat from my locker, running back to the floor to cover her shoulders. When I reached her, she sloughed the coat off of her shoulders.

"You're cold as ice, Naomi. Put it on."

She shook her head no and walked away, down another aisle. She had two tapes in her hands and was stalking down the aisles. I couldn't imagine that she wanted to rent movies right after her play. Obviously, stranger things had happened, but it wasn't Naomi's style. This was a monumental weekend for her, there was no way she was here to get movies. No, this was bigger than that.

"Naomi, what are you doing?" I raised my voice, trying to get through to her, but she continued to ignore me. Finally, she walked to the picks corner, and with a swoop of her free arm, she knocked all of my picks to the floor. The tapes crashed and flew out of their plastic clamshell containers.

First, she placed one new tape on my shelf: *The Jerk* with Steve Martin.

"Oh, I get it. I'm a jerk?"

A snooty expression crossed Naomi's face as she placed another title on my shelf. *Unforgiven* with Clint Eastwood.

"Aren't you going to say anything?" I huffed, waiting for her to respond. "Fine."

I made a fist and shoved my hand against the movies on her shelf. They flew into the corner and tumbled to the floor.

"What are you doing?"

I tilted my head to the side and glared at her. "What do you think I'm doing? Two can play this game!"

Stomping down the aisles, I searched for the perfect movies to put on Naomi's shelf, but I was flustered, overwhelmed, and not sure what to pick. And then, as I walked through the classics section, I found my first title. Naomi was following close behind me, and her heavy dress was whipping against the videos on the bottom shelves. Tapes and cases were flying every which way.

"What is that?" she asked, trying to look over my shoulder as I grabbed the tape, a smug smile on my lips as I marched back to the picks corner.

"*Taming of the Shrew?*" she asked, sounding a little confused. "I don't know what a shrew is, but I know it's not good."

"You're right, it's not."

"Okay, fine," she said, sticking out her chin and marching past me to grab another movie. Following close behind, I hoped that with me breathing down her neck, she would get just as flustered as I had gotten with her right behind me.

No such luck.

With a satisfied look on her face, she grabbed *Better Off Dead* with John Cusack. Her lips curled into a smile as she placed it dramatically on the shelf, then moved her hands around the box like freaking Vanna White.

"Real nice," I said, shaking my head. And since she'd chosen an 80s movie, my brain knew exactly what to choose next. With a cynical grin on my face, I walked to the same section that she'd visited and grabbed a movie that I knew she loved, but Sully informed me that she hated being compared to a certain redheaded character.

The second I placed *The Breakfast Club* on the shelf, she pointed at the box, closing her eyes tight in anger. "If you call me a Claire, I swear to God, I will hurt you."

"I'm just picking movies, I said nothing." I paused and tapped my chin. "Although now that you mention it, I can see the similarities."

"Oh really?"

"Yep." I said, enunciating the 'p' at the end of the word for emphasis. Her cheeks, already a deep shade of pink, turned fire engine red, and she stormed off to a different section of the store. Instead of following her, though, I set off to find another movie of my own. In my mind, this had turned into a race, one I was damn sure going to win. I could hear more tapes getting knocked over by her dress.

"You're going to clean this place up."

"I don't think so! I'm not on the clock!" she yelled back, and I grimaced, knowing she was absolutely right. As I walked back into the classics section, another bratty heroine jumped out at me, and I laughed to myself as I jogged back to the picks corner.

"I do declare, you are a pain in my ass," I said, placing *Gone with the Wind* on the shelf.

"And let me guess, you don't give a damn?" she said, rolling her eyes. "Lame."

She placed *Tombstone* with Val Kilmer and Kurt Russell on my shelf, and I was genuinely confused. "What the hell is this? Are you calling me a cowboy or saying I have tuberculosis? Neither one really makes any sense."

She rolled her eyes again. "Neither. Although you having a case of TB sounds tempting."

She smirked before continuing, "You can't trust *anyone* in that movie...and I kinda want you dead right now."

"I got that from the John Cusack flick. Might want to mix things up a little more, Naomi. Your picks are getting a little redundant."

"Oh, like yours aren't." She flipped her long braid behind her back and stormed away; this time I followed right behind her. Before she could even find a new title, one leapt out at me, and I laughed, grabbing it and hustling back to the shelf. Naomi followed close behind me.

"What is it? I can't see."

I placed it on the shelf and she gasped. "Now you've gone too far."

"Naomi, you have two movies that have me dead, don't you think it's pretty fitting?"

"*Misery*? Freaking *Misery*? She's a psychopath!"

"If the shoe fits," I said, shrugging like the smug asshole that I was.

"Ughhhh!" she yelled out. "I didn't want to do this, but you've pushed me too far. Too fucking far, Ben!"

She came back seconds later, huffing as she walked with the tape behind her back.

What could possibly be so bad that she'd need to hide it before the big reveal? I had to chuckle a little at how quickly everything had escalated. I was just about to suggest we make peace, but my peaceful intentions fell away the second she placed the last tape on the shelf.

The Way We Were.

It was like a punch in the gut. I was frozen in place, the words stolen from my throat as she stood before me, daggers flying from her stone-cold eyes. The tendrils of hair that spilled down her face resembled icicles. The hem of her dress was ruined as she'd dragged it through dirt and snow. Her tiny nostrils flared, and she swallowed hard.

"What is that supposed to mean?" I asked, my heart felt like it was pounding inside my throat.

She ignored my question and produced one of her own. "Why didn't you come to my show?"

"What?" I asked, not sure how to answer, trying to buy myself time—even if only a few seconds.

"You heard me, and I'm *not* going to ask again," she sneered. She literally sneered at me. She looked possessed, crazed, enraged.

"Marley really wanted to see it, and—"

"Bullshit." She shook her head vehemently.

"It's not," I protested weakly.

"You *knew* I wanted you there."

"Did I?" I asked, finding my voice again, finding a little bit of the anger that I'd had a week ago at the party when I watched her flirting with my roommate. "Why didn't you just give the extra ticket to Jeff? Then you'd have the cheering section you deserve."

"What are you talking about?" she spat.

I rolled my eyes. "My roommate. Don't act so inno-cent. You know what I'm talking about."

"You have, like, ten roommates, Ben. I don't know them all."

I crossed my arms in front of my chest. "But you know *him*. Or at least you knew him last weekend."

"What? You mean at the party?"

"Yes."

"That tall guy with the dark hair?"

"You know who he is. Stop pretending."

"Don't you dare turn this around on me because I spent five minutes talking to some random guy at a party. I won't let you pull that shit, especially when you're seeing Jenn."

"Are you kidding me? I'm not doing *anything* with Jenn."

"It certainly looked like you were at the party." She tilted her determined chin.

"Then you weren't really looking, were you?" I demanded, and she stared at me, her face in a permanent sneer as her lungs heaved beneath her dress.

"Why didn't you come to my show?" she demanded again.

"Why is *The Way We Were* on my shelf?" I demanded right back.

"You know why."

Then, I stepped closer to her with narrowed eyes, grabbed the copy of *The Way We Were* from my shelf, and moved it to hers.

Reaching to grab the movie, the tips of her fingers grazed the clamshell, but I blocked her, and she retreated. She tried to get to it from one side of the shelf and then the other, but I blocked her each time.

"You don't get to do that!" she yelled.

"Oh yes, I do!" I tilted my head to the side. "How does that feel, *Hubbell*?"

"Oh my God!" Naomi said, looking up at the ceiling. "You're insane if you think *I'm* the Hubbell. *You* are the Hubbell, Ben. *You!*"

"Just keep telling yourself that," I said, shaking my head

"I thought I was the Hubbell. I thought I was a fool for not kissing you on Christmas, for not telling you how I really felt. But I was wrong."

"Bullshit!"

"You didn't show up for me, Ben!"

"Yeah, so?"

"You took the easy way out and hid here at the store—such a shitty thing to do. And why? Because I talked to your roommate for a few minutes? Are you kidding me?"

"It's more than that," I said, and I could feel my jaw tick as my anger consumed me. "What about Jamal?"

"He's my costar—and one of my best friends. So what?"

"I saw you guys."

It was her turn to narrow her eyes. "What are you talking about?'

"On Valentine's Day...I saw you walk past here. He was nuzzling your neck right after you took a bite of your pizza. Best friends my ass!"

"For your information, I turned him down that night, which caused a whole big thing. He and I were barely speaking until yesterday, and for what? For you! God, I'm so stupid!" She pushed past me and walked the length of the store. I followed her, unable to stop myself.

"For me? What the hell does that mean?"

"What do you think it means, Ben?"

"Ugh, would you just talk to me?" I groaned, feeling like we were spinning in circles like hamsters on a wheel.

"I want to, but—"

"Talk to me."

She closed her eyes tight, and one tear slipped down her cheek. "Fine."

She cleared her throat. "I knew what I wanted, okay? I was ready to be a Katie, ready to fight—to give *this*," she moved her hands in the air between us, "a real chance. I wasn't going to let Jenn or Jamal or anyone get in the way."

"This?" I asked. "Do you mean us?"

She shrugged. "But congratulations, Ben. You saved me the trouble by showing your true colors...tonight, you showed me *exactly* how much I mean to you."

"You wanna talk about true colors? Okay, let's do that. Why did you bring me those pancakes on Christmas?"

"Because you had to work."

"And?"

"And...I wanted you to have a nice Christmas."

"Why?"

She said nothing, swallowing hard.

"You were all alone, and you didn't get to eat your roast duck."

"Stop it. You're avoiding the question. Tell me why, Naomi. Why did you drive down here, bring me food, parade around in a damn elf hat, and then the *second* I show interest, you bail? What the hell was *that*?"

"I didn't bail, you're being ridiculous."

"What do you call it?"

"It was snowing. My mom needed me back home. She's crazy about her traditions."

"Right." I rolled my eyes. "How are we supposed to figure any of this shit out if you won't be honest with me?"

"Fine!" she yelled, throwing her hands up in exasperation. "I got scared, all right? You tried to kiss me, and I just freaked out."

"Why?"

"Why do you think?"

"Did you want to kiss me?"

"Of course, I did." She looked up at the ceiling. "I mean, duh!"

"So why did you run away?"

"You wouldn't understand."

"Don't insult me." I shook my head. "Why did you run away?"

"Because you could destroy me."

"What? I would never hurt—"

She interrupted me, "*Because* when I'm with you I feel…exposed, vulnerable, defenseless, and completely out of control. Like I'm this tiny, little, delicate flower in your hand, and you could crush me with one sudden movement…and I'd be ruined forever."

I was stunned. "What? I don't—I mean, I—"

"I've never felt like that before…but on that day, on that counter, that's how I felt. Like if my lips touched yours, I'd be destroyed. Maybe not now but eventually.

"Why, because I'm about to graduate?"

"No," she said, her voice a whisper. "Because you're you."

I was speechless. I couldn't believe what I was hearing. All of the things that she made me feel, I did the same to her. How was that even possible? She always seemed so much more in control when it came to our arguments, our dynamic, our banter.

I lowered my voice, trying to soften the tension between us. She was more delicate than I'd ever imagined, and I needed her to know she was safe with me. Always safe with me.

"We could destroy each other," I said softly. "You've had your hands wrapped around my heart since the day you started here."

"No," she said, shaking her head as if to say *nice try, buddy.* "I annoyed you."

"You did," I admitted. "And you'd be lying if you said I didn't irritate the living shit out of you, too. We butt heads, it's what we do. I love how strong-willed you are, even when you make me furious."

"Which is often," she reminded me.

"And vice versa," I said with a shrug, "But there's something here, isn't there? I mean, I think we both know there is."

She nodded, and I took her hands in my own. She smiled, looking down at our hands as I caressed her icy fingertips with my thumbs.

"I want to be better than my excuses," she said, her tone turning gentle. And I was brought back to our very first fight when I said that to her. "I did it with Jamal, and now I want to do it with you."

"What do you mean?"

"I'm not going to make excuses anymore. I want you, Ben. I've wanted you for months, and I'm not going to avoid it anymore. I *refuse* to be a Hubbell."

I smiled. "So do I."

I cupped her face with my hands and peered into her eyes. They were welling with tears. "Your skin is ice cold."

She shook her head, her eyes locked with mine. "I don't feel cold anymore."

With a sigh, I stroked her chilled skin with the pads of my thumbs, trying to warm her face the way I warmed her hands. "I'm crazy about you, Naomi. Always have been."

"Then kiss me," she said, swallowing hard. "This time, I'm not going anywhere."

And so, I did. My lips pressed to hers, ever so gently at first, but as her arms wrapped around my back, she opened her mouth just slightly, inviting me in. I wasted no time. Deepening the kiss, I caressed her tongue with mine, and my hand slid to the back of her neck. She moaned as her tongue stroked mine, and her fingers dug frantically into my back. And just as I was about to hoist her up, to have her wrap her legs around me and carry her to the counter, the bell rang over the door. Breathless, we broke apart and stared at the door. The customer, a man in his forties, looked us up and down, then scanned the store, taking in the situation. With a knowing smile, he winked. "I'll come back later."

We laughed, and Naomi pulled me in for another kiss, her fingers roaming through my hair. I poured my desire into her lips, her skin, her hair, my mouth drifting down to kiss her neck as my arms wrapped around her, the tips of my fingers dancing on top of the fabric of her dress. Her skin warmed at my touch, and she shuddered, sighing into my hair as she pulled me close. Her dress was cold, wet, and sticking to her body. I wrapped my arms around her, pulling her close and stroking her hair, trying to warm her up.

"I told you I'm not cold anymore," she murmured, nestling her head into my chest as I rubbed her back and kissed the top of her head as I scanned the store.

"Wow, we really made a mess of the place. Are you really going to make me clean this up all by myself?"

"Well, I mean, I should probably get back to the cast party," she said in her best smart-ass voice.

"Ahhh, right," I said, hugging her tight. "I can't believe you didn't even change out of your costume."

She laughed and then sighed. "I wasn't really thinking too clearly."

We stood in silence, and then I finally said what I'd wanted to say since she walked through the door but was just too proud to say it. "I'm so sorry I missed your show. Really, really I am."

She looked up at me. "I'll forgive you...eventually."

We laughed, and I pulled her in for another kiss. "There's a matinee tomorrow afternoon...maybe I can get you a ticket? That's if my director doesn't kill me for ruining my dress. I may have to stay up all night trying to get the stains out."

I smiled, relieved that this performance wouldn't be lost to me forever. "I wouldn't miss it."

"Good." She pulled away. "Just to warn you, there is kissing. Kind of a lot of it."

"With Jamal?"

She clenched her teeth. "Yeah."

"I suppose I'll have to get used to that, right?"

"What do you mean?"

"Dating an actress? You're going to kiss all sorts of guys in your career. I should probably just rip off the Band-Aid and suffer through it."

"I like the way you think," she said, and I laughed.

"Since when?"

"Shut up and kiss me," Naomi said, going up on her tiptoes and planting another wistful kiss on my lips. And just as I was opening my mouth and inviting her to deepen the kiss, everything came to a screeching halt when Heather's voice pierced the room.

"Ben...what's going on here?"

CHAPTER 19

Naomi

"We're gonna get caught, you know," I murmured between kisses. Ben's lips grazed mine as they curled into a satisfied smile.

"By who? Dutch?" he asked, chuckling under his breath. "He already knows I'm crazy about you."

"I had a feeling," I said with a grin, my lips seeking his once again. I couldn't get enough of him. Couldn't get enough of the touch of his lips, the register of his voice, the way his fingers felt against my skin. I was completely and totally his. And as much as it scared me, it was the happiest I'd ever felt. His lips pressed to mine again as we hid in the corner of the video game room. It was a weekday, and this room was generally empty in the afternoons. And because of that, it had become our place for stolen moments. I pulled away and dragged my fingernails gently against the warm skin of his neck.

"I just don't want you to get into more trouble with Heather."

"Let me worry about that." Ben nuzzled beneath my ear, and goosebumps rose on my arms. "Besides, she's in Maryland, remember?"

"How could I forget?" I asked with a sardonic laugh. "She wanted to murder us both."

When Heather had walked in on Ben and me kissing, she was not pleased...far from it. But she didn't have the luxury of reprimanding Ben for kissing a subordinate since her mom needed her desperately and, because of that, *she* desperately needed Ben to run the store while she was gone. If not for Ben, Spotlight Video would spiral into chaos, and she knew that better than anyone.

"Nah. She was just shocked. I'm sure when she gets back, she'll just pretend she didn't see anything."

"You sound pretty confident," I said, tilting my head to the side and biting down on my lip. I knew it drove Ben crazy whenever I did that move. And so, I didn't do it too often, but every once in a while, I liked the idea of driving him wild.

"That's because I am," he said, raising both eyebrows. As cheesy as it sounds, I was lost in Ben's icy blue eyes, even when he was being playful. In other words, I was a goner.

Pathetic, I know. But ask me if I care.

For the past few days, Ben and I had spent as much time together as humanly possible, including stealing away for mini make out sessions in the store while our coworkers were busy. No matter how much time we spent together, though, like everyone in the honeymoon stage of a relationship, it was never enough. Every stolen moment added to the excitement, the sweetness, and the passion that was growing between us.

And I couldn't get enough.

"Ben!" Sully called from the front desk. "Where are you? We've got a problem up here!"

"I should go," he said, running his fingers through my hair. "Maybe wait a minute before..."

"I know the drill," I said with a wink. "Go on. I'll see you in a minute."

With a contented smile and a squeeze of my hand, Ben pulled away and walked toward the main area of the store. As he rounded the corner, I saw him run his fingers through his hair and fix his collar. He was so cute, even when he didn't mean to be.

For the love of God, Naomi. Get it together.

Putting on my best poker face, I walked slowly into the main area of the store and took the opportunity to visit the picks corner. I had to laugh when I was reminded of the videos Ben and I had placed on each other's shelves. Deciding to harness the cheeseball within me, I returned the tapes on my shelf to their normal spots and started over.

In just minutes, I'd filled my shelf with a sweet message to Ben. I hesitated at first, wondering if our coworkers might figure it out, but then I realized it was incredibly egocentric of me to assume that they were so wrapped up in the ongoing tension between Ben and me, that they would care enough to notice.

And if I knew my coworkers at all, I had nothing to worry about.

I'd chosen my movies...*When Harry Met Sally, Uncle Buck, An Interview with the Vampire,* and *Ice Castles.* With a sigh, I smiled to myself and walked to the counter where Sully and Dutch were in the thick of another great debate.

"Ace, you have to weigh in on this," Sully said, leaning against the counter with his lips pursed in annoyance. And it was then that I noticed it.

"Oh my God," I said, staring at him. "Is that a *blue* shirt?"

He rolled his eyes. "Here we go."

"Is it possible that you've abandoned your all-black protest? Sully, say it ain't so!"

"All right, all right. It just so happens that I'm no longer in mourning. I don't think Kurt would want me to lament publicly over his death anymore—"

"Or, you know...Wendy's having an effect on you."

"Don't look so proud of yourself, Ace." He shook his head, but his reddening cheeks told another story. "I did this of my own accord."

"All right, I respect that."

"But still," Ben interrupted, "the influence of a good woman..."

"Don't even get me started on how amazing that girl is. She finished her latest script this weekend, and I was the first to read it. I'm not sure the current rating system would even allow it to be made. It's *that* messed up."

"Ew."

"No," he said, his eyes uncharacteristically dreamy. "It's *fantastic.*"

"I'm happy for you," I said. And I really was. It was so nice to see the influence that Wendy was having on Sully. Before long, he'd be letting us call him Bryan.

Yeah, right.

I patted him on the arm. "It sounds like you've met your match."

"You'll get there, too, Ace." He winked. "Just keep the faith, okay? Anyway, as I was saying…"

Ben and I locked eyes for the tiniest of moments, both doing our best to hide our smiles. Sully was so preoccupied with his debate with Dutch that he didn't even notice. And since Dutch already knew about Ben and my feelings for each other, I didn't pay him any mind.

"Please tell Dutch he's crazy."

"Why?"

Dutch interrupted, "I think the Star Wars universe needs prequels. You know, like the first three episodes."

"And *I* say, you don't mess with perfection…you'll only screw it up."

Dutch shook his head. "Pop in the first movie. Right now. You'll see it says *Episode IV* right at the top in those yellow letters."

"I know that, nimrod. I've read all the Star Wars books. I still think it's silly to go back. The first few books are boring anyway. Why do you think they started the movies with episode four?"

Dutch shrugged. "No idea, but I'm telling you…George Lucas would be insane not to cash in."

"If he does, he's a sellout. Next thing you'll be saying is he should sell the movies to Disney or some shit."

"Bite your tongue," Ben said. "No way. Lucas is an original."

"That's what I'm saying!" Sully said. "You're only proving my point."

"So, what do you want me to say, exactly?" I asked, not sure how I was supposed to weigh in on this debate. "What are you arguing?"

"Whether or not you predict that Lucas will become a sellout and make the prequels."

"Ahh," I said, pressing my lips together and furrowing my brow. "As much as I love the idea of more *Star Wars*, I know the prequels are boring."

"And how do you know that?" Dutch asked, looking shocked. "Did *you* read the books?"

"As a matter of fact, I *did*. My brother, Jonathan, and I read them together years ago. Nothing gets interesting until *Episode III*."

"I'm impressed," Dutch said with a lazy smile. "I figured you were only into it for Han Solo."

"Whatever." I rolled my eyes. "Harrison Ford is gorgeous, there's no denying it. But my sisters and I are huge *Star Wars* fans. You don't need male anatomy to enjoy the story—and to think that you do is a little moronic."

"Touche," Ben said, looking proud as he leaned back and licked his lips, looking at me like I was good enough to eat. And I loved it.

"So, no...I don't think he'll make the prequels because I think he knows they'd be a big ol' boring disaster."

"There. Case closed," Sully said. "The *actress* has spoken."

I took a fake, dramatic bow.

"Speaking of which," Sully continued, "you must have a lot of extra time on your hands now that you're not rehearsing a million times a week."

"Yeah, it's weird." I didn't want to mention to my coworkers that I had gotten in a ridiculous amount of trouble for wearing my costume out of the auditorium. My director had not only reamed me out for ten minutes straight, but he'd also given me fifty hours of community service to pay to replace it. I'd been spending an hour a day helping him organize costumes, make-up, and props. Truth be told, I didn't mind it at all, but I pretended to have a slight attitude every day when I arrived to keep my ruse going. I was afraid if I showed genuine enthusiasm, Mr. Martin would make me scrub the stage or something ridiculous.

I couldn't figure out why Sully would be curious about my 'free time' unless, of course, he wanted something.

"What's your point?" I narrowed my eyes, and Sully rubbed his hands together like he was hatching a scheme.

"Here's the thing, Ace..."

"Oh my God, spill it."

"I was hoping you could take a couple of shifts off my hands."

"And why is that?"

"Wendy's schedule and mine aren't exactly gelling at the moment. Between classes and our jobs, we hardly see each other during the week."

"So, wait, you want to get out of shifts to spend time with your girlfriend?"

"Yeah?" he said, sounding like it was a question rather than a statement.

"That's adorable, you big softy!"

"Ugh, puh-lease. It's just a couple of shifts, no big deal."

"Got it," I said, grabbing the calendar. "Which ones?"

Sully pointed at a couple of afternoon shifts that I knew didn't conflict with my class schedule. Pausing to make sure that Ben would also be working those shifts, I nodded and put Sully out of his misery.

"I'll do it. But you owe me big time, you got that?"

"Got it. Thanks, I won't forget this."

"I won't let you," I said with a wink, and then my eyes met Ben's, and he smiled in recognition, knowing we'd have two extra shifts together at the store.

"Hey, why didn't you ask me?" Dutch asked.

"Because you're already working one of those shifts." Sully crossed his arms. "Plus, you're not exactly the most reliable person here. If you take my shifts and then forget to come in, Heather and Ben will still be pissed at me."

"Wrong," Ben said, shaking his head.

Dutch's brow was knitted. He was confused and, it seemed, a little bit hurt. "Hey man, I've been better lately."

"It's true," Ben said. "He hasn't been late at all this week."

"Wow, I'm impressed," Sully said, his words dripping in sarcasm. "I asked Naomi because I wanted to ask Naomi. That's it."

"You know," I said, tapping my fingernails against the counter. "Jenn did quit...and Heather hasn't replaced her. Maybe Wendy would like to work here."

Sully looked stunned, like a deer in headlights, and I

wondered if that was too close to home—like maybe Sully was one of those people who compartmentalized different facets of his life. Maybe he didn't want Wendy to get too chummy with his coworkers. Maybe he wanted to be able to make a clean break if things fell apart.

"Ace, you're a genius!" he exclaimed, grabbing me by the shoulders and kissing me on the cheek. I stood there, stunned, realizing I'd misread his expression completely.

"Ben, what do you think?"

"About hiring your girlfriend who writes horror so disturbing it wouldn't be shown in theaters?" Ben asked, one eyebrow raised.

"Exactly," Sully said, his arms out to the sides. "Come on, Ben!"

"Honestly, I think she'd fit in well here," I said, clenching my teeth. "We all met her at the party. She's good people."

"I liked her," Dutch added.

"Why don't you see if she even wants to work here, and I'll talk to Heather about it when she gets back."

"When is she coming back?"

"Tomorrow."

"Sweet," Sully said.

"Until then, remember, it's not a done deal, okay? Heather has final say on new hires, but yes, we do need someone now that Jenn's no longer here."

Sully rubbed his hands together. "Now I'm even more excited that she quit."

"Sully," Ben said with a warning tone.

"Oh, come on, you know we're all thinking it. She was a drag. A *total* drag."

"He's got a point," I said playfully, and Ben shook his head.

"All right, all right, she didn't exactly fit in here. That's true."

Dutch let out a, "Ha! Understatement of the friggin' year, man!"

"Fine, whatever. Yeah, it worked out for everyone."

"You're so diplomatic, man. I love that about you," Dutch said.

"So do I," I said.

"Nah, it's annoying." Sully scoffed. "Sorry, man. No offense."

Ben chuckled, shaking his head. "None taken."

"Okay, so Ace is going to take my shifts, and Ben will talk to Heather. This day is shaping up nicely, I gotta say."

"I'm happy you're happy, *Bryan*," I said, testing the waters.

"Don't push it," he said with playful disdain.

For a moment, I stared at my coworkers in total appreciation. How Jenn could voluntarily quit a job like this with these unique and usually hilarious people was hard for my brain to understand. And if Sully and his girl-friend worked together in the store, maybe it would make mine and Ben's transition to a couple just a little bit easier. At least, I hoped it might. I knew that eventually, we would be forced to tell everyone, especially when they noticed we were no longer bickering like we used to….and our pick shelves were nothing but lovey-dovey movies. In fact, if Sully didn't figure it out by the end of the week, I'd be disappointed in his observational skills.

But, until then, we had a secret that was ours alone.

With stolen moments in the video game room, rushed kisses, and whispered sweetness.

"Oh, wait," Sully said. "Since she and I are already hooked up, would we be grandfathered in?"

"What do you mean?" I asked, quizzically.

"You know, the whole rule about dating coworkers."

"I thought that only applied to the managers," Dutch said. "I hit on Marley for weeks."

"Any luck?" Sully asked.

Dutch shook his head. "Nah! I think I'm a little too wild for her."

Normally I would laugh at Dutch's comment, but I couldn't. I was frozen, staring at Ben, remembering the rule that I'd conveniently pushed to the very back corner of my brain. Self-preservation, I guess.

Ben swallowed hard and glanced my way. "It does only apply to managers."

A knot formed in my belly as I wondered what would happen. Heather was furious with us, and there was a good chance that one, or both of us, would be fired when she returned from Maryland. My stomach dropped at the idea of leaving Spotlight Video. My coworkers had become my on-campus family. They drove me crazy at times, but I could be myself when I was with them. Absolutely, totally myself. And the store, rather than my dorm room, was my home away from home. And I'd be devastated to leave it.

Absolutely, completely, and utterly devastated.

CHAPTER 20

Ben

"I love that Sarah has so many afternoon classes," I said, pulling Naomi closer as we laid on her bed, listening to Sarah McLachlan singing softly from the speakers of the CD player. Her lava lamp glowed from the corner of her room, and I watched as the sunshine yellow bubbles expanded and broke off into little pieces only to come back together again. I'd never had one of those lamps, but after seeing how soothing it could be to watch, I was rethinking this trend. Naomi was nestled into the crook of my neck, and she splayed her hand gently on my chest; the touch of her fingertips to the cotton of my shirt made me shiver a little bit. There was nothing like the feel of Naomi.

Nothing at all.

"Me, too," she said, leaning up on her elbow and

kissing my forehead, my nose, my chin as she slid her leg to cover mine, and her toes rubbed playfully against the tops of my feet. "I hate that we have to go to work soon, though."

"I know."

"We still have an hour, so let's not think about it yet."

"So, what else do you listen to?" I asked, trying to sound casual, not wanting her to know that Sarah McLachlan didn't do it for me. But she was on to me. Narrowing her eyes, she tilted her head to the side.

"Anything but R.E.M.," she said, her voice snarky, and she gave me a devious wink.

A laugh escaped my lips. "Yeah, I figured."

As much as I would have loved for Naomi to bust out an R.E.M. CD from the towering piles on her desk, it was a breath of fresh air to be with a woman of conviction, especially after the Jenn fiasco. Once someone tries to manipulate you through the things that you love, it can feel...strange, gross, odd. Naomi would never pretend to love something that she didn't really love. And it was one of the many things that I loved about her, even when that particular personality trait led to arguments between us.

"You seem to like female singers."

"Yep. Tori, Sheryl Crow. Sarah really likes Ani DiFranco."

"Never heard of her."

"She's edgier. Like she's kind of pissed off a lot of the time. I'm not sure she's my cup of tea, but..." She hovered over my lips. "She's better than Michael Stipe."

"You're such a pain in the ass," I teased, running my fingers through her hair.

"You love it."

"You're right," I said, staring into her softening eyes. "I do."

Naomi sunk into my chest, placing her hands on the pillow beneath me, kissing me hard. Her lips were hungry against mine, and her tongue stroked my own. My hands drifted down to grip her ass as I pulled her closer to me. She sighed into my mouth and moved her hand to grip the side of my face as she kissed me again and again. I was hard beneath her, wanting her more with each passing second. Within minutes, our lungs were heaving, our breath was ragged, and I knew we needed to slow things down—even though that was the last thing I wanted. Forcing myself to decrease the intensity of my kisses, Naomi followed my lead.

"You're amazing," I said, running my fingers through her silky blonde hair as it spilled all around me in waves.

"I can't believe you're here. Like, actually in my bed. It's all so surreal."

"It is. I thought we'd never get here." I bit down on my lip. "Any regrets?"

"Hell no!"

Laughing, I pulled her to my chest, and she relaxed into me. With a sigh, I said, "Same here."

"You want to watch TV or something?"

"Nah. It's all talk shows and People's Court." I paused for a second. "I just realized that even though I know all about the movies you love...and now all the music, I have no idea what television you watch. It's weird."

"I don't talk about TV at the store." She tilted her head

quickly to the side. "But Sarah and I watch some shows together. I know *you're* all about *Seinfeld*."

"Yep." With a laugh, I ran my hand up and down her back. "Well, I don't watch a ton of TV since I'm usually at the store or in class, but...I do love that show. It's probably the only thing I make time to watch."

"Yeah, it's okay. I only watch it because it's on Thursdays. You know, *Must See TV* or whatever."

"But you don't think it's funny?"

"I guess Elaine is pretty funny. And I like Kramer. I can't stand Jerry, though."

"Why?"

"I don't know...I think it's his tone of voice or something. Not sure. There's just something about him that irks me."

"You really need to learn how to form an opinion," I teased, kissing her nose. "Can I try and guess your shows?"

"Sure," she said, raising both eyebrows. "This should be interesting."

"Okay...*Friends* for sure."

"No brainer."

"*Party of Five?*"

"Ooh yes. I tape that every week, and Sarah and I watch it together. She's crazy for Bailey, but I think the older brother is hotter. Plus, he dropped everything to raise his siblings. How sexy is that?"

"You're so boy crazy."

She rolled her eyes. "This should not be a shock to you."

"It isn't."

"Okay, what else?"

"What's that one on MTV? With the girl who dyes her hair really, really red? They use the word *'like'* a lot. The name is on the tip of my tongue, but I can't think of it."

"Oh my God, *My So-Called Life!* I'm completely and totally obsessed with that show. Jordan Catalano...don't even get me started. His eyes are almost as beautiful as yours."

"Almost?" I asked, licking my lips. Naomi placed soft kisses on my lips.

"Almost."

"I had a feeling you liked that show. It's very...you."

"You're pretty good at this, you know."

"I guess you could say I've been studying you for months..." I paused, realizing how that must have sounded. "Not in a Jenn way or anything. Nothing creepy, but you know what I'm trying to say."

My cheeks reddened, and I felt like a moron, but at the same time, I knew I could say just about anything to Naomi. We'd gotten over our biggest hurdle—admitting our real feelings for each other. If we could do that, I knew I could be honest about how closely I'd paid attention to the things that she loved. I loved all the details that made up Naomi Parker, the girl of my dreams. The girl who shocked the hell out of me in the best possible way.

"Studying me, huh? Okay, stalker!" she said, kissing me again, and I tickled her belly. She squirmed at my touch. "Okay, okay! Stop, I am *way* too ticklish."

"Fine." I narrowed my eyes jokingly, and she pressed her hand to my chest.

"No, honestly, I get it. I guess I've been *'studying'* you, too." She put air quotes around the word studying. Then she sighed and looked at the ticking clock, knowing our time together on this lazy afternoon was almost up. Naomi nestled back into my chest.

I cleared my throat. "Tell me about your family. I know it's pretty big."

"Oh yeah. Two brothers, three sisters.

"And you're the…"

"Oldest. I share a room with Sam, she's a senior in high school…*and* she knows all about you."

"Oh, she does?"

"Yep." She smiled wide then bit down on her lower lip. If I wasn't already hard, that move would have done the job. I couldn't get enough of Naomi biting her lip. "You know, girl talk."

"Sure."

"Did your mom ever get over the whole Christmas thing? The roast duck and stuff?"

"Eventually, yeah, but we avoid talking about it. I sent her flowers on Valentine's Day, so I think I got some brownie points there."

"You did?" she asked, her eyes wide and innocent like a doe's.

"Yeah." I shrugged.

"That's so sweet."

"When I was growing up, we just had each other. No grandparents nearby or anything. My mom used to say it was us against the world."

"That sounds like an awful lot of pressure for a kid to have on his shoulders."

"Still is sometimes. But, you know, it's all I really

know. I can't even imagine having a bunch of siblings running around and getting into all my stuff."

"Yeah, that part sucks, but you get used to it. Just imagine if Sully and Dutch were your brothers...and you could never escape them. Ever."

Giving a dramatic shiver, I deadpanned, "I cringe at the thought."

"They're not that bad."

"I'm kidding. They're good guys...they're just...an acquired taste. Like cheap beer."

"They most definitely are. I used to think Sully was the most annoying person on the planet. Now I love the crap out of him. It's funny how life works, isn't it?"

"Wait. I thought *I* was the most annoying person on the planet?" I asked, my tone light so she knew I was only teasing.

"It was a close tie," she said, dragging the pad of her finger down the side of my face, and I closed my eyes. "But not anymore. Now you're my favorite person on the planet."

"On the whole planet?"

She licked her lips. "Yep."

"Well, that's pretty awesome." I kissed her gently. "And I'm pretty certain you're the most talented person on the whole planet."

"Really?" she asked, giving me a sexy grin.

"I can't stop thinking about *Othello*. You were like, unbelievable up there. You know that, right?"

Naomi blushed, which was a difficult thing to accomplish. Fanfare wasn't something she ran from—normally she clamored for it, in fact. But those dusty pink cheeks told me that my opinion mattered. It mattered a lot.

"When I'm up there, I just...I feel larger than life, you know? Like I can seriously do anything, be anyone. It's the most incredible feeling in the world. I crave it constantly."

"It must be hard when a show wraps."

"Ugh, it really is." She placed a hand on her forehead and stared at the ceiling. "It's like a loss, like you have to grieve not being this character anymore. Does that sound strange?"

"Not at all." I shook my head. "It makes sense to me. Whenever I finish a big project, I feel a similar loss. I'm proud of what I did, of course, but starting over with a clean slate for the next project can feel a little daunting."

Naomi shot up in bed. "Yes, exactly! I mean, I'm always wanting that next role, that next big audition, but at the same time, to think I may never be Desdemona again, for real, up on that stage? It's heartbreaking. I was worried you wouldn't get it."

"No, I do. As much as a non-actor can, I guess."

She nodded.

"I'm just so relieved you let me come to the matinee. Seeing you up there was just incredible."

"Even when I was kissing Jamal?"

I winced. "I think I blocked those parts out."

She giggled. "Understandable."

"I can't wait to see you perform again. When will the next show be?"

"I'm going to do a community show back home this summer. Maybe you can come see it?"

"No doubt. I'll be there. Front and center."

"I'm going to hold you to that, you know?"

"I know."

She sighed, glanced again at the clock, and nestled back into my chest.

"Forty-five minutes until we have to go. Ugh."

And then we were silent because we knew that when each of us clocked in for the evening, Heather would be there. And if Heather was there, it meant there was a strong chance that one or both of us would have to answer for our kisses that past Saturday night.

To be clear, I had absolutely no regrets about kissing Naomi, about being with her, about taking that risk with the best job I'd ever had. She was worth all that and more.

"Don't think about it," I whispered. "It'll all be fine."

"I hope you're right."

"I think I am."

* * *

I couldn't stop glancing at the clock.

She was late. Heather was late.

I was hoping that she would have been at the store when I arrived so that if there was anything that needed to be said about my breaking the rules, it could happen without involving Naomi. After all, I was the one who had technically, at least in the eyes of the company, taken advantage of my role as her superior. But if anyone at corporate met Naomi, they would know it was impossible for anyone to be superior to her. She simply didn't allow herself to be belittled, talked down to, or be subject to any abuse of power. She was that headstrong, that tenacious.

She didn't do anything she didn't want to do. But still, policies are not meant to be broken. And so, I was prepared for major consequences when Heather and I finally talked things through. Yes, I was hoping it would be swept under the rug, but I knew the chances were slim. Heather may have had a lot of personal conflicts over the past few months, but she was a dedicated Spotlight employee who didn't stick her neck out unless she was confident that it wouldn't affect her standing in the company in any negative way.

And Naomi and I dating could have consequences. Big ones.

Every quarter, someone from corporate came to the store as a secret shopper to evaluate us. We received marks for customer service, cleanliness of the store, and employee professionalism. Coworkers of mine had been let go for much less than a manager dating a subordinate. Our secret shopper caught a nasty stomach bug in the fourth quarter and wasn't able to evaluate us, so Naomi wasn't as seasoned with the process. I, however, had worked at Spotlight for years...and quite frankly, I was surprised one or more of us hadn't already been let go over the past year...especially Dutch or Sully with their pranks and arguments. Obviously, we'd just gotten lucky, but good luck can only last for so long.

Glancing at the clock again, Heather finally walked through the front door, bundled up in her winter coat, scarf, and hat.

"Yikes, it's freezing out there," she said, plopping two tapes into the return bin and avoiding eye contact.

This is not good.

"Ben, I need to see you in the back room."

"Sure thing," I said, my heart pounding in my chest. Heather didn't use phrases like *I need to see you.* This wasn't going to end well.

"Emmett, hold down the fort, please."

"You got it, boss," Emmett said with a perplexed expression. I knew he was trying to figure out what I could possibly have done to piss her off, considering she had just arrived back from her parents' place. I shook my head, and he pressed his lips together in sympathy before ringing up a customer and leaving me to join Heather in the back.

Swallowing hard, I met her at her desk, where she was seated, her expression hard as stone.

"How's your dad?"

"Better. Thanks for asking." She ran her fingers through her hair. "Look, we need to talk."

"I know." I nodded, scratching the back of my neck.

"I don't think you realize the position you've put me in."

"I know."

"No," she snapped. "You don't. Two words, Ben. Secret. Shopper."

I closed my eyes tight. I'd expected the secret shopper thing to come up, but I didn't expect Heather to be so bitter, so angry. It was very unlike her. Usually, I was considered the 'bad cop' at the store when it came to discipline, rules, and all of that stuff while Heather got to be the nice guy. In fact, I didn't think I'd ever truly seen her angry before.

That is, until this very minute. She was pissed.

She threw her arms out in exasperation. "You were making out in the *middle* of the store. What if corporate had seen that?"

"On a Saturday night? You think they'd send someone then?" I was avoiding the issue, and I knew it. But I was trying to get Heather to calm down, if only for a little bit.

I failed. She only got more upset.

"That's beside the point. What if a customer had called to complain?"

"I didn't think about that."

"Obviously. Because you were thinking with the wrong head."

"Heather," I said, shaking my head.

"Sorry, that was out of line. But, seriously, Ben...I expect something like this from Dutch...or even Sully. But you? I never saw it coming."

"Me neither." I shrugged.

"How could you be so reckless? And what am I supposed to do now?"

"Look, we won't have any more PDA, I swear. No kissing, no holding hands, not even meaningful glances across the store," I said, my tone just a little too impish. Heather glared at me.

"This isn't funny, Ben. And what do you mean, *any more*? You mean you're still seeing her? It wasn't a one-time thing?"

"Definitely not a one-time thing. I'm crazy about her."

"Jesus Christ, Ben." With her teeth gritted, she stood up from her chair and paced the room.

"But we can be discreet. Heather, I promise you. I won't make you look bad."

"You don't understand. For you, this is just a campus job, something to put on your resume before you go off to do special effects or whatever the hell it is."

"Yeah, I know but—"

"This is my career, Ben. I'm *trying* to climb the ladder, which is hard enough to do as a soft-spoken, usually-in-a-good mood woman. You could screw it all up for me. All of it!"

"I wouldn't do that."

Heather ignored me and continued with her rant. "And I'd have to start over...or stay here and *never* get promoted and be a manager of a campus video store for the rest of my life. Do you think I want to be managing kids like Dutch when I'm forty? Huh? Do you?"

"Heather, listen—"

"I'll have to fire one of you."

My mouth went dry. "What?"

"Yep." She placed one hand on her forehead. "And since I don't have anyone else that I'd trust to take your spot, it'll most likely be Naomi."

I heard scuffling near the entrance to the back room, but when I turned, no one was there. I thought I saw a blonde ponytail drift away out of my sight, but I couldn't be sure.

Naomi?

Glancing at my watch, I saw her shift was just about to start. She was probably heading back here to punch in when she heard us talking.

Shit.

"Heather, please don't fire Naomi. It's my fault, I'm the manager here. I'm the one who broke the rules, not her."

"So, you want me to fire you, then?" she asked, and my mouth dropped open. It was bone dry, and even though I opened it to speak, no words came out. I loved my job. Even more than I'd ever realized before that moment.

"One of you *has* to go, Ben. I can't risk corporate finding out about you guys. And although I trust you, I certainly don't trust her. She's a live wire, a total hothead."

"She's really not. Please, Heather, just hear me out. You don't have to fire anyone."

"I'm too pissed to talk about this anymore. Go back to the desk, please."

I stood, stunned, with no idea how the hell I was going to get Naomi or myself out of this mess.

But still, I didn't regret that kiss on the sales floor. Or any of the others that followed—not even for one minute.

I could figure this out…I had to.

CHAPTER 21

Naomi

"Whoa. Naomi, are you okay? You're all pale and stuff," Emmett said as I approached the front desk. His voice startled me from the racing thoughts that terrorized my brain.

I did my best to hide the panic controlling my every thought, but that was never my strong suit. I could dazzle people on the stage, pretending to be another person from another place, another time...but hide my own feelings? I was downright terrible at that.

"Yeah, I...I'm totally fine," I forced out, still in a daze that I couldn't quite pull myself from.

"I don't think so." Emmett hopped down from the desk and walked to me, placing a hand on my arm. He looked to the back room and lowered his voice. "You were fine when you walked in ten minutes ago, but now? Not so much. What is it?"

I shook my head before clearing my throat, feeling myself getting choked up with emotion. "I don't think I can talk about it. Not yet. If I do, I'll start to cry, and I can't do that...not here."

"Oh...I see." Emmett paused. "Does this have anything to do with Ben?"

Surprised, I cocked my head to the side. I could feel the color drain from my cheeks. "Why do you ask?"

"Because Heather looked pissed when she came in today, and she and Ben have been back there talking for at least fifteen minutes—since before you got here."

Yeah, I figured as much.

"Oh, right."

"Are you guys, like...you know, a thing or something?" Emmett asked with a half grin.

Clenching my teeth, I glanced around to see if anyone else was in the store. Fortunately, it was just Emmett and me.

"Yeah."

It felt so good to tell him. I wasn't sure why, but somehow, even though I felt like a huge weight was sitting on my shoulders, just admitting that Ben and I were together made me feel a little bit lighter, and I allowed myself a quick smile.

"Holy crap, this is huge!" Emmett said, eyes wide as he placed both hands on the top of his head.

"Shhh, calm down. No one really knows except Heather, which is not a good thing."

"Oh," Emmett said, his ecstatic expression fell and was taken over by a look of concern, of hesitation.

"She saw us kiss. Here…in the store."

"Oh."

"Is that all you're going to say? Oh?"

"Sorry. So, that must be what they're talking about back there, huh?"

"Yeah."

"Shit."

"I know."

"Do you think he'll get fired?"

Startled, I shook my head. "Bite your tongue."

"Well, I mean…it was technically an abuse of power, right? Manager and subordinate?"

I shook my head, walking to the desk, not wanting to make eye contact with Emmett. "It doesn't feel that way. Not to me."

"I know. It's not like he's a lot older or anything; he's a student, too. It's kind of ridiculous for corporate to even have a rule like that if they're going to let students become managers."

"Good point," I said, fiddling with the hem of my sweater. "What am I gonna do?"

"I don't know," Emmett said with honest eyes. "Maybe you just have to wait to see what Heather does. You and Ben might not have much say in the matter. After all, she is the boss."

Closing my eyes tight, I drew in a deep breath. "I already know what she said. I went back there to clock in and I heard them. I don't think they saw me, but I heard some of it. It's not good."

"Oh." Emmett swallowed and scratched his forehead. "Do, uh…do you want to talk about it?"

"No," I said, shaking my head. "I'm sorry. It's not that I don't trust you, I just…don't feel ready. It's overwhelming."

"Got it. Whatever you need, just know I'm here, okay? If you ever need to talk or anything, I'm here."

"Thanks, Emmett. You've always been a good friend to me." My tone was softer than normal, and I placed my hand on his arm, squeezing just a bit as I spoke.

Emmett looked down at his arm, and then at me. His expression was pure disappointment. "Hey, don't talk like that."

"Like what?"

"Like you're giving up or something."

"I didn't mean to. I think I'm just a little stunned, my brain is still trying to catch up."

"Makes sense. You must be happy, though…about Ben, I mean."

A feeling of warmth spread through my chest just at the mention of his name. "I am. Ridiculously happy, actually."

"I knew you liked him…I mean, I guess we all did."

"I was that obvious, huh?"

"Yep. Not that his poker face was *any* better than yours. That guy was a goner the day you set foot in here. I saw it from the beginning."

"That's nice to hear. I honestly didn't think we'd ever get together," I said, tapping my finger against the countertop, trying so hard to focus on the excitement of my new relationship with Ben. But I was terrified that no matter who Heather fired, it would change everything. If I was fired, I would miss this place more than I'd ever missed anything in my life. Of course, I'd find another job —that wasn't the point. This place was different, these people were *my* people. And I hated the idea of only walking through those doors as a customer. In fact, it made me sick to even think about it.

On the other hand, Ben had worked so hard...for years. The last thing I wanted was for him to lose the job that he loved because he got involved with me. What kind of resentment would that lead to between us? Would we be doomed before we even had a real chance to begin? That thought alone made me cringe.

"I know what that's like," Emmett said, his normally upbeat voice suddenly sad, melancholy, contemplative.

"What do you mean?" I asked. I was so lost in my own thoughts I could barely remember what we were even discussing before I'd spaced out. Emmett gave me a tight-lipped smile and pulled out his Bubble Tape.

"I know what it's like to be into someone for a really long time. And feel like it'll never amount to anything."

"Oh, Emmett," I whispered, knowing exactly what he was trying to tell me. The only other person who chewed Bubble Tape in this store was Marley.

"How long have you liked her?"

He sighed. "A long time."

"But you haven't asked her out or anything. Have you?"

He shook his head no. "It could ruin everything—our friendship, I mean. How could we keep working together if I asked her out and she wasn't interested? I mean, it's not like with you and Ben—that was obvious...to everyone."

"Not to *me*."

"And obviously, not to Heather either," Emmett said with a sardonic laugh. "But she has no idea how I feel about her. I guess I have a better poker face than you guys...which I used to think was a good thing. Now I'm not so sure."

He looked down at the bright pink container, then shoved it back into his pocket.

"I think you two would be really cute together."

"Sully doesn't think I have a chance."

"Sully's a moron."

Emmett laughed. "Good point."

"Maybe you just need to up your game a little bit, you know? Like, show her you're interested without being obvious. I can help you."

"Really?"

"Sure."

"Thanks, Naomi. But, please don't tell anyone. Sully knows, but that's it.

"Of course," I said, closing my mouth and pretending to lock my lips and throw away the key. He smiled, looking relieved.

"Emmett, if it's okay, I'm just going to put some tapes away. I need to clear my head. Thanks for the distraction, though. It was nice to think about someone else's drama for a few minutes."

"Of course. Happy to help," Emmett said sarcastically, then he looked past me to the back room. "It looks like their meeting is over. Ben's coming our way."

All the more reason to grab a stack of tapes and head in the opposite direction.

I wasn't ready to talk about what Heather said...especially with Ben. Quickly, I grabbed the nearest stack of tapes and walked in the opposite direction. Ben must have needed clarity, too, because he didn't follow me immediately. It wasn't until a few minutes had passed and I was almost out of videos that he met me near the children's section.

"Hey," he said, his hands in his pockets.

"Hey," I said, avoiding eye contact and focusing only on the row of Scooby-Doo movies in front of me.

Awkward.

"Did you, uh, did you just get here?" His eyes were pensive. Maybe he suspected that I'd heard something. "You haven't clocked in."

"Oh crap. Yeah, I was late," I lied. "So, I totally forgot to clock in. Hopefully Heather won't be too mad."

Passing him the small stack of kid's videos, I walked quickly toward the back room. "I'd better do that so I actually get paid for today. Thanks for the heads-up."

"Sure." I heard him say behind me, his voice sounding relieved. And I'm sure it's because he didn't want me to know what Heather had said. He didn't want to talk about the Heather fiasco any more than I did.

Thank God.

As I approached the back room, I knew I had to get some distance, had to get away from the store. So, rather than walking to the time clock, I made eye contact with Heather and walked to her desk.

"Naomi," she said, her voice cold.

"I, uh…I know I just got here, but I'm not feeling well. Would it be okay if I went home?"

She looked relieved. "Sure. Feel better."

"Thanks."

Walking back to the front desk, I grabbed my coat and scarf from the spot where I had crammed them. Ben turned to me in confusion, his face pale, like he'd seen a ghost.

"Wait, where are you going?"

"I don't feel so good."

Technically, it wasn't a lie. Since I'd heard Ben and Heather talking, I'd been fighting nausea. But I knew I was perfectly healthy—nothing that a can of pop wouldn't fix.

"Oh," he murmured. "Do you need me to take you home?"

"No, no." I waved him away. "I'll just hop on a bus."

"You sure?" Ben asked, his soulful blue eyes pained.

"Definitely. I'll call you tomorrow."

"All right."

HOURS LATER, after stewing in my dorm room for far too long, I knew I needed to talk to someone. Sarah had an APO service project and wouldn't be home for a while, and if I was being real, she wasn't the person I wanted anyway. That person was at home.

Grabbing the clunky yellow phone from Sarah's desk, I called my house.

"What do you want?" Jonathan asked before I even had a chance to say hello.

"What do you mean? How did you know it was me?"

"Mom and Dad got caller ID."

"Finally! Now, go get Sam."

"Why?"

"Why do you think, dumbass? I need to talk to her."

I could hear my mom talking in the background. Jonathan huffed into the phone. "Mom wants to know if you're eating enough."

"Tell her yes."

"Yes! She had two bacon double cheeseburgers for dinner."

"Shut up, Jonathan."

"Make me."

"You're so immature. Now, go get Sam, you little shit."

"Sam!" Jonathan yelled directly into the phone. Wincing, I pulled the receiver away from my ear, vowing to make him pay for his shitty attitude when I came home for spring break.

"I was just thinking about you," Sam said. "How is Ben? Give me all the juicy updates. "

"Everything's great…sort of."

"What does that mean? Trouble already?"

"No, not like that. He's wonderful, and he makes me really happy."

"Then what is it?"

"Heather saw us kiss, remember?"

"Oh right. But then you didn't get in trouble or anything, so I figured—"

"That's only because she was out of town. She couldn't

do anything from Maryland. She needed us in the store, covering for her."

"Ah, that makes sense. So, now what—she's back?"

"Yep." I nodded, looking up at the ceiling, willing my tears to go back into the ducts instead of spilling down my face, but it was no use. "And now everything's totally screwed up."

"Why? I don't understand. Did you get fired? Did Ben get fired?"

"Not yet. But she's going to fire one of us...I think it's inevitable."

"Shit, Nay, that sucks. I'm sorry." She paused. "Well, maybe she'll fire Ben."

My stomach twisted. "Why does everyone keep saying that? I don't want that. I'm crazy about him, I don't want to be the reason he loses his job!"

"I know that, but you also want to keep working there, right?"

"One hundred and ten percent. I'd be lost without that place."

"Maybe she'll change her mind. Maybe she just had to blow off some steam, yell at you guys a little bit, and then she'll get over it. You did say she has to leave town a lot for her family...maybe she'll realize she'd only be screwing herself over if she fired you. You're a good employee."

"So is Ben. He's the best. He's worked there for years, Sam. Years."

"He's also graduating in May."

"So?"

"So, he's probably already applying for real jobs after graduation, right?"

"We, uh...we actually haven't discussed that. So, I don't know. Either way, I wouldn't want him leaving like that."

"Like what?"

"In disgrace, in shame."

"Nay, it's not the 1800s. It's a video store gig, for god's sake."

"Sam! You know what I'm trying to say. He's worked too hard for too long. This isn't fair to him, and no matter what happens, things will never be the same again. One or both of us will lose our jobs, and there will be this pink elephant in the room, like, all the time."

"Ooh, can the elephant wear a silver boa?"

"Why are you being like this?"

"Because I don't know why you even called me. It's obvious what you're going to do."

"How can you say that? I don't have a clue what's going to happen."

"Somehow, I doubt that, big sister."

"You know, I was planning to kick Jonathan's ass during spring break, but now it looks like I'll be focusing on you."

She chuckled. "Bring it on. You know I love you, Nay. But I have a huge physics test tomorrow, and I need to study. I really can't stay on long."

"Wow, okay. I feel the love all the way over here, let me tell you."

"I'm sorry, but I got waitlisted at U of I. I need to up my game. I promise I'll call you this weekend, okay?"

"Fine, okay. Good luck on your test."

"Thanks. I love you."

"Yep, love you, too."

Hanging up the phone, I paced the room, wondering how the hell Samantha could possibly know what I was going to do about this work disaster. I didn't even know if there was anything I *could* do.

But then it hit me, and I stopped dead in my tracks. As I stared at the Calvin Klein poster on the back of our wooden door, I knew exactly what to do. And I would have no regrets.

Turns out my sister knew me pretty damn well.

Better than I even knew myself.

CHAPTER 22

Ben

*I*t was hard to concentrate. After my fateful discussion with Heather and Naomi leaving just minutes after she got to work, I was struggling to keep my mind on the customers, the video returns, and reining Sully in.

His latest debate with Emmett? Whether or not Pauly Shore was worthy of his fame. I literally couldn't think of anything I cared less about. And yet, the debate continued.

"The guy's a moron."

"Sully."

"I'm serious. Who did this idiot sleep with to get his career?" he asked, holding up the display box for *Son-in-Law* that a customer had left at the desk. "He plays the same stupid guy in every freaking movie. He has no range whatsoever."

"Sure, I mean, that's his thing. But, c'mon, this picture? It's genius. Anyone who looks at that immediately knows what they're referencing," Emmett said, pointing at the box. Pauly was holding a pitchfork and standing in front of a barn with Carla Gugino, posing like that famous painting of the farmer and his wife. It was ridiculous, but I had to agree with Emmett. The marketing was brilliant.

"It's just a box, Polaroid."

"And it's funny."

"This," Sully said with an elongated blink. "You thought this trash was funny?"

"Well, yeah," Emmett said. "He's ridiculous and every-thing, of course, but he makes me laugh because you never know what craziness will come out of his mouth. And I love the whole fish-out-of-water thing where this city boy is spending time on a farm, making a fool of himself."

"Ben, help me out here." Sully was always looking for validation from the other employees when he argued with someone—anyone—over movies, actors, music...basically anything that involved pop culture. He wanted Emmett to see that he was constantly outnumbered when it came to his opinions. Emmett never seemed to care, though. Not one bit.

"Haven't seen it yet," I answered. "But I kind of liked *Encino Man.*"

"Oh, God. Don't even get me started. That shit's even worse."

"Mouth," I snapped.

"Sorry. But really, a caveman found in modern-day America? Talk about reaching."

"That's what makes it fun-ny! It's not supposed to be realistic, man. It's meant to be silly, crazy, weird," Emmett said, exasperated, then changed his tone of voice to give his best Pauly impression. *"No weezing the ju-uice."*

"Ugh, I don't know you," Sully muttered, shaking his head slowly. "And if you rent that new one of his, I will ban you from our dorm room."

Emmett's eyes brightened. "Wait, there's a new one?"

Sully rolled his eyes. "Ugh. Yes, Emmett. It's on the new release wall...you know, the one where he joins the army. And acts like an idiot...as opposed to the one where he goes to a farm and acts like an idiot...or finds a caveman and—"

"Acts like an idiot," I finished his sentence with an amused laugh.

"Exactly. Ben gets it."

"Oh, man!" Emmett ran to the new release wall, stopping almost halfway through the alphabet. *"In the Army Now*! I forgot this one was out. I've probably walked past this box a thousand times and didn't see it. Thanks, Sully!" he yelled.

"No Pauly Freaking Shore! You put that movie in my VCR and I'm going to murder you in your sleep. You know that, right?" Sully yelled right back.

Emmett laughed as he walked back to the desk, tape in hand and shaking his head. "Wendy's rubbing off on you."

"Not really," Sully argued, and when he saw the tape, his entire body tensed. "And why is that tape in your hand?"

"I don't think you've ever threatened to actually *end* my life before... especially over something as insignificant as a Pauly Shore movie. Not that I'm worried or anything. You're just mixing things up, I get it. Women can have a powerful effect on the male brain."

"Or maybe it's just the natural evolution of Sully." Sully shrugged. "And I hate when you sound like a biologist."

"I hate when you refer to yourself in the third person," Emmett deadpanned. "Hate it. And you know my dad's a scientist. I can't help it."

"Well," Sully continued, "*Sully* hates when you like moronic sh—I mean, *stuff* like this. Sorry, Ben."

"How on earth do you two live together?" I asked. They looked at me like deer in headlights.

"What do you mean?" Sully asked with an impatient sneer. A look of disdain on his face. "He's my *best friend*."

"I know, but...you two are always arguing."

Emmett shook his head. "Just about stupid stuff, though."

"Not, like, real-life stuff, man. It's no big thing."

"Oh," I said, taken aback. "I'm sorry, I didn't realize."

"And we're not arguing. It's a debate—a healthy sharing of ideas and concepts with a hint of social commentary," Sully said, sounding like he was writing a dissertation or something.

Emmett rolled his eyes. "I hate when *you* sound like a professor."

"Deal with it."

"Never mind," I said, shaking my head. "I guess I misunderstood."

"Obviously."

"Wait, I thought she went home," Emmett said staring through the glass windows, looking confused. Within seconds, the bell above the door rang, and Naomi came storming into the store, her eyes as crazed as the night of her performance. No costume this time, but it was still bringing me back to that night in a big way. She was up to something. Something big, and my stomach churned at the thought. She studied the front desk, her eyes scanning the store.

"What are you doing here?" I asked, hopping off the platform behind the desk and walking toward her. She ripped the wool hat off her head.

"Where's Heather?"

"I thought you were sick," Sully said. "Don't bring your germs over here. I've got tests next week."

"Shut up, Sully."

"Wait," I said, putting my hands up, not understanding what the hell was happening. "What's going on? Why do you want to see Heather?"

"Don't worry about it."

I raised an eyebrow, my cheeks getting hot. "Naomi."

She swallowed hard, her eyes wide and determined. "Where is she?"

"She left," I said, lying through my teeth. She narrowed her eyes, then let out a sardonic laugh.

"You're a terrible liar."

"She's in the back," Sully said, crossing his arms and leaning back into the counter to watch us with an amused smile on his face. He just needed a box of popcorn and he'd look like a pig in shit.

"Shut up, Sully!" I snapped, my nose flaring as I glared at him. He only shrugged.

"Thanks, Sully," Naomi said, and she stormed past me.

"Naomi!" I yelled behind her. "Naomi, stop!"

I caught up to her just as she crossed the threshold of the back room. Grabbing her shoulder, I looked into her eyes. "Don't do this."

"You don't even know what I'm doing."

And then I realized, she was right. I had *no* idea what she was about to do, but no matter what it was, I didn't want her to mess anything up for herself with Heather, especially now that I knew Heather wasn't going anywhere anytime soon. She was going to be part of Spotlight Video for the long haul, and even if that meant that she was promoted to a district manager, Naomi would still be her employee. I didn't want her to screw anything up.

But it may be too late.

"Heather, I need to speak to you."

Heather looked up from her desk, her expression completely impassive. "What is it?"

"Fire me," Naomi said before swallowing hard and closing her eyes tight. "Please."

"Naomi, stop!"

"What?" Heather said, looking as confused as I was. "You want me to fire you?"

"Respectfully, yes. Please…please fire me."

"You can't be serious," Heather scoffed before looking at me. "Is this a joke?"

I shook my head, retracing my steps and wishing I'd just talked to Naomi after Heather and I had talked. Then maybe this wouldn't be happening. Then she wouldn't be screwing up. She wouldn't be saying these things that I *knew* she'd regret.

"I thought you loved this job," Heather said.

Naomi's eyes softened. "I do. More than you know."

"Then I don't understand."

"Look," Naomi said, placing her hands on her hips. "I heard you guys this afternoon. I know you're going to fire one of us, and as much as I love this place, I think it should be me."

"Naomi, stop talking," I snapped.

You're going to ruin everything!

"No, Ben," Naomi said, her eyes welling with tears. "It's my fault we kissed in the store—"

"No, it's not!"

"You've worked here for years, and I refuse to be the reason that you leave."

"Naomi—"

She raised her determined chin. "Just let me do this."

Heather cleared her throat. "Listen, as much as I would like to accommodate your request, Naomi. I'm afraid it's impossible."

"What?" Naomi asked in disbelief, looking back and forth between Heather and me. "Why not?"

Heather looked in my direction, and I closed my eyes tight.

Here we go.

"Because Ben already gave his two weeks' notice."

"What?" Naomi stalked toward me, her blue eyes angry, betrayed. "Why would you do that?"

"It doesn't matter. It's done," I said. "Please just...stop talking, okay?"

"No! Ben, why would you do that?" One tear rolled down her scarlet cheek.

An awkward pause fell over the room as Naomi, Heather, and I all looked back and forth at one another. I didn't want to spill my heart in front of Heather, but if I had to, then so be it.

I opened my mouth to speak and then Heather put me out of my misery. "I'm going to make sure those idiots haven't burned the place down. You two...well, take a few minutes, okay?"

She left the room, closing the door behind her. Naomi and I stared at each other in silence.

"Why did you quit?" she demanded.

"It was the right thing to do."

"Ben, you love this place. It's part of who you are."

"Think about it. I'm graduating in two months. I've started applying for full-time jobs."

"So, you can still work here, too."

I tilted my head toward her. "I've had my time here. It's your time now."

"Oh my God, stop it. You have to tell Heather that you changed your mind. Otherwise, we'll never have a chance this way."

"What? Why do you say that?"

"It'll be this uncomfortable topic we can never get past. And what if you end up resenting me? You had a good thing going. And here comes Little Miss Naomi, who swoops in wearing her stupid, freaking, ridiculous costume and spoils everything!" She was flustered and not making much sense. I had to laugh. Then I placed a hand on her cheek.

"If you really think that I could resent you for a decision that *I* made, then you have no idea how I feel about you. No idea at all."

Her eyes were pained, and she shook her head. "I guess I don't."

"Naomi, I'm crazy about you. That's not going to change—especially not over something like this."

"You don't know that."

"Just hear me out. This is your first year here, and you bonded with those idiots from the very start—probably more than I ever have. These are your people."

"But so are you. You are my people, Ben. You're my favorite person, and I can't let you do this."

"It's already done. And it's going to be just fine," I said cupping her face in my hands and slowly wiping away her tears with the pads of my thumbs. "Now, stop being your stubborn self and just go with it. I promise you'll thank me later."

She fell into my arms, her shoulders shaking as she cried. "I *cannot* believe you did this. Heather must want to kill you."

"Probably." I chuckled. "Someone else will step up."

"Who...Dutch?"

"That would be something to see."

"That would be *frightening*."

I pulled her closer and kissed the top of her head. "That was really cute, what you did. Storming in here and sacrificing yourself like that."

"Oh, stop it," she said, nudging my chest with her hand.

"It was brave, Naomi."

"I would've found another job."

"That's not the point."

"I know." She sighed. "You realize all those guys are going to hate me, right? I'll be the girl who made Ben leave Spotlight Video. They'll curse the day I was born."

"Nah, they all know my days here are numbered. The longest I would have stayed is through the summer."

"Maybe you still can. Maybe Heather will change her mind."

"I don't think so. But you know what? That's okay. I've made peace with it. You should, too."

"It just feels so...final."

"Nah, it's a new beginning."

"And you won't resent me?"

"Not a chance."

"You promise?"

"Yes, Naomi. I swear to you. No resentment, no regrets."

Her lips curled into a smile, and she went up on her tiptoes, kissing me gently. "Thank you."

"And we'll just say you owe me one." I gave her a mischievous wink.

"Oh my God." She rolled her eyes. "Are you going to hold that over my head forever?'

"Maybe."

She sighed. "Ahhh...and so it begins."

We laughed, and I pulled her in for a kiss. As my lips pressed to hers, I ran my fingers through her hair, knowing that no job could ever mean more to me than her. Yes, it was early for us. Yes, there would still be many obstacles ahead of us since I was leaving school just as she was getting started. But I had to have faith that we would figure it all out.

And the fact that I had three promising interviews in Chicago didn't hurt a thing.

Naomi and I would be okay. And Spotlight Video would always be an important part of my college experience and, if I was honest with myself, a huge part of *me*. And no matter why I had to make my exit, I would always be grateful for the imprint it made on my life.

And having Naomi Parker as my girlfriend?

That was just the icing on the cake.

CHAPTER 23

Naomi

$\mathcal{I}$t was Ben's last day at the store, and I was in no mood for it. In fact, I was moody as hell. Emmett and Dutch were tolerant of my pouty behavior. Emmett even let me play *Ice Castles* for the second time that day.

"Ace, you *have* to stop moping around. It's not like he dumped you or something. C'mon, you're depressing the hell out of all of us."

"Sully—"

"No, no, hear me out because I know what I'm talking about. Ben quit a gig at the best place in town…for you. You should be flattered."

"I *am*."

"Could've fooled me. I mean, the least you can do is be happy, show him a little gratitude."

"Don't you get it? The thought of him leaving makes me sick to my stomach. And I can't even bring myself to look at Heather anymore."

"It's not her fault you two hooked up. She's just doing her job. And you haven't even apologized to the rest of us, you know…"

"Apologized to you? For liking Ben?"

"For getting him fired," Dutch said, kicking his feet against the counter and narrowing his eyes. "We'll miss him, you know."

"He'll still come around."

"Well, sure, as Naomi's boyfriend." Dutch hopped down from the desk and changed his voice to sound like Ben. "Tell Naomi I'm here to pick her up. Tell Naomi I came by. Yada, yada, yada."

"I can hear it already, and I'm getting nauseous just thinking about it."

"Sully!"

"Ace!"

"Listen, Dutch…I tried, okay? I tried to save his job, but there was nothing I could do. He'd already made up his mind."

"I know, I know." He huffed, not looking me in the eye. "It still sucks."

"I know it does. And I'm sorry. If I could change it, I would."

"What about me?" Sully pressed. "What about my apology? That guy is like a brother to me."

Emmett shook his head. "You're so full of it."

"Fine, I apologize to you all, okay? I'm sorry that I fell for him."

"No, you're not."

Pressing my hands to my chest like a Disney princess, I batted my eyelashes and sighed while an uncontrollable smile took over my face. "You're right, I'm not. He's wonderful."

"Ew. You're gross," Sully said with a smirk, and I cracked up. I loved getting Sully all riled up.

"Don't even! Wendy hasn't started here yet."

"So?"

"So, once she does, you'll see what it's like."

"No," he said, his expression arrogant as he pretended to dust off his shoulder. "Because I have class."

"Riiiight."

"*And*—Heather already knows that we're dating, and she's still willing to hire Wendy. I can't take Ben's job, but who cares? As long as I'm not her boss, it's all good. Apples and oranges, Ace."

I knew he was right. Our situations were very different. Regular store associates weren't encouraged to date each other, but there weren't any rules about it either... it was just the managers who were under tight restrictions.

"Ugh, when did you get so annoying?"

"Only since birth." He glanced down at the calendar. "He'll be here in ten minutes. I expect a major attitude adjustment before then."

"Sir, yes, sir," I said sarcastically, rolling my eyes and grabbing tapes from the bin.

"You know, speaking of Heather. She's late for her shift. And she was moody as hell yesterday. Not sure what's going on there."

"Probably feels guilty," Emmett said. "I mean, I would. Ben's her best employee."

"After me, of course," Sully said, and we all rolled our eyes.

"Puh-lease."

"It's a joke, people. Relax." He looked at his watch. "Eight minutes, Ace. Get your game face on."

Waving him away, I grabbed a stack of videos and walked the store, returning each tape to its spot, willing myself to change my attitude and put my best foot forward on Ben's last day. He didn't know it, but we were planning to take him out for a drink after work. Luckily, Heather was closing, so the guys and I were able to avoid asking her to join us.

Approaching the picks corner, I smiled, seeing that Ben and I had both placed *Only You* on our shelves that week. We'd rented it the previous weekend and loved it. Robert Downey Jr. and Marisa Tomei were just...ahh, perfection. And it was the first romantic film that Ben and I had watched all tangled up together in his bed—eating popcorn and candy. The movie was so good that we waited until the credits to start making out. Most of the time, we barely made it halfway through a movie. But this time we watched the entire thing. With a sigh, I thought about how much better my life was now that Ben was mine and not just the guy that stirred my heart and frustrated my mind. He was mine, and I was his, and, funny enough, we barely fought anymore. Although everyone around us, especially our coworkers, knew that would never last.

But for the moment, it was blissful, and I was soaking it

all in. I just had to remind myself that even when he'd clocked out tonight for the last time, it wasn't going to change anything between us. He'd promised me that. And he had two interviews lined up after spring break. Lucky for me, both of the production companies were in Chicago, so Ben wouldn't be too far away. I would never want anyone to stand in the way of my dreams, so I refused to stand in the way of his. But the thought of losing him so quickly after finally getting together pained my heart, so I was relieved when he told me that he'd decided not to apply to any west coast locations. Not because of me, thank God, because I wouldn't have felt right about that, but because he wanted to get some experience with a smaller company first, to build up his resume before taking the plunge. The planner in me hoped that he'd be ready in just a few more years...then we could go together. But I knew I was getting ahead of myself.

"Aww, are those for me? You shouldn't have," I heard Sully say from the desk, and Ben, who'd just entered the store, replied.

"I didn't."

"She's putting movies back."

"Got it. I'll find her."

"I'm over here," I called from the dollar rental section. When Ben rounded the corner of shelves, I saw them. The biggest bouquet of flowers I'd ever seen!

"Are these for me?"

"Yep." He looked so proud as he handed them to me, giving me a peck on the lips.

"Ahh, PDA," I said jokingly.

"What is she gonna do, fire me?" he said with a wink.

"But it's your last day, not mine. Why are you giving *me* a gift?"

He shrugged. "I just felt like it. And I know you're taking this really hard, so I just thought…you know. Why not? A beautiful woman always deserves beautiful flowers."

"I like the sound of that." I smiled, giving him another kiss. "Thank you, Ben. So much."

"Of course. I'm going to clock in. Want me to put them back there?"

"Nah, I'll put them up front. The guys need to see how to treat a woman." I winked.

"Sounds good," Ben said with a laugh as he walked away.

The bell above the door rang again as I was walking back to the desk. It was Heather, and she looked like hell. Her hair was disheveled, and she had bags under her eyes. She was wearing plaid pajama pants and not a stitch of make-up. Very un-Heather.

"Hey," she said to me. "Is Ben here?"

"Yeah, he's clocking in."

"Good. I need to talk to him. You, too."

"Oh," I said, placing the flowers on the counter.

"What are those for?" she asked.

"They're from Ben. Just…well, just because."

She closed her eyes and pressed her lips into a thin line. "Fine. Whatever. Come with me."

Glancing back at the guys, I grimaced. Dutch made a confused face, Sully's mouth dropped, and Emmett shrugged. None of us could figure out what the hell was happening.

Maybe she'd found someone to replace me, too. Maybe those flowers would turn into 'sorry-you-got-fired' flowers. My heart started pounding in my chest as I followed Heather to the back room, terrified of where this confrontation might lead. It was bad enough that Ben had quit, but I was finally making peace with it—sort of—and would be devastated to lose my job as well.

"Good, there you are," Heather said to Ben, who stopped dead in his tracks as he saw her, and I knew exactly what he was thinking about her appearance. His cheeks grew pale, and I knew his brain was trying to figure out her intent just as I was.

"I need to talk to you both," she continued. "Have a seat."

Ben and I sat next to each other, and I swallowed hard, my mouth suddenly dry as a bone. With my heart still pounding a mile a minute, I resisted the urge to reach for Ben's hand. If she wasn't planning to fire me, I didn't want to tempt her into considering it.

"What's going on? Is your mom okay?"

"Yeah," Heather said, pulling off her coat and running her fingers through her hair. "She's fine. But, uh, I've been thinking a lot about stuff. In fact, I haven't really slept at all in the past three days and, uh…I'm not really sure how to say this."

Oh my God. I'm toast.

"I haven't exactly been the best boss," Heather said, shaking her head and pressing her lips together. "I know I've been gone a lot, heading home to help my parents.

And you took the reins, Ben. You saved my ass so many times."

Ben and I glanced at one another, both in shock.

"I was just doing my job," Ben said.

"Yeah, and you do it well. Please tell me you haven't found something else yet." Heather's eyes were desperate as she pulled her brows toward one another.

"No." He shook his head. "I'm starting to interview for full-time work since graduation is only a couple months away, so I figured I could just take a break."

Heather threw her head back. "Oh, thank God."

"What's going on, Heather?"

"Look, I was mad, okay? I was, like, really pissed at you for doing that in the store. I expected it from others but not from you, and I went off. But if you guys will promise to be on your best behavior...I'm talking, like, prudish, not-even-holding-hands in the store behavior so that we don't get busted by a secret shopper, then I'd like to ask you back. If you'll consider it, anyway."

"Really?"

Ben and I locked eyes again, and I swear my heart flew right out my chest and soared around the room. I couldn't believe my ears.

"Really," Heather said. "I'm never going to find someone to fill your shoes. And I know I'll have to eventually when you've got a career and stuff, but for now...I'd like you to stay on in whatever capacity you're willing. Even if it's only for a couple more months."

"You're serious?" Ben asked, his cheeks returning to their normal, gorgeous shade.

"As a heart attack," Heather said.

"Well, yeah. I mean, of course. You know I love this place," Ben said.

Heather closed her eyes. "Oh, thank God."

"You keep saying that," I blurted out, then wrinkled my nose, realizing it probably wasn't the best response to Heather finally getting her head on straight and realizing how valuable Ben really was to the store.

"Yeah," she said, looking slightly annoyed but trying to rein herself in. "I'm just...I'm really relieved. That's all."

"I am, too."

"So, let's get you back on the schedule," Heather said, wasting no time at all. "I'll grab it from the front and be right back."

She flew past us, and I jumped out of my seat, hugging Ben with all my might. "I can't believe this!"

"I know. I think I'm still in shock."

"Same here." I pressed my hand to the side of my head. "But I'm so freaking happy, I can't even tell you."

"I know," Ben said, pressing his forehead to mine. "Me, too."

Resisting the urge to kiss him, I placed both of my hands on his cheeks. "It's nice to have you back."

"Thanks."

"I'll go tell the guys. They probably won't believe me, so I may need your backup when you finish here."

"Okay." Ben nodded, running his hand through his hair, his bright blue eyes still looking stunned. "I'll be up there soon."

* * *

HOURS LATER, Ben and I were surrounded by Emmett, Sully, and Dutch at a campus bar. We'd found a wooden corner booth and were about to toast Heather's change of heart.

"So, originally we were going to wish you good luck with everything and commemorate your last day," Emmett began, lifting his bottle of Corona into the air. "But now...well, now we can celebrate your first day? I mean your second first day?"

"Here's to Heather getting her head out of her ass," Sully said, raising his glass of Guinness.

"Well said, my friend." I giggled, clinking my amaretto stone sour to everyone's drinks.

"And to your continued employment at Spotlight Video," Emmett said. "I hope you won't leave us too soon."

"We'll see how the job market treats ya, Ben," Dutch said. "Is it wrong that I'm hoping you don't get anything for a while?"

"I mean, *kind of.*" Ben shook his head and laughed.

"Sorry, man. Just don't want to see you go. Like ever."

"Let's not think about that." I shook my head and took a sip of my drink before grabbing the little plastic sword from the glass and pulling the maraschino cherries off with my teeth. "Right now, let's just celebrate Ben and how lucky the store is to have him."

"Exactly," Emmett said.

"Hey, man, did you guys see what we're getting next week?" Sully asked. "*Shawshank Redemption.* That movie is badass. Too bad we can't play it in the store."

"I haven't seen it," Dutch said after letting out a burp.

"Oh, you have to," Emmett said. "It's brilliant. But yeah, definitely not allowed to play it at work."

"Morgan Freeman has the best voice on the planet," I said.

"Bullshit," Sully said. "No one compares to James Earl Jones."

"Does everything have to be an argument with you?" I asked.

"It's not an argument, it's a debate," Ben said, placing his arm around my shoulder.

"Thank you!" Sully said, throwing both of his hands out. "You finally get it, man!"

"What is he talking about?"

"I'll tell you later." Ben smiled. "But I have to agree with Naomi. Freeman gets my vote. Dutch?"

"Darth Vader, man. No comparison. Emmett?"

Emmett's brow was knitted as he supported his chin with his hand, his elbow resting on the wood of the table. "I'm not sure."

"We're not asking you to vote in the next election or anything. It's just a question," I said, my voice snarky but playful.

"Fine, then I have to go with Freeman."

"Are you kidding me right now?" Sully's eyes were as large as saucers. "You're the biggest Star Wars fan I know."

"One has nothing to do with the other."

"Like hell, it doesn't."

"Sully, we're just comparing voices, not characters."

Leaning in to nuzzle my nose against his ear, I whispered to Ben. "Aren't you glad you won't miss any of these highly controversial yet vastly important debates?"

"You have no idea," he said, turning to kiss me on the lips.

"Get a room," Sully scoffed, but secretly gave us a wink before pounding the rest of his Guinness.

"Oh no," Ben said, looking around me to the corner of the booth.

"What is it?"

"We forgot about the flowers."

And instead of being upset, I smiled…and I laughed, thinking of that line in *Ice Castles*, one of the movies that brought us together in the store. My favorite line in that entire movie…a line that always made me think of Ben. And I just couldn't stop smiling.

"What is it?"

"We forgot about the flowers," I repeated, tilting my forehead to him. His confusion turned to recognition, and his smile matched my own.

"I get it." He sighed, kissing me again. "Maybe we can stop at the store on the way back to your place. Heather should be there for another hour."

"Can we rent *Ice Castles*?"

Ben nodded. "Absolutely.

EPILOGUE

Ben

June, 1995

"Y ou guys are officially obsessed," I said as I walked into the store, and *Dumb & Dumber* was playing on every TV…again.

"Dude, I've been waiting for this to come out on video for months. You know this," Sully said as he wiped down the counters with cleaning solution. He was wearing the bright yellow gloves that we kept in the back. "Heather said I can play it as much as I want if I clean the bathrooms. I'm just waiting for this part to be over before I start. Hence the gloves."

"You hate cleaning the bathrooms."

"Oh, I know, but c'mon," Sully said with a twitch of his

shoulder as he stared at the screen like he was waiting for something to happen. "Still a no-brainer."

"*Mock!*" he yelled along with Jim Carrey on the TV above him.

"*Yeah!*" Dutch sang.

"*Ing!*"

"*Yeah!*"

"*Bird!*"

"*Yeah!*"

"*Yeah.*"

"*Yeah!*"

They gave each other a high five as they cracked up.

"Ouch, that rubber glove hurts, man."

"Oh." Sully looked at the yellow rubber gloves. "Sorry, Dutch."

"I can't handle you guys," I lied. As much as they sometimes annoyed me, I was going to miss little moments like this with my goofy coworkers. I would miss their antics and how they could argue over the tiniest of details. I'd never known anyone like Dutch, Sully, and Emmett. I would miss them more than I wanted to admit. The store would be really quiet when they left for summer vacation.

"You're in luck. They're about to clock out, and we can change the movie," Naomi said as she emerged from the back room, giving me a sexy wink.

I lived for those winks.

"Not me," Sully said. "I'm waiting for Emmett. We have to pack up our room after his shift. Can't believe this is my last day in this store.'"

"Not for good," Dutch said. "Just until September, man."

"Yeah, yeah, I know."

"Are you and Emmett rooming together again next year?" Naomi asked.

"Yep. We're moving to the towers." Sully looked rather proud of himself.

"Ooh, fancy." Naomi wiggled her eyebrows. "How'd you score that?"

Lurie Towers was the hardest housing to obtain on campus. You had to be a junior or a senior, and there was a ridiculously long waitlist to get in.

"I know people," Sully said, looking smug.

"Whatever." Naomi waved him away, rolling her eyes.

"Where's Emmett?"

"I'm right here," Emmett said, emerging from the video game room. "Heather had me rearrange all the Sega games."

"Wow, you, too?" I asked.

"What do you mean?" Naomi asked, puzzled, and Emmett laughed.

"Yep," Emmett admitted. "Me, too."

"She's really cashing in on your obsession with this movie." I turned to Naomi. "They're selling their souls for Jim Carrey."

"Huh?"

"Heather's giving us chores so that we can keep the movie on repeat," Emmett said, popping open his Bubble Tape container and pulling out a nice, long stretch of pink gum. "But little does she know I like organizing things. So, no big deal."

"I should've made *you* clean the bathrooms."

"Nope. Not happening."

"Wimp," Sully said, grabbing his caddy filled with cleaners as he walked to the bathroom. "I'll be back in a few. Pray for me."

"When's your last shift, Dutch?" I asked. It was finally hitting me that so many of my friends would be leaving campus...some even leaving the state.

"Tomorrow morning," he said. "Then I'm outta here! What about you, Naomi?"

"Today."

"Wow, end of an era, huh?" Dutch teased, winking at Ben and me.

"Yeah, I guess it is," Naomi said, turning to me with misty eyes. "But we'll still see each other a lot. My dad is going to let me use the car more this summer."

"Sweet," Dutch said.

"And I'll drive to her place. I'm actually meeting her family this weekend." I said, smiling at Naomi and resisting the urge to pull her close. I wanted to respect Heather's rules while I was still employed.

"That should be interesting," Dutch said, nudging my arm. "Don't do anything I wouldn't do."

Gritting my teeth, I nodded. "Solid advice."

"Oh, congrats on the new job, man," Dutch said. "I keep meaning to tell you that."

"Thanks," I said. I'd gotten a full-time position as a special effects artist for a production studio in downtown Chicago called Madison Avenue Studios. It was a small studio, tiny compared to those in L.A., but that didn't bother me. Everyone has to start somewhere, and I was more than ready to pay my dues in the industry.

"When do you start?"

"After the Fourth of July holiday."

"Excited?"

"Yeah," I said. "It's a great place to get my feet wet, and the pay is good, especially for right out of school. Most of their movies go straight to video, which is...ironic considering I won't be here to brag about them."

"We'll do that *for* you," Naomi said with a wink. "You'd better believe if a movie you had a hand in comes through those doors, it's going to get played. A lot. I'll even clean the bathrooms to make it happen."

Holy shit. She is crazy about me.

"Wow. Thanks," I said. "Still, it'll be a shame not to be here. But...onward and upward, right?"

"Absolutely."

"Are you moving to the city then?"

"Not yet. Some of my roommates are here for one more year, so I'm going to stay on the lease until they're ready to graduate. Then, I'll see. The commute shouldn't be too bad if I hop on the 'L'. Plus, our rent is so cheap compared to downtown. I need to save a little bit to afford it down there."

"And you'll be closer to me this way," Naomi said with a wink.

"Yes, an added bonus."

Sully strolled back from the bathroom, wiping the back of his forehead with his bare arm.

"You're done already?"

"It's just a toilet and a sink, dude. What's the problem?"

"It felt like you just walked back there to start cleaning."

Sully altered the register of his voice and made a

phone signal with his hand. "Pick up the clue phone. Hello!"

"Pick up the *clue phone*? Is that another Wendy-ism?"

Sully, although definitely an original when it came to personality, had started to adopt some of his girlfriend's mannerisms and phrases. We lovingly called them Wendy-isms when they reared their ugly heads. Not that we disliked Wendy. She was actually pretty awesome, and a Chicago native, so she'd be working the store all summer while most of the students went home. She was quickly becoming part of our work family, but that didn't mean we teased him any less when he picked up a new phrase or figure of speech from her.

Sully laughed. "Nah, her roommate, actually. She annoys me most of the time, but I like the clue phone thing. It's like something my little sister would say. And I actually miss that kid. Don't repeat that because I will deny it."

"I'm going to call your little sister as soon as you clock out. Her name is Brittany, right?" Naomi teased.

"Whatever, Ace."

The bell above the door rang as Marley came running into the store. "You guys!"

Marley, although a very sweet girl, wasn't usually so boisterous. We all stared at her in shock as we took in this new, louder version of our normally meek coworker.

"What's going on?" Naomi asked.

"It's happening!"

"What's happening?"

My parents *finally* agreed to let me live in the dorms next year. And a spot opened up today. We just got the call before I left for my shift! I move in Labor Day weekend. I can't believe it. I've wanted this…well, forever!"

We all knew that Marley was in desperate need of some distance from her strict parents. She'd been begging them to let her start her sophomore year in the dorms, but they'd held out until her second-semester grades were good enough for their liking. Fortunately for Marley, she'd aced the semester, and they'd obviously agreed to let her live away from home…even if it was only across town. For her, it was a gigantic step toward independence.

"Marley, I'm so happy for you," Naomi said, giving her a hug. Marley beamed.

"And, I'm getting my older brother's old computer. So, I'll actually have my *own* computer *in* the dorms. I'm in heaven right now. Heaven!"

Marley had a dreamy look in her eye as she shoved her purse under the counter.

"You know we have lockers in the back."

"Oh, Ben, give it a rest," Sully said. "They're never going to use those lockers."

"Ugh."

"So, what do you need a computer for? They have computer labs in every dorm. Big ones."

"I know, but…" Marley bit down on her lip. "Never mind."

"No, what is it?" Naomi pressed.

"I don't want to use those computers. I kinda…need privacy when I'm using it."

"Oh my god, are you watching porn?" Dutch shrieked, his eyes stretching in disbelief.

Marley looked mortified. "Shh, there are customers in the store, Dutch."

"Oh, sorry."

"And of course not. Do you really think I'd spend hours in the kitchen making you cookies and brownies if I was just going to watch that stuff anyway? I don't think so." She shook her head as she crossed her arms.

"I don't know." Dutch shrugged. "Maybe you like computer porn better than video porn."

"Would you stop saying porn?" Marley said, her cheeks growing a deep shade of red. Dutch had a real talent for embarrassing the poor girl.

"Then, what do you need privacy for then?" Emmett asked, his brow knitted.

"Well, so…here's the thing. We got AOL."

"You did?" Naomi asked. "*Your* parents got AOL?"

"Why is that so shocking?" Marley asked, taken aback.

"No, it's just…" Naomi hesitated. "From everything you've told us, they seem a little strict."

"Oh, right. Yeah, but my brother needed internet for his Master's program since he's in technology, so they signed up. And now I can talk to *all kinds* of people." She bit down on her lower lip again, her eyes looking a little guilty.

"You're acting weird," Dutch said.

"Are you meeting guys online, Marley?" Naomi asked, looking as shocked as I felt. That was the last thing I expected Marley to do with an AOL account. I figured she'd get a pen pal in Japan or something.

"I mean…yeah. Is that bad?" Marley asked, clenching her teeth.

Naomi shook her head. "No, just a little surprising."

"They have these chat rooms," Marley began. "And you can talk to people all over the world. I'm talking to this guy in London right now. I don't know him that well, but he sounds really smart."

"Just be careful," Emmett said. "Anyone can go online."

"Oh, I know. But, I mean, he's in London." Marley shrugged. "It's fun."

"What's the chap's name?" Sully asked, using his worst British accent.

"Simon."

"Don't get too attached. Once you're out on your own, there'll be plenty of fish in the virtual sea," Sully teased as he glanced at Emmett.

"Oh, I know. But I mean…it's fun. On the other hand, I'm definitely staying up way too late. I talk to Simon before he goes to his classes, so I'm up until about three or four every night. I'm starting to feel it." Marley yawned, leaning against the counter. Then she shook her head quickly. "Oh wait, I forgot to clock in. I'll be right back!"

When she walked away, Emmett pulled the bubble tape out of his pocket and looked at it. "London," he said under his breath, and I tilted my head to the side.

"She'll be fine, Emmett."

He wouldn't make eye contact with me. He just stood there, shaking his head as he shoved the pink container back in his pocket.

"What's up with you?" I asked. "You're being weird."

Naomi leaned over and whispered in my ear. "He likes her."

"Naomi," Emmett said, pressing his hand to his forehead as he looked up at the ceiling in angst.

"Sorry. But Ben won't say anything."

"Fine. Whatever."

"So, ask her out," I said.

"I'm leaving in *two* days," Emmett said. "I won't be back until Labor Day weekend. What would be the point?"

"Unless…" Sully said, tapping his chin.

"Shut up, Sully. You've already told me I don't have a chance with her. More times than I can even count."

"I was just kidding around," Sully said, looking guilty. "C'mon, Polaroid!"

"It's a lost cause, anyway," Emmett said. "Maybe I'll hook up with someone at home. Get my mind off her."

"Rebounds never work," Naomi said with a kind smile. "At least not in the long run. Just ask her out."

"No way." Emmett shook his head. "Maybe some distance is all I need."

"Distance," Sully whispered, and his lips curved into a devious smile. His arm shot out against Emmett's chest. "That's it!"

"What?"

"Dude," he said, turning to Emmett. "I've got an idea."

THE SPOTLIGHT VIDEO SERIES

Be Kind, Rewind
Blank Tapes (coming spring of 2022)
Late Fees (coming summer of 2022)

For more information about The Spotlight Video Series,
click here:
https://www.ladybosspress.com/spotlight-video

The following preview has been approved for all audiences...

Coming, Spring 2022

Blank Tapes
　　Book 2 in the Spotlight Video Series,

The year is 1995, and Marley Gallagher is obsessed with her new computer...and the guys she meets in AOL chat rooms—they're the perfect escape from her introverted nature and strict upbringing. A townie, and a shy one at that, Marley is finally embracing a little independence as she moves into her first dorm. The chat rooms online offer her the chance to reinvent herself and maybe fall in love in the process. The only problem is, she's so focused on the guys on her computer screen, she doesn't see the one who's right in front of her nose...her coworker at Spotlight Video, Emmett.

Emmett Roberts has been in love with Marley since their first shift together. And it's obvious to everyone but Marley. Not wanting to ruin their friendship or make things really awkward if she turns him down, Emmett avoids asking her out in person. With a little help from his friends at work, though, he devises a plan to win her heart. But, when Marley discovers that her latest online love interest is actually her coworker in disguise, will Emmett lose his chances with her altogether?

ACKNOWLEDGMENTS

I want to give a HUGE thank you to my beta readers: **Deb Bresloff, Pamela Carrion, Kelly Sisulak, Laurie Darter, Megan Kapusta, Beth Suit, Stacy Brown, Shannon Allen, and Jaime Davison.** I am TRULY grateful for each of you and all the time and energy you gave to reading and giving feedback on this crazy band of misfits at Spotlight Video. You are all awesome and have given me your unique perspectives on the story, the time period, and the characters. You are all wonderful!!

Deb Bresloff- with each and every book, you are always happy to lend an ear, brainstorm, and support me however you can. Thank you for loving Naomi and Ben and helping me make this story uniquely its own.

Pamela Carrion- As always, I feel very lucky to have you in my corner. Thank you for loving these crazies and for encouraging and supporting me! You are truly awesome!

Tiffany King- Thanks for all the awesome video store chats as we reminisced about the simpler days—returning tapes to the shelves and using the old-fashioned credit card sliders! Those chats helped me to shape this story into what it is!

Beth Ehemann- Thank you for believing in this series

before I even knew it would be a series! I am so grateful for your genuine enthusiasm and support.

Kristen Proby-- I am so happy to be an author with Lady Boss Press and will always be grateful for this opportunity you have given me. Thank you so much for taking a chance on me!

Lori Francis- You truly go above and beyond for all of the LBP authors. Thank you for all that you have done for me!

Thank you to **Michelle Preast** for the absolutely perfect cover! You are so wonderful to work with, and your creativity continues to dazzle me!

Thank you to **Jaime Ryter** for your mad editing skills! I've never had so much fun reading an editor's comments before, and I'm looking forward to working with you again!

Thank you to my **readers** for reading and supporting me and my writing. I hope you enjoyed this story, and I can't wait to continue this series.

Thank you to my beautiful daughter, **Audrey**, for your excitement about this story. Every day you would ask, "How's your book coming along?" and you made my heart soar. Your support, encouragement, and excitement are so vibrant and so meaningful to your momma. Absolutely priceless! When you do read this, I hope that you'll enjoy it—and that it gives you a glimpse into what life was like during my beloved 90s. You are such a gift to me, darling girl, and I'm grateful for you every day!

And finally thank you to my husband, **Chris**, who has supported me and every dream I've ever had. Thank you for believing in me, my love! I'm so lucky that you're mine.

ABOUT THE AUTHOR

Melissa Brown is a pop culture maniac and hopeless romantic—in fact, you'll find (way too many) pop culture references in her books! She lives in the Chicago suburbs with her husband and children and has an unhealthy obsession with both *The Office* and *Ted Lasso*.

Melissa enjoys writing contemporary romance and romantic suspense.

CONNECT WITH MELISSA BROWN ONLINE:

Website:
www.melissabrownbooks.com

Facebook Page:
www.facebook.com/MelissaBrownAuthor

Facebook reader group (Books with Brownie):
https://www.facebook.com/groups/127591530753685/

Amazon Author Profile:
http://bit.ly/melbrownie

Goodreads Author Profile:
www.goodreads.com/melissabrown

Instagram:
Melbrownie77

CONNECT WITH MELISSA BROWN ONLINE:

Twitter:
@LissaLou77